ANTICHRIST

A Story About Heartache

R.B. Batson

PAGE PUBLISHING
Conneaut Lake, PA

First originally published by Page Publishing 2023

ISBN 979-8-88654-777-1 (pbk)
ISBN 979-8-88654-789-4 (digital)

Printed in the United States of America

TO MY BELOVED FAMILY

CHAPTER 1

TRAVIS MARX WAS ABOUT THE SAME AS ANY OTHER eighth grader at the county high school he attended. His big problem was that he had made the mistake of being born into a teetotaling cult and had to read books in order to have science explained to him. This made him less popular among his peers, and his family tended to mock him mercilessly when he would get irritated with their limited understanding of the globalizing procession away from backward rural and Southern Bible Belt nonsense. They wanted him to fit in with the popular cliques with the extracurricular activities his parents expected him to participate in. One thing they wanted him to do was to pad his résumé for college, and the second was they did not want him hanging out with the marginalized and downtrodden in their community whose family was not well-connected in that community by showing up at a proper church. Everyone in his class was horrible that year, and the high schoolers did not seem to have a clear picture either. His brother, Hank Marx Jr., was one of those airheads. He would do anything he was told to do to be popular and looked like an ass every time he started an argument. The whole way of life that the community was holding on to was temporary, and the big dramas of life in that small rural community made it a hellscape. The youth group and leaders at his church did nothing to make heaven and an eternity with them look like a better deal.

This was 2008, and the economic forecast looked grim. He was glad that his junior varsity wrestling season had come to an end with his having made the call to not be there for spring training because it looked like his brother needed to join it for popularity purposes. He did not want to have a conventional American life. Everything his family was conditioning him for did not feel like it would help him have upward social mobility and instead would only get him indebted and feeling hopeless so that he prayed to God. Travis didn't pray to God. He liked to take matters into his own hands and show human agency, but he did not exactly hate God if he existed. He did not understand the Trinity when it was explained to him as a youngster in vacation Bible school and stopped taking the Old Testament seriously at the end of third grade. He did not understand why a simple Unitarian stance and an openness to nineteenth-century Protestant liberalism was no longer good enough for his family.

Some of his father's family who had moved from Germany still acted normal, and he thought his mother from India would have married for a better life, but obviously she hadn't. It did not help that the town was on the coastline of North Carolina, and everything the teetotalers were doing there to try to put Olde Towne, North Carolina, on the map was utterly pretentious and made it difficult for people like Travis to leave the area as anything other than a refugee when the world as they knew it was ending, and there was not going to be a Second Coming of Christ on the horizon anytime soon. Travis had German relatives who talked like that up North. If he would not be that abrasive to delicate Bible-thumping ears, then a lynch mob would not get started. At the same time, many other people were fooling themselves and behaving with malice toward those they expected to take care of them when the gray matter would leave their brains. Their own gossip and disingenuous customs were not resulting in anybody else there being particularly religious; it just made them sincere about keeping the Christian label or else they dabbled in Wicca or some New Age nonsense that he was perceptive enough to know the adults loved for those people as opposed to being an established religious minority.

He was having difficulty with his parents not giving up on him being involved in the Restoration Church denomination in town. He had invited a friend to a youth group activity, but he did not want to go himself, and Travis understood why their evangelistic efforts went nowhere here and really wished they would stop going to poor countries to mess those people up next. It was obvious that they were not going to outgrow their cultlike sect origins and be more like the conservative Baptist and Methodist denominations in these towns. Everybody in town knew they thought they were the only ones going to heaven, and they vouched for their cultlike status by being selective about what they accepted in written history. Southern Baptists were just as bad about that. He was, in fact, tired of his parents and the lies of the adults in his life about what would help him be successful. They were all participating in social decay and were expecting the impoverishment in the developing world that neoliberal globalization created to allow them to take their socially decaying religious rituals to other people who needed better things to hope for and to work toward. Travis Marx stopped acting religious when that was not in his beautiful nature and started having fun in the eighth grade, much to the chagrin of his parents and brother.

It was then that he had a talk with God; God, of course, did not answer back. He went to talk about Eastern religious teachings to his new friends who looked past his preppy clothes his parents made him wear and saw him for the apostate he basically was and loved him for it. They were quick to tell him that those were not a thing for White converts. If he wanted to do something different, he needed to do the California New Age movement and buy their books at the local bookstore. After checking out a book on world religions at the school library and hearing enough of his Wiccan New Age friends talk, he decided that any philosophy that worked for the collective good of humanity had been lopped in with the major world religions a long time ago and humankind on planet earth had since then cared nothing about doing what was best for humankind collectively.

Some of the things these people were reading from the local bookstore were only taken seriously by what most people globally would consider to be weirdos. He was glad to have them as friends, being eccentric and feeling the heat for it himself. There was one person he was close friends with who basically perceived a lot of the things he did; he had the misfortune of dropping from the wrestling team before the season ended but at least had the bragging rights of knowing this community was full of crap. He had knowledge about a lot of things that Travis would never have thought to inquire about—what some might call the deep things of Satan. He was glad that his family had access to the computer internet and found out interesting information on the World Wide Web he would not have found at the school library. He found information from university-funded studies that vouched with no statistical margin of error that things like lucid dreaming were actually achievable and verifiable and that Eastern meditation was as effective in altering a person's level of consciousness awake or asleep as indigenous ethnobotany and that certain fungi had the capability to produce. He could not find any scientifically valid studies on time travel, and his friend had to explain to him that one article he read was actually the plot of the Philadelphia Experiment and that no secret government projects had ever been undertaken for time travel. The project that occurred as was planned was the Manhattan Project. He also realized that everything he read about how to develop telekinesis was not going to help him manipulate matter; that apparently was a joke.

He did feel like there should be something to clairaudience among the fields of extrasensory perception. He had friends who claimed to be clairvoyants and to see things like auras, but clairaudience was basically the same thing as telepathy as far as he knew, so it seemed to him like it needed to be a thing. A race of telepaths could correct all the misfortune in the world. There were no government studies on telepathy available to him on the World Wide Web. It appeared the idea was as much of a joke to the government as telekinesis and time travel, but not investigating foreign aircraft. His friend Demarcus told him that there were probably downed Soviet aircraft and that he might very well find out someday that the

Pentagon had invested some money in frivolous things like nuclear fission, time travel, telekinesis, and telepathy and been horrified by the results and backed up off that to channel its own energies into endless proxy wars with the Soviets and regime changes to become the world's greatest cultural exporter since the French as the world's police force. An idea Americans associated with incredible hulk-like superhero strength and a force for liberty rather than a green group of armed peacekeepers. A fable now in the eyes of the rest of the world unlike the Hollywood superhero movies with CGI explosions they were turning up at theaters to see.

One night before Thanksgiving, Travis had one of his talks to the God who never responded back and said, "You know, if you give me the ability to hear people's thoughts, you know, if they are secrets that are not too great and that person seems like they can get out of hand without intervention, I may actually keep talking to you."

Travis heard thunder and looked out the window, but there was no lightning. "Are you sure that is what you want?" Travis spun his head around and saw a dark-indigo silhouette at the door. It had horns that were conical, and you could see the whites of its eyes. The beast had magical red eyes that twinkled at him with what could either be delight or malice. It appeared about seven feet tall and was covered in wispy long dark-indigo fur.

"What the hell are you?" Travis inquired.

"I have been watching you for a while and listening to your thoughts even longer. I can give you that which you desire. Just ask me for telepathy."

Travis didn't have to think twice. "I would like to have telepathy."

"Your wish is granted," said the Big Blue Guy. "Now I am going to show you what that will cost you."

You just offered it for free, Travis thought.

"That is not how it works. Look out the window." Travis gulped and turned his head to the right to look out the window, and he saw what looked like a film roll traveling off from the window up into storm clouds extremely high up in altitude. "Everyone who has ever known you is going to hate you," said the Big Blue Guy.

5

Travis did not know what to make of what just happened. He was looking out the window, seeing the film roll continuing to travel upward, and the Big Blue Guy was no longer visible. He knew things could not possibly be that bad; he would go to sleep and not remember what he had just seen.

When Travis awoke the morning before Thanksgiving, he heard a man's voice; when he managed to blink his eyes awake, he saw a person there in his room who, although not family, looked familiar, like Zod from the Superman comics. *I will be your guide. You can trust me to teach you how to be a powerful telepath and move around the hidden realm.* The man was dressed in rubber and had an oiled beard. He looked like he might be sadistic but possibly a fun guy.

Why are you making a thing out of this supernatural gift this way? asked Travis.

Because there's a lot you need to get right once you start on this journey or else you do not start on it at all. You can come up with an avatar later. I am the Vegan Sadist. I also wanted to share with you that sometimes when people die, they decide to stay here in this realm, and I think you may have seen one of those people last night. He was being a jerk.

Really, I don't remember.

You should try to remember who the bad guys are. I think that guy was one of them.

I don't have a lot to do today. I was going to read and listen to music mostly before Wednesday evening services.

That can be the next time I show up. There are two people you need to know about.

Okay.

Travis went about his day as usual, staying in an upbeat mood even though most people deteriorated over the holiday season until spring forward. His brother was not at home, and his mother had to work at the library and his father for an architecture firm. It was not going to be great at school anymore during these years. At least until he had to go to church and see some more of the people he thought were useless; he could have it easy. He went downstairs and found Viviane, his mother, a naturalized citizen from India who had given him his brown eyes and black hair, already working on the

Thanksgiving dinner and Hank, his father, a German American, home with her. She said he had rescued her from the fourth-world Adivasi family she was born into before leaving India with the assistance of Christian missionaries with Hank and changing her name after learning better English. She had got a library science degree and worked even though Hank made beaucoup bucks in sustainable architecture as a capitalist Libertarian, double-talking Republican type with chauvinist comments in private and at church.

The day was subdued compared to what it had been before they bought his brother a car for his sixteenth birthday, and he had not been given a curfew. The other Marx brother was a complete saint, of course. The day with the two of them had not been odd compared to usual despite the appearance of the Big Blue Guy last night. She was preparing the same things she usually did a day in advance. He had a bowl of cereal and headed back upstairs to read a random young adult novel, and by the time his dad got home, he was dressed and ready for church.

When he and his parents got out of the parked car, he headed to his age group's Bible study. He had an hour before class ended to listen to a pointless discussion and not need to interject a radical idea hopefully. Sometimes it was worth it, and sometimes not. As the first thirty minutes passed by, he became increasingly aware his mouth was dry in a way he would not otherwise have been bothered by; and the last thirty minutes, he was increasingly aware of needing to pee in a way he would not otherwise have been bothered by. The bell buzzed; he got up and walked out. And after leaving the bathroom, all the church folk had started the slow amble on down to the auditorium; and while he was heading there, the Vegan Sadist appeared again. *I know that guy from last night was lying. I have looked at your whole life, and you have a good one. I am about to show you your future wife.*

Is she one of the two people I need to know about?

He heard the thoughts of someone else then. *That kid cannot possibly be trying to get on this thing we have going on here. That is like, literally, the first thought I have heard from his small noggin all night long about a single one of us here. He needs to leave while he can.*

7

Who would that be, Mommy?

Travis reached the end of the hall and saw a tall woman with red hair, glasses, and wearing a pantsuit with a girl about eleven years old, two years younger than him, next to her. The girl had a unibrow.

That little girl will be your wife. I know it, said the Vegan Sadist.

"Oh, hell no!" said Travis out loud.

"Kid cusses. That is the big thing not to do. Look! He made that girl cry!" said one of the useless old people everyone was waiting to die off.

Mommy, I heard both of those people. That person there I can see, and he was vicious to me out loud came from the crying young girl whose name Travis did not catch. Her lips were not moving, her mother was glaring, and the girl caught it quick and stopped crying.

We can get that separated for her, the woman messaged in his direction. *You do not need to make a thing out of this. I do not like what you are about, Travis.*

The Vegan Sadist had the idea, not me. I don't want this any more than you do.

And that one should have no business coming into a church. I guarantee you that one is a demon.

I don't think people really do your thing on that side, Travis thought at her.

They need to. You can reach the lost with it. At least that is what I told Ophelia it was for.

If it is the mischievous purpose, then you are good to stay here, said the Vegan Sadist.

What do you mean? the older woman asked Zod.

The playful telepath had left and had no more words to offer.

I am going to be keeping my eyes on you, thought the older woman.

Me too! piped in Ophelia.

CHAPTER 2

TRAVIS HAD JUST GOT BACK FROM HIS FIRST DAY at seminary. He knew he was new to the church, and this local seminary *was* rebranded for open-minded scholars, so he thought they might be fine with his Unitarian Universalist inclinations. He would give it a go for a history and counseling double major degree. He had a geography major and a minor in anthropology with his undergraduate degree and thrived in the social sciences. He had arranged a day to volunteer at Habitat for Humanity before music lessons his parents gave him assistance financing, and he volunteered at a regional art museum as a museum guide, being conversational in German, Dutch, and French as well as English. At that museum with the language, art, and music appreciation lessons his parents had paid for on his behalf since he was in high school, he had got to the point where he was leading guided tours. They—the people at the museum, of course—were impressed by his application of his knowledge of contemporary art and his restraint in dissing the capitalist and anti-humanist system that made the American art market larger than that in Europe, as well as his intermediate proficiency in German, Dutch, and French.

He had read the syllabus and was prioritizing how he would meet school deadlines around his obligations and be in a position to work the next year if his art was not selling because it was no longer edgy enough because after all, this was advanced material, and he did not want to drop out. He had his reasons. He was going to have to make some effort to attend church fairly regularly, despite that being the least appealing thing about his new religion to him. So he decided to go to the Bible study at his parents' church that night. He had read the first chapter to his counseling course textbook and decided that degree program was going to be complete refuse or waste, but at least his parents couldn't send him to a counselor when his behavior became increasingly eccentric and tacky in their eyes. He was enjoying reading his history coursework, if not the way it was taught. All the recent theologians were blatantly heretical, and that made it a blast for Travis when he needed to speed-read and go party later.

He walked into that church and immediately heard Morgen Blossom telling other telepaths to watch out for Travis, that he was not what he appeared. He walked into the auditorium for the adult classes and saw Ophelia sitting with her mother. She had grown up into a gorgeous redhead and had her unibrow fixed. *I did not think he would come back here. He hasn't been here in such a long while.*

It is okay. This starts up when I am stressed out and starting something new. It will go away.

Won't! thought a snarky young female voice.

That is not the only one who has been watching you today. I listened in on your thoughts while you were at school, thought Dr. Strangeglove, a new telepath, at Travis.

It's not a thing.

Of course, it's a thing. We got it started with a few people we knew would do it right. All you ever think about is sex and sacrilege.

Is Mr. Blossom one of them?

No.

Travis sniggered.

Inappropriate, thought the male voice.

I guess we just don't listen to the preacher give his Bible study.

You could. We would correct you if your thoughts were not sola scriptura. Then an instructor at the school turned his head in Travis's direction and gave him a sly smile.

Travis did not like that. He practiced his mindfulness and focused on his breathing. He stood for the singing and did not sing. He bowed his head in prayer the first twenty seconds and then lifted it, wishing they had a liturgy to shorten the prayers and the sermon. When it was over, he drove home and went to sleep.

He got up easily and made tea. He read a chapter in the second of his three books for one of the courses he had on Mondays and Wednesdays; and then he was going to make it to an afternoon class, read the syllabus later, and make it to the museum to lead a tour, his only one this week. He did not hear anyone talking to him again. It did not happen to him on Friday when he had Habitat for Humanity.

When he got to music lessons that afternoon, he could hear familiar spirits he wished he did not have to deal with from the moment he walked into the parlor of his instructor's music studio, liberal telepaths.

I can't believe he is going to go through with this, said a dull, droning, so annoying man's voice.

There isn't any need for that. Travis does not give a damn about sticking with dogma. He will learn from liberal theologians in his paperwork. He isn't studying to be a preacher.

"Come on in, Travis," said Viola.

"I want to show you the song I was working on this week."

"We can do that after scales. Do you need me to play them for you?"

"Are we doing piano or voice first?"

"Whichever one you want."

"I would rather do voice."

"Let's run scales."

"Si-ii-ii-ii-ii," Travis cooed for all to hear as his voice climbed up to E5. She was trying to get his voice to sing like a Bollywood artist, having moved on from Broadway repertoire; they needed him to have a magical voice recital with glissando and street dancing.

"That doesn't sound pretty," said someone in the waiting parlor out loud. "I don't really want to make a point of that by this year's recital. It will be lost on people here. They do not care about anything authentic from the Indian subcontinent. They don't even do yoga right. Let's work on the song we have for now."

Travis was singing words he had seen translated and learned to emote through phonetics, while Viola hit the drum underneath her as the karaoke version of the song played on CD. They moved on to a piano lesson where he was playing "All I Ask of You" from *The Phantom of the Opera*, which he had sung before at a voice recital in a duet. It sounded beautiful on piano. He was doing well; this was a skill he was going to have mastered the way he wanted before he left town for good.

"Praise God for my mother having kept the piano keys in operable condition."

I don't think you understand what to praise God for and what to thank your mother for. Either that or you need to do a better job of practicing mindfulness and play Weber superbly came a demonic voice that sounded like Viola but obviously was not. *I guarantee you it was. I also don't like the songs you are writing. You need to focus on Broadway and the Great American Songbook and stop making poppy songs that are weird. It isn't what it's about.*

I think it is.

"Trust me. Do Broadway. That's it for today!" exclaimed Viola. "I think you will do well with those two for now. I would like to find you something better for the recital."

Travis left, aware that whatever it was that followed him in there was not going to leave him alone until he was adjusted to seminary.

Opposite, it said.

Travis arrived at the museum of modern and contemporary art in Charleston on Saturday forty-five minutes before he was supposed to receive instruction in how to lead group tours through the next exhibit. After showing his membership card, he entered the sprawling galleries, empty except for a few visitors and security personnel moving about the museum patrolling and never having to intervene. He went to the gallery that had needed a replacement collection for a while; he would be able to ask his questions before he had to field questions from museum visitors when he got around to this gallery. It was a new contemporary traveling showcase from a European artists' collective; Zeer Goede was what they called themselves. They were Dutch and not interested in the COBRA arts collective because there was not enough money in it for them. He was not always presumptive. Having a brother who continuously made an ass of himself being presumptive, he knew such mistakes should be avoided. He could not help thinking that this exhibit was going to be crass and vulgar. He had noticed that recently and thought the museum was starting to go downhill.

When he walked into the most spacious gallery, he moved to the white space off to his left and, walking into it, noticed a ten-foot-tall Big Blue Fuzzy Monster with goat horns and friendly eyes standing confidently with his left and right feet spread apart in what appeared to be the beginning of a plié and his right palm clutching a pimp's cane. He was not sure what to make of it. Looking over to his left on the museum wall and not one of the temporary walls that went up in these spaces, he saw a skeletal sculpture dressed in a red cape standing on top of a pile of ceramic skulls.

This is unlike anything I have ever seen before, he thought.

He walked over to a wall to look at a painting sandwiched between two metal busts of sailors reaching out of the wall with their faces contorted in agony and saw a family of four sitting for what appeared to be a church directory photo blown up into 36″ × 60″ dimensions. The girls in the middle were twins sharing a distinctive unibrow facial feature. He walked around that wall and saw an LED projection of a scene from *Rosemary's Baby* on the other side with the words "Hail Satan," captioned underneath it in Art Deco lettering. "I do not remember those lines being anywhere in the movie."

"How recently have you watched it, Travis?" said Annette, a friendly but dominant woman who happened to be part of the museum's management and the biggest she-pimp in town.

Travis told Annette, the museum volunteer coordinator, that he was totally perplexed and had no idea how he was going to field questions from an audience. He didn't even know what this was about. The exhibit promotional said the artists' collective was about waking people up to the impermanence of America.

"That is what this is about. We are the only museum in the state that carries contemporary art and art that other museums might consider pornographic. The others would not have visitors interested in it. If you notice a group of people not being receptive to changing notions of right and wrong, they can be directed to the museum of sculpture from the Orient or the museum of African pottery, or if they are like your mother, you can direct them to the museum of the Flemish master artists here in Charleston.

"I probably know how to handle it. I read a book on contemporary art from Oxford University Press."

"That is great. We will have an exhibit on Dada and Surrealism in the spring here, and you would be the best docent guide to explain that exhibit. It is fun being Travis."

"That's right, Annette."

When Travis was done at the museum and driving home, he was glad he had not had an encounter with a telepath his entire time there, dead or alive, and he was wondering how he was going to read that into his reading material at seminary and have honest, quality paperwork. Maybe if he combined Christianity with Tibetan Buddhism, he could handle the existence of telepathy and keep knowledge of it to just a few people. He could be a heretic in his paperwork as a history major, but his counseling major teachers were asses and would ensure that he did not get a 4.0. He really did not want to be in school the next two years, but it was helping him get along with his parents, so he would try and be glad that telepaths had not started traveling across space as of yet. He had voice lessons the next day and had not heard from any of the church people, at least not anything that sounded demonic in nature, since he was not a regular church attendee and they had not been provoked to it yet.

He headed off to Habitat for Humanity ReStore early that morning and walked in to see Matthew and Luke were having downtime as paid employees. They usually only required volunteers for build days, and he did not want to participate there or work at their office if it meant carrying health insurance, which his father was still doing for him for now. He thought he might be alright never doing that and relying on natural healer fixes instead. Since they were understaffed there now, he was dropping by to set out arrivals. He was probably going to find a new place to volunteer. There really wasn't anything good in town to help a brother out, but he might try Meals on Wheels next.

Matthew asked him how he was liking his coursework at school. He told him one major was probably going to be more informative than the other if he wanted anything to grow from the seeds the instructors were planting, and that was the history major; the other was only good for knowing how to handle other mental health professionals who, more often than not, lacked a moral compass. Matthew, originally from Ohio, chuckled and said, "That works for a dirt cheap degree. Just make sure it isn't your only iron in the fire while you are working on it."

Kevin, who was a choir director at the most liberal United Methodist Church in town and originally from Ontario, piped in, "There are other ways to handle it: you could show up at a different church. You don't want to become too liberal, then you'll end up like Canada. There are good things about your area that I like."

"I like French Canada as well as Ontario. I think it would be nice if our peaceful revolution would look more like the French one. It should be less of a bloodbath not having a monarchy to bow to anymore. I do not think you have the slightest clue what these people are about. Hopefully, they chase you away. I would love to bring the Northwest or Northeast down South. They will not have it."

He left without any intention of going to the most liberal United Methodist Church in town and very hopeful that Habitat for Humanity would go away with the Green New Deal and Economic Bill of Rights. If it turned out the books he was reading were malarkey, he might read faster than he was thinking he could last week, dropping all the nonsense and volunteer more. Partying wasn't getting him references.

He mentioned this to Viola briefly between his Bollywood mating ritual song and dance and his sweet rendition of "All I Ask of You" on the piano and had a pleasant lesson not discussing experimental songwriting and no telepathic progress for the week. *I actually have noticed you practicing more mindfulness* came a womanly thought from nowhere.

That doesn't count.

"Are we good enough to move on?"

"Did we just start this last week?"

"It may have been the week before."

"Let's give it one more week. I can see you doing well at long piano pieces by the time you are through with school here. We can also pick a different one for the spring recital."

"Is it possible to go from playing that to 'Clair de lune' by the spring?"

"Well, now that your lesson is over, you can go look for that in my library or something like it."

After ten minutes, he finally found a book full of the works of Claude Debussy. Other than the occasional random music book, it was all musical theater and Rod Stewart / Barry Manilow let's-all-do-the-Great-American-Songbook-type material she had in her library. The people in the area must have taught her not to invest in classical piano pieces and Bollywood dance number music books.

"See anything in there different from what you have seen before?"

"I may not care about voice lessons in a year," said Travis.

"Well, we'll do whatever you want this year while we have double lessons, but that is what there is a demand for here."

He drove home. He stopped and had a Ridiculous Burger at Burger Hut. He was, after all, a vegan and despised fast food, but he would make an exception for Burger Hut's Ridiculous Burger. And then he went home, singing. He went upstairs and wondered what there would be to do on the weekend if his gas money wasn't going to restaurants and books right now, and then he read through his course books mostly. Midway through the night, it dawned on him that he was not going to understand the material if he did not start taking the words of liberal scientists and economists seriously, and then he would end his twenties much smarter than he ended his teen years. He might even be able to read literature critically like a master's degree-holding intellectual and connect the processes of the universe into a grand theory of everything. He could not hold dogmatically to Christian religion if that religion could never become a philosophy, and his school did admit people from all religious backgrounds so that it could receive federal funding. He was going to read some of the great literary masterpieces during this period. He might even study math, economics, finance, chemistry, and physics. He might end up studying the life sciences and keeping animals, a windowsill garden, and growing oyster mushrooms. He also might decide not to do that.

It was an election cycle. In the end half of 2019, he was not worried about who might or might not get the Democratic nomination. He knew that he would not vote for any contender the next year bought out by special interests. The sinister potential of a kleptocracy to remove the social safety net for the 99 percent due to Citizens United had him more worried than President Hampton being the fourth in a line of three presidents to get eight years. He knew that it was important to keep economic and environmental justice as well as democratic reform and women's rights rolled out properly from his one year as a registered socialist. From his one year as a registered socialist, he knew that it was important to emphasize the ongoing battle against racial injustice in order to get a socialist alternative to the current horrifying socioeconomic mode in America, but he did think Senator MacDonald was a capitalist at heart. He had promised that the last failed Democratic nominee was going to cancel student loan debt when they had said no such thing, and he could see him saying that there would be substantive criminal justice and prison reform done this next time when the establishment candidate they'd hand the nomination to this time would say he would do no such things in a meaningful way.

Racism would continue and people of color would get hate the next four years regardless of who'd become president from the parties of War and Wall Street. He secretly wished that religious attendance would go down for good as well as people paying attention to the mainstream media after they had misled people time and again. He also secretly wished that the family unit would disappear, but that was not an issue that pollsters were even asking about in 2019. It seemed like all the Democrats cared about tacking onto the Republican Party platform were platitudes about lifting wages, guaranteeing job creation, and solvent social security with the agenda to promote buying American. Travis had never seen them get results from these empty promises as the debt soared under them and people did not buy as much and job creation simply didn't happen with inflation and economic collapse on the horizon.

As for the Christians who would need to adapt? Who knew, maybe they would get investors to make an app for life management. They might even allow emergent monism from nineteenth-century German protestant liberalism into the progressive church, or you could even leave the church if they couldn't ever get a clue. His family was horrible to him the summers he behaved irreligiously, but he knew they would improve later. He prayed to God that they would put an end to the structural violence of capitalism without rules and stop focusing on a few abortions every year as the reason to go to church and support the duopoly because that was not convincing people to care about voting for a particular candidate, to talk about the latest lies the American media was injecting into the debate, or to care about the most blessed sacrament. He had been reading John Milton's *Paradise Lost* and realized that he had a book his mother thought was as important as Dante's *Inferno*, and one of them was blatantly a heretic, like William Blake. Milton and Blake did their own thing, and that was why they were beloved by the literary scholars.

He went downstairs to talk with his parents about how Milton got away with being a heretic in seventeenth-century England and had a volume apparently comparable to Dante's *Inferno*, and they told him that he did not know what he was talking about. Milton and Blake were deeply religious, and everyone knew that. He was going to have to not be hopeful that they would improve later and not expect them to be able to discuss innovations in economics and finance, current events in Europe, musical industry shenanigans, philosophical conundrums, or the continuous problem of the commodification of art plaguing contemporary art with them. That was not the type of discussion that went on at their dinner parties; they didn't even serve drinks. He just needed to leave the house before they became too desperate to hold on to America. He would do better doing that with model looks. He needed to get sexy quick. "I am singing a Bollywood song and dance number," said Travis.

"I wish you would get over dancing. It looks as bad as cursing to our friends," said his mom.

"I would love to be able to play Claude Debussy on the piano. I should definitely have my best piano recital ever this year."

"I don't think that's something our son Travis is capable of doing now, Hank, do you?" said Viviane.

"Travis is an ass for not trying to be me and doing my thing."

Travis stopped having conversations with his parents that night. If they ever mistook his kindness for approval of their parenting, he was brusque in turn, and they accused him of being manic. He needed less of them around him the rest of his life if they thought that was their purpose for him as his parents.

He went to church again on a Sunday night. It was the first time in eight weeks, about halfway to Thanksgiving.

"Tonight, I know we all have our minds on the political turmoil in the world, and I just wanted to let you all rest assured—"

I wish he would stop talking too.

What are you about? Travis thought.

I think I know what this is about. Look down there at that little old lady. She is a widow, and she gave money to the church today, and I bet she didn't have a lot. They, the men leading, want for you all to give to the collection plate to keep missions going. Does anybody care? Could you not give to a charity, or is it wrong to give to a charity that competes with the church? Maybe you could vote in candidates who take away the government's ability to interfere with what should be in the hands of the church and not big government and tell people that the church will actually take care of you and see how that goes.

She was rotten then, thought Dr. Freemoney.

Who is she?

A divorced Baptist. Now she attends here and there. They don't think like we wanted them to once they have telepathy apparently.

Maybe you should stop trying to make it Christian telepathy. Make universalist telepathy a thing.

I don't think it has anything to do with that.

I am probably not going to come back here. I thought you were like me and tired of this nonsense. That woman there does not work. Her daughter will not want to until she has to, and when you are that widow down there, you will throw the dollars at the collection plate because it is what your husband would have wanted you to do even if they are dismantling her social security.

That is a pathetic group of people posing as the devout.

You are right.

That woman is an adulteress. I guarantee you, Travis. You can hear her talk, and she talks like a whore, Morgen Blossom thought.

You whore yourself out all the time you powerless bitch woman. You whore yourself out to the billionaire class, the media, and the men you let in to preach nonsense like this.

She probably had an abortion at some point. Do that from now on.

That instructor is a prick.

Agreed. I am coming up to the balcony so that you can see me.

A pretty blonde woman in her midthirties ascended the stairs, and upon reaching the balcony's landing, she tossed her hair over her shoulder with a flick of her wrist and gave a sprightly smile. Her teeth sparkled, and her eyes were full of blasphemy. Travis gave her a knowing wink.

"That is a good kid. I may come back for more," she said out loud.

Travis was glad when the sermon was over. The preacher was fired up about the progressive menace sweeping the Northern States and taking youth away from the church. By the time he issued the invitation, he had a bit of spittle on his face from his rabid ravings about the godless Liberal Democrats.

I don't want this to continue any more than this, yet I cannot bring myself to look away. These people are clowning around when they talk about church unity. Everybody else is looking at them and thinking, Well, who the hell are you? Do you have as many members as the Anglican Communion, the Eastern Orthodox, the Roman Catholics? Well then, who the hell do you think you are? *Anyway, that's how I am about it. Just stay at home and read those books your partying money is going toward now. You might not even have to put on pants most Sundays as you get older.*

I like that idea.

"See you in two weeks?" she said out loud as she spoke a second time.

"I will see you later." Travis did not know whether telepathy had occurred; he did like what he was hearing though.

Travis stayed away from the church during the two weeks and wrapped up his schoolwork six weeks before Thanksgiving. He decided to start attending a mosque after reading the Zahar, a text on Sufi Islam. He asked the imam there if he needed to read the Koran in order to know the will of Allah, and he was instructed that he only needed to accept Allah as supreme lord and he would need to profess Muhammad as his most important prophet.

"Is it because he was more practical than the others?"

"Yes, you would find that in the Koran if you read it. A lot of imams in the West believe that the civil law was an accommodation to the circumstances in which the word was revealed to Muhammad."

"Does that apply to the ceremonial and moral law?'

"Are you a Jew?"

"No. I was raised a Christian, but I was told I was not doing it right, so I am looking for something else."

"Were you in the Orthodox communion?"

"No, not really."

"Well, okay, that's fine. Muhammad had interactions with Jews who keep those proscriptions, and most of the Sunni Muslims—which is 80 percent of them, including those here—adhere to what he proscribed in the ceremonial and moral law the same way most Jews keep what Moses proscribed there as if they are binding for Allah's people everywhere. The Eastern Orthodox have more of a resemblance to Judaism than the modern Roman Catholic Church, which is the big one in the West. Muhammad had dealings with them as a merchant while the Catholic Church was warring and decimating the Roman economy. Christians in the East were different from those in the West and were bickering about a lot of things that did not matter tremendously to most people in Asia. The Jews, for the most part, had been doing the same before them. Muhammad thought they behaved better than the animists around him, and he had the correct heart for Allah to reveal to him the Word the way it was handed down originally."

"Will I understand it if I read it?"

"No, you would not. You need more guidance. You do need to know that there is a call to prayer in Muslim countries, and in Saudi Arabia, Shi'ites are banned from doing the hajj. If you are going to be a mystic, then do it with the proper imam explaining the Koran and Asian culture to you. There is only so much you can expect them to do now."

"What else is mandatory?"

"You must fast during Ramadan and give to the mosque."

"I could do that. I would prefer to be a Sufi."

"From observing you now, I think that is enough for us to work with you. Then you can do the hajj someday."

"We will be praying soon. The men will be praying over there."

Travis had fun with the predominantly Asian and half-Asian Muslim community that day. He had fun with Ranveer, Sanjay, and Sundar. The three of them were also in their midtwenties and unmarried.

On his way back from the mosque, Travis saw a Help Wanted sign at a five-and-dime-type general store. He walked in and asked for an application to fill out and return and headed back to his parents' house. He sat down at his parents' place and talked with them about getting work and moving out and traveling and seeing where he would want to live after he got his master's degree. He did not tell them he was a closet Muslim and lied about how quickly he was wanting to leave the area. He got work before Black Friday and continued going to the mosque. He decided to move in with Ranveer as his roommate and to travel to Savannah with Ranveer, Sanjay, and Sundar for the Christmas break. Ranveer was a good guy like Travis. He was not quick to respond and presumptive. It was harder to get an emotional outburst from Ranveer. It made it much easier for both of their parents when they dropped by, and it made it easier for Travis if some of the Christians he stopped talking to dropped by to pester him.

Sanjay, Sundar, and the two of them were planning on cutting loose in Savannah. After knowing them this long, he figured Sanjay and Sundar would be the most useful at making a Christmas holiday in the South a fun trip, as they were party animals year-round and did not discuss their alcohol consumption and sexual pastimes openly.

When Thanksgiving arrived, Hank Marx Jr. had flown in to see his family. He had a few conversations with his parents, his mother in particular, that involved complaints that bordered on agonized wailing. Travis wondered what was bothering his brother, but given that they never had any conversations together, he figured if it was important, Hank Jr. would let everybody know.

On Wednesday night, when his mother was cooking and she was talking with Travis, she had started discouraging any talk of Travis leaving the area. Travis asked her if the talk of leaving the area had Hank Jr. going off the deep end.

"Does Hank Jr. want me to stay here with you in North Carolina so that he can continue being independent as you age?"

"Of course, I want that," said Hank Jr. "And luckily for me, she will let me have anything that I want even if it means throwing you to the wolves."

"You're not like that, Viviane."

"Let me tell you how that is. I basically would."

"Yet you expect me to stay here and take good care of you when you are aging?"

"That is how it has always been done."

"Not in Germany, but I agree with Hank Jr. as well," said Hank Sr. while sitting in front of the news. "I particularly do not like the idea of you being independent. That cannot happen when a wave of radicalism is sweeping the country. The last reason I would have moved to America was to watch it become Europe."

"Look, if you know how that is for me with Europe, you need to back down," said Travis.

"I would never for you," said Hank Sr.

"It would have been better if you had killed yourself ten years ago," said Hank Jr.

"I agree with Hank Jr. None of your attempts were serious enough," said Hank Marx Sr.

"And I agree with your father," said Viviane.

"*You* are a bitch. You should never have left India."

"Then you would never have been born."

"I am going to get away from you. I will return when he is not here. As long as you promise me that you will not just have him fly in to try to set everything aright, then I will see you face-to-face again. You did not backstab me anywhere near as bad as the other two. You are just a victim of the patriarchal, colonial, capitalist, imperialist experiment known as America. I am going to have to leave to stay safe. I am already not going to be seeing you at Christmas. I am telling you now that I will not be having Thanksgiving with you."

"Dude, I don't care. *You* are my least favorite son. If you are going to kill yourself, pick a more effective method."

"You don't mean that, Viviane."

"*You* are a fool. I always mean what I say and say what I mean."

"I still love you," said Travis.

"Apology accepted," said Viviane.

"That's not what I meant. I definitely need to leave. Do not follow me. I will get a restraining order."

"You could kill yourself," said Hank Jr.

"You could go to the hospital and then to church and vote for a capitalist," said Hank Sr.

"*You* are both fools if you thought I would repeat mistakes like that for you."

Travis left the house and drove fifty minutes to get to Ecstasy Beach, South Carolina, where he had been living with Ranveer.

"I do not know which state I am going to vote in now," Travis said to Ranveer as he got settled and talked to him on the phone.

"Luckily, that's a year away," Ranveer told Travis, trying to console him.

"I am going to work the weekend and eat at a buffet on Thanksgiving."

"That's what I would do."

On Thanksgiving Day, Travis ate at Crackerjack's, a Southern buffet chain. He arrived home and saw dancing gnomes in the parking lot outside the apartment. He went in to piss in the apartment's toilet, and when he cut on the light, the Big Blue Guy was there. *Remember that I have everything under control.*

Travis puked in the toilet and pissed before he flushed. "I think I am never going to eat another vegetable again."

Travis went to bed and worked the weekend. He was not bothered by everything that was on his mind. He liked that he was able to compartmentalize so very well.

When the semester had ended for Ranveer and Sundar, Travis and Sanjay had arranged time off work to spend the winter break in Savannah at a cheap motel. They drove through Charleston, and while they were doing that, Travis had the idea to stop and see Oliver Gupta. "I would like to touch base with a family friend and see if he will let me spend some time in Charleston this spring."

"Have you called him already? I just got over you being vegan. I do not want to deal with you if you start acting like an idiot."

"I have called him. Mr. Gupta likes to deviate from convention. I don't see anything wrong with it if he is still following my advice."

When they pulled up to Mr. Gupta's house midday, another car was parked outside of Mr. Gupta's house, and Mr. Gupta was in the driveway waving goodbye to a college-aged guy.

"Travis, I would stay away from that old queer. You are about that guy's age. That is the wrong thing to do in the wrong place at the wrong time."

"He said he was going older and Whiter now. I wanted to see before I asked to stay with him."

"Are you going to blackmail him?"

"It wouldn't work with Mr. Gupta. He doesn't care about anything."

"You've never done it with a guy?"

"No, I did it with a girl. I still haven't met anyone as fun. Mr. Gupta was trying out grooming when I knew him at a younger age, and he was cool when I said no and advised him to date older. I am glad I put a stop to it. "Hey, Mr. Gupta! Are you done? I was wondering if you are still good with letting me stay with you because I need a place in Charleston for a week this spring."

"You're just as good as gay," he heard from the car.

"Thanks for sharing," Mr. Gupta said to Travis's Muslims who had not driven away yet. "Are you really going to come over to visit in the spring?"

"It all depends on whether I continue the museum docent opportunity after I am done with school in the spring now that I have a place to stay. I cannot stay at Ranveer's forever, so I may as well rent somewhere. I still have a place to stay this year while I finish up early next semester as a distance learner."

Travis went back to the car and got in.

Sanjay was the first to speak, "I heard everything you just said. Please tell me you don't sympathize with those people."

"I actually like them."

"Then you are a gay vegetarian and not a Muslim. Something's got to give. It is not consistent."

"I didn't say that I fall in love with them. I have friendships with them."

Sanjay was angry. "Sundar and I will show you the gayest thing you can ever do once you are a Sunni Muslim. You can only do it with White girls, and you cannot tell anyone."

"That's not right of them," said Ranveer. "You are wrecking a lot of notions that are pretty entrenched in the West already. Travis, *you* do everyone a favor and leave your support for LGBTQI+ rights at not allowing discrimination against them in health care, education, housing, and employment and allowing them to give blood, and you can be a good Muslim sooner. They are being bad Muslims. White people are not any better to use as whores than Asians. Every one of you is going to make this a pathetic trip."

"I'm turning on the radio," said Sundar.

CHAPTER 3

THEY ARRIVED AT THE MOTEL THEY HAD RENTED AT six o'clock and then went into a Moroccan restaurant. There was a belly dancer shimmying for the dinner guests. He sat down with his Muslim brothers. He had a helping of shakshuka from the breakfast menu even though it was dinnertime. They were all sitting on low couches and eating with their right hands. The belly dancer weaved her way through the crowd over to Travis and his friends, and she swiveled her hips a bit, much to their delight.

Travis asked her, "What made you decide to become a belly dancer?"

"I had to. My father didn't believe me when I told him I didn't need him and could make it alone. He tried to control me with stupid things I did not want. I have been a dancer ever since."

"I am a dancer, and I think like you about stuff like that. I have a father and brother who try to control me with stupid things I don't want."

"Take my advice and do whatever it takes for them to finally understand you mean it."

"Even if I have to leave the country?"

"Yep."

"Okay."

"Say you left because you had to. The right people will understand. They didn't believe me either when I said I didn't care. That
was around the time it became my go-to line about everything. They
were oblivious about it all. I was polite, and it was actually them
being dense. I didn't want to say 'Screw you, I am leaving anyway'
and throw that plate of shakshuka I made for Baba over his head.
I do know I am happier because I decided to do that one evening.
When somebody tells you that they don't care, it's probably because
they don't care."

"I agree with you."

"You get a kiss!"

The gorgeous belly dancer puckered her plump lips while Travis
leaned in and kissed her as Sundar said out loud, "That is wrong,
Travis. That's not how we are. You are acting disgracefully."

"I think you have the problem," Travis said to Sundar, raising
his voice.

"Agreed," said Ranveer.

The dancer danced and sang to the beat of drums. Gradually
the conversation started returning to normal. "I like this place. Even
if it has no vegan options, it is the closest thing to a nightclub in the
Middle East or India that we are going to find in Savannah."

"We can head to Atlanta after Christmas Day, and there will be
more there."

"You can be back here tomorrow on Christmas Day. There's not
a lot else open then."

As they left the restaurant, they noticed a homeless person outside. He was obviously homeless, not getting to shave and all, but he
had awareness in his eyes and not bewilderment or violence. One of
his friends said, "If you don't watch out, you could be as bad off as
that guy there. He wasn't resourceful early enough, and that bimbo
in there you were praising for her mistakes cannot possibly be that
either."

"I guarantee you she's resourceful. She has a good intellect. If you
want a dependent, submissive relationship partner in the West, date a
girl without a good intellect and never worry about them threatening
to divorce over your disapproval of their career decisions."

"That shouldn't be a thing."

"Well, here it goes hand in hand with your acceptance of pre-marital sex. I don't see how that does not benefit everyone."

"An independent woman is a bitch."

"Opposite. A dependent and submissive relationship partner is a bitch."

"It should be both then, and that is a thing."

"I think you will like seeing Senator Buffet in town on Christmas Eve. The Democrats are a capitalist party. She has a chance at securing the nomination. If we are not going to vote for a socialist third party, I would like to see how she gets a crowd fired up."

Travis walked over to the homeless guy and asked him, "Why are you out on the streets?"

"I am always out on the streets when I cannot get my Navane filled."

"Is it because you are not functional, or do you have a bad family that keeps requesting a more severe diagnosis?"

"I wouldn't call my family bad. I think the fundamentalist menace in the Deep South, which includes many health-care workers and social workers, is conspiring against me, and I left the house rather than give them ammo to call me a paranoid schizophrenic next. I did not have anything arranged in advance that I needed to have done first."

"Don't contact them. I'll give you some money for a Greyhound bus, and you can start arranging to head up North."

"That's obviously the thing to do," said Sanjay.

"I think he did that well. He could get a job up North if he wanted to work. He's not like the others and ready to commit theft. He is a wandering, restless soul who is probably underbanked and needs his debit card."

"I have that."

"That's a good kid," Travis said and went off together with his friends.

"They are obviously wreaking havoc instead," said another of his Muslim friends.

"If you really want to see Senator Buffet give her speech today at Forsyth Park outside of the Cathedral of Saint John the Baptist, we need to head there soon. You need to know that woman is definitely a disgraceful person who won't accept her place in the cosmic order. We could find something else to do tonight after dinner. We could pick up a whore."

"It's still not too late to pick a good centrist candidate and not a radical woman no one likes claiming to be a unity candidate. I think that by the end of it all you will want a candidate for patriarchy from the center," Ranveer said to Travis.

"I think I know how it will be if you all do not pick a unity candidate with me. I know the history of the Democratic Party, and that hurts them not having bold reforms to keep markets strong even if they get in the White House for eight more years if the economy is lurching at a sustainable rate and not enough full-time jobs are available to everyone who wants to work. They will be known as the party that wrecked the American economy when there is no fabled recovery after the next crash they hit us with in twelve years.

"Have you actually heard her give a stump speech? She would throw it right back at the president when he is using his divisive rhetoric."

"I think I know how that goes. That is not how Democrats get elected."

They walked into the open square where many young people were standing to hear all about the senator's plans for capitalism with rules and ending the kleptocracy that kept the system working in favor of labor exploiters.

After five minutes of another person speaking to introduce her, Senator Buffet hopped up onto the stage and boldly declared that in order to get anything done in DC, they would need to pass comprehensive reforms and take back all the wealth the oligarchy had stolen from the middle class. "We the workers will not continually be exploited by the American billionaire class, and our message of 'Where will you hide with your toys while we go looking for you?' is all over the media now. My campaign will not take money from Big Oil, Big Pharma, Big Ag, and Big Tech, along with bankers engaging in financial speculation, but it sure has made a difference taking money from the tobacco industry and the few gun manufacturers behaving responsibly that we do not want to put out of business seizing their corporate charters and assets in getting ads up in early voting states, and we are polling very high right now. Who says you cannot take money from a political action committee?

"I am here to tell you that what Americans want now more than ever is big structural, financial, and economic overhaul. That is why I have doubled down recently on the importance of ending the fractional reserve method for issuing debt that I do not see middle-class families paying off soon. I also know that it does not sell well to pitch a tax on the middle class, which is why I started my campaign with six pillars for financing the economic overhaul. First, cut corporate welfare. Second, tax corporate profits as part of keeping CEOs from getting money through theft. I call it what it is. Third, start a progressive wealth tax and a progressive income tax to start offering public goods to be sold at a profit to the government. Fourth, I will make it so that the estate tax is restored. Fifth, I will make it so that everybody must pay into social security. And sixth, I will start a stock sale tax. With these taxes, I can guarantee everyone who is able to work a living-wage job. They will have a secure retirement. They will have ten million green housing units available to them and public broadband. I will make sure everyone who wants access to health care, childcare, and a college education can obtain those public goods as well."

She continued, "There is another candidate in the race who is talking about raising the minimum wage to $20 and lowering the workweek to thirty hours and providing thirty million jobs and twenty million new green buildings and starting a guaranteed income above poverty (UBI) program and guaranteeing new green housing to all who want access to that. We need to face the facts that a land value tax and a financial transactions tax are polling low, because once you throw those in, you have a steady-state economy with no new growth. Taxes slow down the economy, and we must keep rolling according to the polling. Capitalism is polling higher than socialism. See, I am very much for remaking the economy, but I know I would hear a lot of complaining from centrist Democrats in Congress about losing seats. Personally, I think it would be a positive experience for them if they voted for comprehensive legislation even if they went away for a six-year period where we had no supermajority. When they pass legislation that is not comprehensive, it is ineffective and can be undone. The centrists give the socialists the ammo to declare Democrats to be enabling fascism to lay claim to your vote. That's plain stupid. For a lot of those guys and gals, it is about power. I sure would hate to be them now having lost touch with the middle class. They have pulled the floor out from under them. They are, in effect, working class if they are carrying a lot of debt and will realize it soon. You don't have to worry about that with me. I am conscientious even when I am rooting out corruption in DC and destroying reputations. If they've lost their reputation because of me, it's only because they deserved it."

"Karma is a bitch!" flashed across the LED screen.

On the LED screen in the back flashed her campaign slogan: "Only the Best for America!"

"Now is the time where I take questions from the audience." She grabbed the microphone from its position and walked around the stage pointing at people and asking them what was on their mind.

A White girl in her twenties was handed a microphone, and she asked Senator Buffet why they should listen to her message when she was not a Democrat until she was in her thirties. "Well, you see the thing is, you are never wrong when you decide to move further to the left. Whether that be on progressive reforms, constitutional challenges that require passing an amendment, or even morality. I always like to remind everybody that I was a lawyer for the ACLU before I taught at Brown, and I have had two hundred endorsements from the most left-leaning lawyers and teachers in the country. I am not only courting devout Christians from the South. I am a senator from Rhode Island. I believe I need a much broader coalition of voters than that to get elected. I have, however, not ignored you and am here on Christmas Eve of all occasions. A vote for me is a vote for someone who would never just ignore what others might consider flyover territory."

An eighteen-year-old White girl asked her what made her think she was electable.

"You see… Now I have never been asked a question as direct as that from a Southerner before…but I do have what I think is the perfect response. Never ever back off from what you have already done and said unless you are becoming more liberal and confrontational. There is no reason to do that at all. It is not the direction the world is heading in. Also remember to be tough as nails. When you have fascism on the rise as economic markets are collapsing and all those people enabling them with half-assed attempts at passing good bills, you must be one tough broad. If anybody tries to climb over me, even if it is in the form of interrupting at a debate, I will shred that mother to pieces. Can I get a hell yeah?"

"Hell yeah!" said the audience.

"Hell yeah!" said the LED screen in the background.

"I cannot handle this," said Sundar. "I knew Savannah was starting to draw pagan butterflies, but that is way too much. She didn't have to go over the top doing that outside of a house of worship bought by the state. They are not even that callous in Europe. That person should not be rising in the polls because she is like this. She will lose momentum after Michigan votes. Even if religious attendance is down in cities in the Midwest and South, you cannot be flagrantly irreverent like that and get into the White House as a radical leftist, at least not yet. You should not like her for being like this. Even if she made it to the top 3, how is that going to help society? She probably does not allow religious liberty. At least if she says she does, it is not the way they think it should be guaranteed them down here. What type of example is she setting for our young women who want to run for office? When did Americans decide to run a godless Jezebel hussy for president?"

"The Americans would get an awesome president if they finally had a president like that!" Travis said.

"Travis, nobody wants an old lady with a heart for evil running the country, not the most powerful one in the world. Stop encouraging women to act like that."

"But she wants to redirect spending from the Pentagon to reinvest in rebuilding the consumer base in addition to redistributing wealth. That means the military will not be a big-enough industry to threaten countries like Iran, and those Islamic republics like those in Pakistan and other countries get left alone and can have secular democracies of their own making. The reactions against the West with Sharia law would go away."

"Travis, are you okay with raising a good girl? Because that is what most mosque-goers expect in the end from people who do not practice abstinence who want to observe official Islamic rites such as weddings and funerals. They will want your daughters to practice abstinence, wear head coverings, and not participate in sports. They have a double standard even if they started more liberal than the followers of Jesus did."

"Would you like to go see that exotic dancer? She may give us all BJs if we come on the outside."

"You are wrong to talk like that, Sanjay, and you are wrong to ask me about whether or not I will back off challenging patriarchy, Ranveer. I do not want children, and I sleep with pro-choice girls who expel the unwanted clump of cells from their womb. You can get over patriarchy in the West, and it is not difficult for oppressed people to migrate and seek asylum."

"*I* will let you have it then. Most will not. At some point, you need to go live your own life away from the mosque."

"You will let me have what?"

"That you are a closet Muslim. You are like that belly dancer. Sanjay, you need to leave those people alone. They live outside the mainstream anyway in the Middle East and Asia. Your callous remarks don't intimidate them."

"Who lives outside the mainstream? Rotten people?"

"Entertainers. Entertaining people."

"You probably can get an adult entertainer here in Savannah, Georgia, but she may not look like that dancer. Promise me that if you bring a girl back to your motel room, she gets paid and you use protection unless it is oral, with you probably having hep C already."

"That makes sense, not the part where you were lecturing me like I was the douchebag all night. I was not going to coerce her into it. I honestly don't mind paying a whore, but I guess it will cost less to get one just to pleasure me and Sundar."

"Ranveer and I will be going to our motel room. With the Gothic feel of Savannah at the holidays and the mood in the city right now, I like walking through it on Christmas Eve a bit before I head back."

"Okay, dude, I thought getting a White chick to boss around would be more fun."

"It'll give you a break for a moment. You haven't got a good night's sleep in three nights. You'll be realistic in the morning about the plausibility of socialism here in the land of opportunity."

Travis went walking along the riverfront starting at a higher-end hotel a few blocks from their motel at midnight with Ranveer, and then they walked back to their motel. He unlocked the door to their room, and he went to bed with the door locked. He woke up at 10:00 a.m. hungry and with no nearby places to get breakfast. He walked by the other motel room, and Sanjay and Sundar were in the room still asleep with a topless White girl in Sundar's bed smoking. "She got to live out a fantasy last night—devil's three-way."

"I was not aware that was a thing."

"In the West, we can make it one. No homo. Also, Ranveer was up earlier and took the car to go get us our fast-food breakfast and then sent out a text saying he would be getting back soon after he was done ordering. He got you an egg biscuit. That was at 8:30 a.m."

"Okay. I will go get a drink from a vending machine here, and we can decide where to go today. Have you checked out Tybee Island?"

"I have not."

"We could go there today and then again tomorrow when the businesses are open before heading to Atlanta."

They drove to Tybee Island. They stopped at a restaurant that was modeled after a tropical inn/dive from a Hemingway novel. It was situated on a lot of acreage around marshes leading out to the ocean just before you reach the city of Tybee Island. There were waterfowl all over the marsh along with sojourners such as sandhill cranes. There were also cats loose and roaming around the property.

"This joint is about like a wildlife refuge."

"I thought it might be necessary to have bell collars on the cats if they roamed around all the time."

"I don't see any migrant songbirds here that cats are likely to kill and eat for the sport of it, so I would say it's probably fine for its Hemingway theme."

"Oysters are good to eat in months that have an *r* in them. You avoid food poisoning that way. It's a problem with all the oysters and has been for decades. Polluting industries may have something to do with it. If it's in that organism, you don't feel sick along with it unless you do it in the summer."

"Do they not have a vegetarian option?"

"They may. Why not go pescatarian for a moment? It's just a liberal vegetarian."

"I would rather have a fried catfish sandwich if I did that."

"Travis, why would you do that? Fish are more sentient than oysters. Let's get a bucket of oysters," Ranveer offered.

The waiter stopped by and took their drink requests and took their orders. Sanjay, the shortest and plumpest of the group, tried a po'boy sandwich. Sundar had calamari, as he noted that it was also part of the phylum Mollusca, along with oysters, and better suited for their plans today. They ordered some side dishes associated with Gullah cuisine. They drank the alcohol and used the gift of gab. They headed over to Tybee Island, where most of the fast-food restaurants were closed for Christmas Day. They walked on the beach as the cold Atlantic surf rolled up and crested higher than what he had seen in the Carolinas and Virginia Beach, the farthest he had ever been along the Atlantic coast.

"Is a storm in the forecast? Because the sky is a normal shade of blue for this time of year, and I do not see any rain."

"Scattered thunderstorms may be arriving later."

"Well, okay, I have not seen the waves rise that high at this time of year before."

He saw a lot of starfish, sea urchins, and sand dollars on the beach.

"I actually know how to tell if those are alive or dead," said Sanjay. "This sand dollar is alive. I can tell it is because it is brown and velvety. This one over here that is bleached out and smooth, having lost its spindly tentacles for moving around, is dead and is safe for pocketing. This starfish has those even if it is not moving. I do not want to take it. That one over there may be different."

They walked over fifteen feet to look at it. "It doesn't move. I can take it and dry it out, but when it starts to smell, it is rank. We can get rid of it. I will try to find a dead sea urchin or two and another dead sand dollar. A dead sea urchin has no spines. Look for the ones that have actually lost the urchin in them. They are definitely dead."

When they had collected a few specimens of dead sea creatures for beach cleanup, they headed back into Savannah on the night of the year when it was the least active. They sat down in front of the TV and watched *Indiana Jones* movies, as those were the least Christian-themed classics that appeared on the American TV stations each year. When they had wrapped up *Temple of Doom* and *The Last Crusade*, they went back to the Moroccan restaurant for dinner, and that dancer had returned for her Christmas concert. She started by singing "Touch Me" by the Doors, and she danced to the beat of the drums. Travis and the guys were enjoying the show she was putting on for her Christmas guests. She sang "(I've Had) the Time of My Life," the theme song from *Dirty Dancing*, and then arrived over to talk with the group.

"What did you think of my numbers tonight?"

"I loved them," Travis told her. "You did something awesome then."

"Travis likes a desi girl," said Sundar.

"I will give you my number, Travis—that is, in case you ever come back through Savannah during busier times for the people here and would like to meet some locals. The summer tourist season is better for that than the holiday shopping period."

They wrapped up the meal and were back at the hotel by ten o'clock and asleep by eleven o'clock. When they woke up, they made plans to leave for Atlanta before driving all night through Florence, South Carolina, to Ecstasy Beach in time for Ranveer and Travis to start their next semester. They packed up and left the hotel quickly and crossed the state to get to Atlanta in four hours. They found their hotel room. Travis knew them well enough by this time to know that they would not be the type to do a trolley tour in Savannah, but he talked them into checking out the Atlanta High Museum of Art the day they arrived before going downtown to window-shop, possibly hit up some after-the-season sales and eat at a pizza parlor. They had tickets to see the Atlanta Hawks play an NBA game the next night. The Atlanta Museum of Art had a traveling exhibition on Woodstock as well as one on the Vietnam War that caught their interest. It started to dawn on them why he liked to volunteer at the museum and be around the artists.

"It is as tough to make it as an artist working in the fine arts media as it is in the music industry or in the theater. I would love to have an exhibition of my own someday as well as act and sing on the stage. It is a fun crowd to run with, but it is exclusive. It is difficult to capture any momentum without having a degree in the fine arts. My parents are not like that about letting me get an arts degree."

"That's all of us as well. They want it to be something prestigious and reverent. Sundar already has his law degree. Ranveer is working on a graduate degree in biology, hoping to get a patent and skip med school. Sanjay is taking the full seven years allowed to get a degree in English and wants to be an English professor."

"I have my counseling degree. There is more money in the American art market. It is anti-humanist, and that bothers me because I think the wealthy Americans have got that started and want to keep it going badly and not lose money the way European billionaires have had to part with it through structures that don't produce more profits for them."

"Oh, that was a rambling William Faulkner-type sentence," Sanjay said.

"It would be great to have a team to bring my drawings and mathematically designed art constructions to life in a traveling exhibition."

"Let's go and see where the men's clothing stores are downtown. I don't want to buy that as much as I want pizza."

"I am the same. The tickets to the game were expensive."

"The Hornets will beat the Hawks. That always happens. The Hawks don't have the same luck recruiting a lot of talent as the Hornets."

"The Hornets win against newer teams. They are more fun to see playing at home now than the Hawks are. Support NC. That's where I'm from."

When they had finished eating, they headed back to their hotel room and looked through a visitor's guide in order to try to find out what to pack into tomorrow's day before they left.

"Apparently, a place called Stone Mountain is a popular draw, but I don't know if it's for White Southerners or people of color plus foreigners."

"I just checked, and it is. Find something better to do. I don't know if there is anything we would be interested in after the game ends, and it starts at eight. There may be another state park to stop at and walk through on the way to South Carolina. We need to go to the game."

The Hornets beat the Hawks. The score lifted twenty points in favor of the visiting team the last quarter, but the home team kept their score in the fifties. And in basketball, it could get really high in the last quarter if one team would get worn out.

"That was a good game," Sanjay said. "We can start heading back home."

They arrived back in Ecstasy Beach, South Carolina, in the evening. He and Ranveer got into their cars and drove back to their apartment. He had ended up with a better holiday season than he would've had he been at home. He did want to know when he would be seeing the Big Blue Guy next.

CHAPTER 4

Travis continued work on his counseling degree from his apartment with Ranveer in Ecstasy Beach. He was planning to wrap up his coursework and leave the South for good, but he needed to check the country out a bit more. He had booked a reservation to a New Age retreat outside of Fresno, California, and was going to investigate the lives of people in California and Oregon on spring break. He would check out Yosemite as well since he would be driving through there. He preferred flying into Portland. He had also decided to check out New England and was going to need to go on a road trip to find out what he must about places to go to escape his family once and for all.

In February, it was convenient for Ranveer to let him out of his rental agreement. He moved back in with Viviane and Hank Sr., and they had begun making snide remarks about him where he could hear and had started acting like they were not. He knew not to call them on it while he was living with them. Once before, when he had his hospitalization, he heard that a guy with a lower intellect than him had his family change his diagnosis from bipolar to paranoid schizophrenic when he was making decisions they did not approve of but that at the same time his family wanted to look like they were involved in rehabilitating their child. At the same time, they did everything they possibly could to encourage a suicide on the part of the guy by controlling his life in ways parents should be reported for doing. They would not help him open a bank account. They would not help him be successful unless he held their ridiculous worldview and would sabotage him in his endeavors locally there in town, hoping that he would realize he needed to nurse them through their dying years before he magically subsisted off state support. They were openly hostile to him and spread lies about him, and the hospital counselors went along with it once his family had secured a diagnosis of paranoid schizophrenic, reporting paranoia that he did not agree should be a part of his records.

He decided to volunteer with the Community Action Agency's Meals on Wheels program once he was back in town and would continue that along with his museum docent responsibility in Charleston on an irregular basis as well as receive voice and piano lessons from Viola again after a three-month hiatus. He dutifully applied himself to the miserable coursework, completely aware that he was majoring in heresy. His instructors said that his work was good enough to get A grades and that he was doing the right thing citing sources even if they were not evangelical Christian sources. He ended the semester in March because his counseling degree was a lightweight one. Then he left on his road trip to go check out the Berkshires and Boston and to drive up by the Great Lakes and see Niagara Falls in Buffalo, New York, before driving Interstate 90 across the state to the Massachusetts Turnpike outside of Albany.

He packed up the bare necessities he needed to take if he was going to be returning. He then drove across North Carolina and into Knoxville, Tennessee, and then into Lexington, Kentucky. He knew that he could get a passport and airfare to Europe and be content with that purchase instead of leaving his car there in North Carolina to die. He was hopeful that in the meantime, he could be carless in Portland and not have to carry auto insurance and get car repairs and gas and to pay less for city transport. The inconvenience of having to ride the bus or light-rail and wait to leave the neighborhood and to know which one to be in at which times did not bother Travis. City life in America seemed more genuine than rural life in America at this time. He drove on through Lexington and in through Cincinnati as the state of Ohio was busy doing intensive repairs to its roads.

When he got off the bridge in Cincinnati, he got to drive through some pretty towns in Ohio that resembled older European hamlets until he drove into Columbus, Ohio. That city was having issues with homeless vagrants arriving on the streets in the morning after heading off them for warmth in the evening. Many were taking to the streets begging. Many were congregating outside motels and other parking lots looking for vehicles to break into. People who were living out of their cars and not doing it at national and state parks were running a risk if they did not make sure every door was locked each time they got out of their cars, and they were running a risk if they parked at a motel and were not keeping their motel door locked.

Travis had brought a lot of food with him and a comforter and pillows for bundling in the colder weather. He was thinking about sleeping out of his car. He was still going to check out what living out of a motel in the wrong part of the city in an economic recession would look like. He checked into a motel frequented by sex workers and old nymphomaniacs as he entered Columbus.

He woke up at 1:00 p.m. his first day in Columbus; and he saw, much to his delight, that an old nymphomaniac dealing with what might or might not be a long battle with madness, depending on her intellectual capacity, had parked next to him and had been opening her car doors and shutting them all morning. When he opened the door to his hotel room and decided what he needed to bring in from his car, he noticed that she had got out and locked the door electronically with the keypad on her key ring and said out loud, "That is all you should have to do," as if she was the most important person in his world. She looked used up and haggard and smelled of smoke.

Travis got his laptop out of his backpack in his car and set it out and started his language lessons. He took a break to read in one of them.

Apparently, the old nymphomaniac had rented a hotel room upstairs above his head and was inviting all the teenage boys of Columbus, Ohio, over to her hotel room if they wanted her to make men out of them. Upon speaking to the hotel manager, he found out that she had rented this room herself and was playing at she-pimping. He wouldn't reveal whether she had done it before. She had the group of guys walking by his room as he had his language lessons, making remarks such as "Looks like you could get some behind," "There is plenty better to do than wasting your time here in Columbus this way," and "There's a whore upstairs if you have cash."

He was making his way through an entire unit in all his languages and reading despite the constant sounds coming from upstairs as the local teenage guys had their way with her. He couldn't imagine a teenage guy would want to have sex with her, even if they were not raised in Christian community, but that was what they were doing. He went to get bean burritos during her whoring, and she was at it when he got back. He took a break to get pizza, and she was at her whoring still. He settled in for an early bedtime so that he could leave and be on the road to get to Buffalo, New York, and see Niagara Falls tomorrow, and she started her whoring up again. It was a tremendous accomplishment for her; he was certain of that. This was just how she spent her weekends. He did not have any idea why it wasn't going on still when he got up and checked out the next day, but at least the homeless vagrants who had been staring at his car from the parking lot across the street all day yesterday had not shown up yet today.

He left Columbus for Cleveland, and on the other side of town, the road markers were not clear. He found his way to the other side of Erie, Pennsylvania—the side that faces Buffalo, New York—and he drove on into New York on the Great Lakes. The change in the climate was noticeable by the vineyards that had sprung up on the New York countryside on his way to Niagara Falls. There was a much more noticeable live-and-let-live attitude of tolerance and less of a pretentious small-town busybody air about the entire state that was missing in the last two states he had been through. It made him reluctant to head back down South without a good reason. He had seen this in the media since he was a kid, and it was observably true. Even if the taxes were higher in those states, it paid off when the people there minded their own business.

There are a few religious nuts up here. A small few. They will lay claim to you. You must make certain to clarify for them repeatedly how you are not one of them. They will not understand why you are not as enamored of them as they are. If lies get started concerning you, everybody knows who is getting it started. They think that, perhaps, by lying about you while not knowing you, then you will decide to spend eternity with them. These people are nuts. And who, Travis, do you say I am?

That voice in my head I call my intuition.

Oh. Others call me God. They do anything I tell them to do.

He saw something in the rearview mirror. It was the Big Blue Guy sitting in the back seat.

Between the two of us, I am okay that you don't think I am God, and I am okay that you don't really trust me and do anything I tell you to do. I am having the time of my life with the others.

Travis drove along Highway 99 to Buffalo and remained mindful that he had a few hours of daylight to check out Niagara Falls on the US side. He took pictures of it, including one of himself at it. Then he grabbed a bite to eat and headed on out of town. Buffalo was not an extremely large American city to drive through though it did have many big buildings in its downtown area. It also had some nice residential properties, and it had some neighborhoods in decline as he headed on his way out of the city. He saw that there were many more businesses doing well there than in some of the other big cities he had seen in the South and the Midwest so far. He noticed that many of the smaller cities along the Great Lakes in Ohio and Pennsylvania were doing well keeping their small businesses around.

He left Buffalo and merged onto Interstate 90 across New York. He had a very long drive ahead of him. He paid a $6 fee to pass across the state of New York to the Massachusetts Turnpike, which was Interstate 90 in Massachusetts. He made a pit stop at one of the service areas for a bite to eat and left the interstate in Syracuse to get gas not too awfully long after getting it in Buffalo. He stayed the night in Albany. The next day, he grabbed I-90 to the Massachusetts Turnpike and started to leave the state. He drove out of New York and into Massachusetts and found himself in the Appalachians. He traveled through the Berkshires. He left Berkshire County and entered Hampden County, where the city of Springfield, Massachusetts, is situated. He had a room booked at an inn in a hamlet outside of the city. It was a chain inn and not a small-business inn like some of those he had seen in Ohio as he traveled. After he checked in, he grabbed a bite to eat, and then he headed on down to plant his feet in Connecticut. He then drove all around Hampden County on both sides of the interstate. He found that there were two churches like his parents' in that county. He also saw many others and had the impression that the odd evangelical churches in Western Massachusetts had more competition still from the mainline evangelical Protestants, the Orthodox, and particularly, the Catholic Church than was the case in the South.

People might go to church on Sunday morning if they felt like it, but they might also go fishing or go to work, and it was far from being an oppressive theocracy. The same could not be said for many towns in the Deep South. His own hometown of Olde Towne, North Carolina, used to be as bad before the workforce started to leave and the town was left with wealthy businesses that employed a few people, such as his father's sustainable architecture firm, and property owners on a beach that got storm-battered more frequently than Ecstasy Beach in South Carolina. He had found out that the area had started a local currency. He went into one of the regional bank branches that he saw carried BerkShares and saw that many business owners in the area still carried them. He saw boutique stores filling the main streets on the side of Hampden County above I-90, and even if not all of them were green businesses with community-owned debt issued by independent community development banks, the area had more small businesses that had not been boarded up during the economic recession. Some had Help Wanted signs out. This region kept money in its community and did not bring in a lot of chain stores. It was also a beautiful area.

As he drove through the county, he noticed that there was a gorgeous panorama of tree-covered hills dropping off slowly to the South as far as the eye could see. He spent his time there and found many quality items to fill the trunk of his car with before he left the area, and he had many pleasant interactions with retail associates. Some people there were losing it as well, but late capitalism's madness had not penetrated the country this far North. The peace disrupters would be dishonest, lying-ass, ignorant sons of bitches who could not handle it when their falsified worldview would crumble around them and the only thing they'd find worth persevering over was destroying anyone else whose way of life actually made sense. *Well,* Travis thought to himself, *I don't have every intolerant bigot from nowhere towns in the South chasing me up here just yet. Something must be drawing their hearts to the South. It may be the land itself. It may be that elsewhere, slavery is gone with the wind. When they do start arriving, they need to go to reeducation camps immediately.*

You still have that New Age retreat out West and all the ideas that get tossed out on the West Coast to stay to check out, said the Big Blue Guy / extradimensional traveler aka God to fundamentalists.

Travis rose early the day he left the Berkshires. He did not go there to party. He was heading to Boston next, and there was so much to do in Boston. There was also a lot to see if you did it in the daylight. The way he had planned his trip, he was expecting to see a city with more variety than he had seen on the East Coast, but he had not been to New York yet. He was looking forward to living it up with a different crowd from the roadhouse White trash that filled the atmosphere of expensive clubs he had been to in the South. He knew that there was a Whiteness to Boston and that there was roadhouse White trash in Boston as well. The Whiteness of Boston even among the usually devout Catholic presence was firmly established to him a few days after arriving there, but there was also a progressive Ivy League school and a wide generational divide where it was also present. Any other Southerners who found themselves this far up North would be fish out of water. They would be missing the theocratic modus operandi that prevailed in the Deep South and in Tennessee and in North Carolina where they had at least managed to accrue some wealth off selling scenery such as the Great Smokies and other ideas.

My god, I cannot stand those people. I would rather do anything else than winter down South, especially some place like Mexico. I will take out a debt consolidation loan with a low monthly payment for five years to help me make the payment on my apartment lease and pay for my car's taxes and somehow make more money next year. I am so over all that BS. God, if you even care, please keep the nuts in the Hispanic communities and the nuts in the White working classes who think there is more to church life than there actually is away from me. Do it for my safety. I do not, for the life of me, understand why they think I still care about the same things they are hung up on. If you need them to fill a purpose, please direct them to fill it far away from me. I simply do not care about them. Amen, Travis prayed at the end of his thought.

The Big Blue Guy did not respond.

Travis had gone to the club. He had ten ounces of weed in his possession at his hotel for the moment and one ounce on him when he went out. He found some Canadians to go to a Bruins game with at the Ice Arena and was hoping he could make it to Fenway Park for a Boston Red Sox game at some point in the summer. He did need to leave and head home soon. He was not up here to stay and was not going to blow through his money at the hotel to meet more acquaintances before heading back home.

He got back to North Carolina late and was still planning on heading back out in April. His parents gave him frosty stares the entire week he was in before he headed back out, and he had no idea why. He had used up every last bit of the Mary Jane before he crossed state lines.

CHAPTER 5

IT WAS APRIL. TRAVIS HAD ARRIVED AT THE PORTLAND Airport, picked up his luggage, and had taken a train to a car rental location. After he had picked up his car rental and checked into his hotel, he drove to check out a few apartments he had looked at renting. He had a few interviews he had been accepted to go to. All but one of them were at chain stores; the other was at a nightclub for him to work at as a shirtless bartender. The prices of the apartments were all about the same as was the pay for the part-time positions he was looking at. He would need to arrange two of those before making a deposit on an apartment, and he had enough wiggle room to determine how to locate near whichever neighborhood was closest to his workplaces, which needed to be in the commercial district. This was something he would not have attempted had he not had the resources necessary to flee his family and their nonsense, having gone along with it long enough. So much for Boston; he needed to go car-free.

He would not need to have a car with him in this area because they had done very well with regional development and public transport. In a week, he had made all his interviews and left the hotel to go to California. He got to arrange a two-week vacation in April for himself as a student switching to being a distance learner his second semester. Having his coursework completed for the year, hopefully forever, and getting ready to end his position at the museum of art after the exhibition on Dada and Surrealist artists, He was ready for a move, even though he planned on doing Meals on Wheels twice more. He drove across the state line into Northern California where there was a retreat at a resort for that week where he could learn from old-school New Age maestros everything that he knew he needed to explore next. He was going to spend five days in a series of in-person classes. After all the reading he had done on the New Age movement after giving up on Christianity and Islam as incompatible with progress and after noticing their practitioners in the South behaving as saboteurs of socialism, he was looking into the occult to see if he could find a better philosophy of life. He had to take two weeks off practicing his Hindi Bollywood song for his voice recital, and he hoped he would not lose vocal strength. He was also taking two weeks off from practicing "Clair de lune." He would probably be able to sing in the community chorus in town that Viola was helping him prepare to sing in; he just could not sing Christian songs or sing in a church. He was certain he would have a tremendous degree of social and economic mobility after moving to the West Coast.

He drove into the resort and found trees and ferns and vegetables in raised beds and verdant lawns that were probably there for natural healer remedy or regenerative gardening classes. He glimpsed people in clothing doing tai chi on a bare patch of lawn. He parked, registered at the front desk, and received his key and set his baggage down in his hotel room. He brushed his teeth and trimmed his beard and set out to make it to the group orientation and social. He noticed variety with instructional and meditative classes about like a medium-sized conference and was not sure what to expect. A lot of the titles of the instructional classes made no sense to him. He had not read any books by these authors. He knew he was going to be participating in the Kundalini yoga class on Tuesday and Thursday. The brochure claimed that Kundalini yoga was an offshoot of African Kemetic yoga, which was practiced in Atlantis. He made his way into the orientation on time and noticed that he was one of about a dozen people that were there. He briefly gave an introduction. He stated that he was a spiritual seeker moving to Portland and needed a better philosophy of life. The speaker whose name tag said Reina told everyone that if they were here on a spiritual journey, they had many options with people giving classes this week and that there were many training sessions going on year-round. Those changed from time to time, and that was an excellent way to spend a week if you returned with an open mind when you wanted to stay long enough to get a certification.

Some of the people that gave introductions were there for a spiritual journey, some were there for learning about ideas for green living that were not covered in the mainstream media and to take beginner's instruction for a month, and some were open to both. The orientation was brief, and then there were drinks, and Reina had left. "Does anybody here drink ayahuasca tea?" said a guy named Don, who had apparently left a casino operation recently.

"I'm not sure. You may not need it for your spiritual experience," said a woman who introduced herself as Valerie. "How would you feel if you felt you had experienced samadhi and you had to mention having done it on ayahuasca tea?"

"Yeah, bro, save that for later," said a man who introduced himself as Raul. Travis could tell immediately that Raul was a man on a mission. He was on a mission to change people's political views.

"We do have champagne. It is much sweeter. It doesn't have the same liftoff though," said Valerie.

"I have actually taken ayahuasca before, and you may need to hug a tree shortly after taking it. Otherwise, you may feel like you have lifted off and actually come to lying on the ground," replied Raul.

"You drink it enough and you can do it in a lawn chair like a Long Island iced tea," said Valerie. "What are you taking tomorrow as a class?"

"I was going to go to the class on the messengers from the Pleiades," said Travis.

"What are those?" Raul asked.

"How do you not know about that part of our awakening?" interjected Valerie.

"If I were you, I would go to the class on egregores. They are forms our collective thoughts take on. There may not be anything to these messengers. Then you can hear the talk on the abuses of Big Ag and Big Pharma on Wednesday night," said Raul.

"Do we really need that? I thought it was Big Oil and the Big Banks causing the economy to lose steam. I also thought it would be enough to provide affordable health care and childcare and that we did not need eco socialism," said Travis.

"Do you not think we need a Green New Deal that provides a universal jobs guarantee, a universal pension system, a universal guaranteed income, and a universal housing guarantee as well as a guarantee to make college and health care free for many more Americans? Who really needs a slow-growth economy from one of the parties of War and Wall Street over that garbage deal? Do you think we should let the Republicans send this socioeconomic mode directly to its crash collision at seventy-five miles per hour and not suffer twelve more Occupy years with the Democrats?" inquired Raul.

"What do you think should be done, Raul?" asked Travis.

"He thinks you should vote for the Independent Left Unity ticket," said Valerie.

"That would be great, but honestly, how much legislation can you expect to get passed on a direct democracy and a moral economy with a blue congress and presidential administration? It probably is only the progressive income tax, progressive wealth tax, and raising social security that are popular when people are polled now," said Don.

"That will not get us what we need to have a more egalitarian and peaceful society. You should also throw in restoring the estate tax, and you must cut corporate welfare and have land value, financial transaction, and corporate profits taxes bare minimum to keep those programs going continuously."

"There are not that many people where I am heading back who care about all those extra taxes. They also do not care about ecology even though it was noticeably hotter there the past two years than it ever has been before, and they do not care about peace or else they would have voted for Senator Buffet. And they certainly do not care about non-hierarchy judging by how many of them attend male-controlled churches. I know Vice President Libby will not do what he needs to do with Big Oil and the Big Banks. People down South do not care about global temperatures rising and are more than happy to be conscripted. They are very hardy people, and if you want to keep them in the union, then you need to back off all the rest of that."

"You are awesome when you make it concise," said Valerie.

"I actually do not think that about Travis right now if he backs off the other things that quickly when Senator MacDonald drops out of the race each time. All the Democrats care about is power. If the number of nonvoters goes up each time, they throw an election that would solve everything. You should make it all those things I just mentioned, and you should add more things. Public banking and public money are being discussed along with a land value tax and financial transactions tax to keep a steady-state controlled economy sustainable and issuing money with a debt it can pay off. You should also make it so that when real reforms go through, technology can be harnessed in ways the workers of the cooperative commonwealth have discussed and decided is useful to them. You should also invest in regenerative agriculture and waste-to-energy programs. You should start moving that way because the billionaire class collectively isn't going to do anything but create more problems to solve. There is no profit without having created a problem. The debt must be paid off in the end, and they have pushed the middle class and the working class to the catastrophic brink. They say the economy is healthy and robust now because there is high GDP and a lot of goods waiting to be sold. The variable in the equation that economists are missing is that people are buying less because the economic forecast looks disastrous. Because of the fractional reserve system of printing money, there are now $1,400 trillion in outstanding debt waiting to collapse. That amount of money is equivalent to ten times the gross domestic product of the entire planet." Raul looked angry but not hostile.

"What else can be done?" Travis sighed.

"You should live frugally. This mistake of the previous life span is going to hit us in our own. It is not just for millennials. There are going to be baby boomers who are affected by it as well," said Valerie.

"Is it important to be tacking on a host of health care and agricultural policy overhauls in addition to refusing to vote without options?" asked Travis.

"The Republicans and Democrats are bought out by a banking cartel and are not serious about climate change. The guy giving a talk on Wednesday night knows that there is double that number of bad players in the economy. Big Ag and Big Pharma must be starved of money or else they are going to take out more of their consumer base, pushing them into wage slavery," said Raul.

"So they would increase the minimum wage if they had a super-majority vote and that still would not be enough to increase consumption?" asked Travis.

"They could do that by executive order. Health care, education, housing, and energy costs would continue soaring along with inflation, and the government would go bankrupt, and it would not make a difference raising the amount of social security people receive."

"It is the Annunaki taking revenge on humans. The billionaires are not smart. They think they are benevolent and a force for good through neoliberalism, so they do anything that the Annunaki tell them to do, and they have resented us for a long time," interjected Valerie. The Annunaki were Sumerian gods that likely were alien visitors.

"You do not really need those older wealthy people controlling you, Travis. If you would vote for Vice President Libby, then you could get all the Americans on board with recycling and composting the same as in Europe," said a German woman named Olivia.

"Germans care about recycling and composting more than we do?"

"They also have fewer cars on the road in the frugal five and have automated bus fleets. They have electric high-speed rail, and they also have postal buses that carry passengers, at least in Switzerland and Austria. If you have a German language email, you can send messages in the post. There is high public use of recycling services, and people will send off commonly bought recyclable items and household waste to be converted into energy or compost. They are further ahead of us in economic and social progress over there."

"Well, I guess I will go to the class on Wednesday night."

"That's great. We have better Wednesday night class discussions than most spiritual seekers."

"How about I check out both of those on Monday and Wednesday and do Kundalini yoga and natural healing classes on Tuesday and Thursday?"

"Would you like to join us in the cafeteria?" said the woman who introduced herself as Olivia. "We have beer, lemonade, hard and soft drinks, juice drinks, and water."

"That would be nice."

"Does anybody have an idea about what the new developments are in the messages people have been receiving from extradimensional beings?" asked Don.

"There is a lot going on there that may prove factual, and there may be much there where people are just being fooled with. It was the same with fortune-telling cards like the tarot and *I Ching* and crystal ball revelations for people who lacked clairvoyance. Some of the psychics who are getting information from extradimensional beings are not the scholarly and scientific types and are prone to primitive shamanistic methods and mystical mistakes. You must take the best of what they have to offer and move on. The great thing about it is that it is the most popular movement for universalism across ancient religious traditions, and it can be compatible with natural healing, which is my line of specialty. A lot of the men here get involved with energy healing while at the same time some can lead a séance and help people with past life regressions."

"That is fine. That seems like a mind's framework for true liberation."

"You have the correct attitude."

"I have already been seeking out lucid dreams." Lucid dreaming was when an individual would become aware they were dreaming from within the dream.

"That was a good place to start if you already had scholarly knowledge on ancient wisdom and science. That is not controversial outside of backward families and communities. Some people participate in primitive shamanism and outdated mystical orders of the world's major religions and cannot remove all the dross we do not need as a global community. That is the type of New Age spirituality we try to cultivate here," Olivia finished.

Travis went to sleep and had his third experience in lucid dreaming and, for the first time, conversed with another sleep world visitor in French. He didn't wake up to record it in a dream journal, which was altogether lovely, because it wasn't always the best to wake up after drinks. He woke up refreshed, popped a brown seaweed supplement capsule, and washed it down with water. He slipped on his clothes and got his hair presentable, forgot that he missed his opportunity to shower since he normally did that at night, and headed down to breakfast glad that it wasn't a hot day and that he didn't need to exercise. He poured himself a glass of orange juice and filled his plate with a cream cheese Danish and blueberry muffin.

"Do you eat like that all the time?" asked Valerie.

"Oh no, I do not. I do not really have a sweet tooth."

"That first workshop will be coming up soon."

"So you said you were training to be a doula at a gentle birth clinic as well as a natural healer veterinarian."

"Well, yes, I was, one of those courses you would be good to show up for, I believe. It used to just be a medicine woman thing here, but I will let you know I think it helps out sustainable homesteaders as well as animal caretakers. The lady who is talking to us today about the messengers from the Pleiades is also very much in favor of holistic health. She doesn't allow herself vaccinations or give blood, and she would never be an organ donor. She knows that hospitals are necessary for surgeries, but she has been able to avoid them like a lot of other people. I don't know how it is for you—you know, where you are from, have a bit of a drawl thing going on there—but many people on the West Coast are able to get by not driving a car. That is the ideal for green living. Especially when you are older, it goes a long way in protecting you from other drivers. I don't know. It may be that case with 5G and driverless buses when people care about that coming to the states. Maybe mostly buses and trains fix that, but where are the jobs there when they get automated? I tried to look up the status of seaweed as an alternative to plastic last night, but I was drunk and forgot the resort does not have internet access. Anyway, they have made it impossible to be a freelance midwife basically everywhere, but you can do it at a gentle birth clinic under the supervision of a doctor. You can even give birth underwater. The doctor has to be there for that. Otherwise, you would only need to go get them if they came out suboptimal, like with an umbilical cord wrapped around their neck. When women guide women through birth, mortality is lower. You can even bring the other kids in to watch you do it."

"That is cool. Though you should send the kids out if the umbilical cord is wrapped around the baby's neck."

"Oh, there's no need for that. Women have even given birth before at gentle birth clinics for camera crews. There is a movie here in our DVD library called *Gentle Birth Choices*. You could watch it in the rec room. There is nothing in it truly shocking, Travis. You need to know that for a fact. It is true that doctors make billions of dollars circumcising young males every year, but I prefer my sandwiches cut if you know what I mean."

"I do not know that that matters. It seems like it is more of a religious liberty lawsuit waiting to happen than criminalizing corporal punishment in all situations. One is a national law in many countries, and I have not seen that happen with the other apart from female genital mutilation. I do not think it is necessary to keep circumcision. I saw that movie, and I know there is not a good argument in favor of it. I would like to do that class tomorrow morning with you."

"Well, we'll be glad to have you and teach you what we know in two days, and then it is up to you to do some reading after speaking with people who actually have tried it and seen what works and doesn't."

"The course this morning deals directly with extradimensional beings, Pleiadeans being one of them. The course this afternoon—"

"You won't get anything from that. The guy who teaches that is an anus. He talks down to people your age the same way that Reina would have had she not left last night. She is much more personable to conventional people, has got more money out of it than most, yet somehow, she will agree with you on just about anything you want to promote through her network."

As Travis and Valerie went to their morning class, they watched an aged and refined woman who looked like she might have belonged to the beat generation before deciding to stay and join in with the New Age counterculture walk into the room and proceed to talk about the changing model of physics in the universe and how it looked to physicists, as if superstring theory was going to become a plausible theory of everything and that quantum nuclear physics—which had been the main emphasis of researchers since the Cold War Space Race, which only accounted for four dimensions—was now officially an antiquated paradigm and now many people were coming to an understanding that there were eleven dimensions. "There were twenty-two dimensions for the math behind $-mc \times mc$ and its resulting tachyon. We tied up and removed the tachyon with spinning strings, which gave us superstrings because of supersymmetry and supergravity and therefore, actually eleven dimensions. Take my word for it." She also told them that they had the ability to expand their own individual consciousness and travel to the ninth dimension. Travis watched the woman talk, and she sounded convincing as she left it at nine and speculated about ten and eleven. She got into a discussion about her spirit guides and how they were messengers from the constellation of the Pleiades. She also emphasized the importance of living in harmony with two-dimensional life for individuals with three-dimensional consciousness; the microbial world of Protista, prokaryotes, and eukaryotes; and that being in a harmonious relationship with Mother Earth and her first colonizers allowed people to get over sickness from them quicker and not carry diseases to other people.

Travis was on his phone looking up what string theory entailed and speculated that string particles in both light and dark matter and light and dark energy vibrated at higher frequencies up the ladder until they reached the top, which might be where the math was in the realm of the philosophy department for now. He liked some of what she had to offer for an explanation for where these extradimensional beings were coming from and what they were up to. He was worried about the fourth-dimensional beings (they were being called Annunaki now.) They apparently had succeeded in placing a cabal of the wealthy in a few positions of power globally by exploiting their pathetically conditioned-to-be-individualistic egos to use them to help take out the overpopulated working classes often as pathetically conditioned to be individualistic and cruel.

"The world's wealthiest people are overconsuming, and the world's poorest are stabbing one another in the backs so that they can be part of a few to join their ranks. The Annunaki have never been so happy. We must work with the Pleiadeans to return the world to normal before the end of three-dimensional life so that a new epoch for three-dimensional life emerging from prehistoric mycelium that seeded the planet does not have to occur for the sake of the goddess. The replacement of human and plant life could be conducted on the planet before our sun turned into a red dwarf. The Annunaki have had a long-standing prejudice against humanity since we rejected the prediluvian civilization of Atlantis and accepted Romanized religion with its one patriarchal God and no goddess and its inconvenient lack of a belief in reincarnation.

"That is when the Annunaki became fed up with us once and for all, and we lost access to the technology of our ancient civilizations, which was better than anything Rome had to offer, including their take on Christianity. That was when many people tried to make life easier by giving themselves one manifestation in matter and an eternity in the bliss of the heaven of the pleroma. They have seen no reason to have a benevolent attitude toward our human population the same as the Pleiadeans who are naturally benevolent and compassionate like the goddess of the dimension of light. They are closer to her in the hierarchy of consciousness. Sometimes they show us what the future holds, and I believe we are experiencing a crisis where in this New Age, many people will die at the hands of right-wing fascists before we can all either get along and have our evolution in consciousness or return later looking different, possibly upon a newly seeded planet to start again."

She guided the group through a meditation to help them contact the first dimension—a crystal at the center of everything. She guided them through a meditation to help them contact the second dimension—the dimension of microbial life and a dimension of energy. She guided them through a meditation to help them make contact with the third dimension of emotion perfectly and then took them into the fourth dimension, where emotion was flat and the beings were apathetic. Then she took them into the fifth dimension, where the apathetic but beautiful Annunaki were flattened by the benevolent and altruistic Pleiadeans.

"That was a spectacular first lesson. I am glad that I made it to the fifth dimension in my meditations the first day."

"If you have been lucid dreaming, then you have to already be receptive enough to broaden your mind to contact the fifth dimension. My guides told me you were ready, and you did what I would have expected a good student to do all day."

"Now is there going to be any Jungian subconscious voodoo tacked onto this series, or have the New Agers moved beyond that?"

"I would say you would have a clue if you thought I did not care about modern psychological theories. However, some do still mention him in the community. He was an improvement on Freud, and as we enter the New Age, we will find that our previous understanding of the social sciences was immature. We have the information shared with us that we can handle when we as humanity are mature enough to handle it. Sometimes we have taken miracles of science and turned them into a curse, but we are continuously making breakthroughs with our collective intuition. A big problem right now with the socioeconomic mode is that groundbreaking scientific discoveries are being made all the time and they are not reported on in major journals or are not given the press they deserve because there is not enough profit for the investors. The American Medical Association, the Department of Health and Human Services, the Centers for Disease Control and Prevention, and the World Health Organization will not discuss treatment options that do not entail long-term management. They do not care about finding a cure for an illness anymore if they used to not so long ago when smallpox was eradicated. Be glad the next speaker is only giving an hour-long lecture after dinner. He has an unpopular idea with egregores."

"Thank you for bringing me up to speed. It was a pleasure meeting you."

They went together out of the conference hall to the commons and sat down at a table to play board games. Don showed up and got everyone to agree to play Jenga. They also painted and played a game with dice and one with Styrofoam noodles, a version of tic-tac-toe, a sack race, and a game of cornhole. Don beat every other player down, including Travis, whom he got on tic-tac-toe. All the time he would not stop rambling about a nonsense topic no one cared about from his days in the casino industry, and they were more than happy to head back inside for their dinner. Travis was the only one who had not filled out a menu ticket to send to the kitchens, so he had more of the same food. It was cereals and raw fruits and veggies by default. He did make sure that they knew to add eggs and dairy tomorrow; oh well, at least it wasn't pureed food like people in the memory unit at a nursing home would need to have. It still wasn't filling.

"I don't like Don. You know, as a person," said Valerie.

"Is that not a little inappropriate?"

"I thought you might be the same."

"I am not going to respond to something like that."

There was a momentary silence, and then Travis realized he needed to go upstairs briefly to brush his teeth or possibly strike up conversation with another group tonight.

"Well, I won't push that any further. I wish we hadn't taken luncheon and dinner earlier than the other groups today. I might have been able to introduce you to some other people before your week was over," offered Valerie.

"I would have done all right with some of the people at the field day party had Don not been there. I am almost through eating. I will need something more filling from the snack bar later tonight. What is the big thing that old guys come here to learn to be certified in?"

"Oh, I bet they usually try out energy healing first. Some may be able to help with past life regressions and help people find animal guides. Most of them wouldn't like Don the way he is right now."

"I may try to get certification in something like that next year. Do men teach Kundalini yoga?"

"As a matter of fact, they do."

He had finished and was heading upstairs, glad that air-conditioning and heating came along with the electricity, meals, and snacks included at the resort but not expecting them to have doubled down so strongly on removing all traces of corporate advertising to the point that there was not only no internet service outside of an office space and personal cellphones but also no in-room television or magazines in the library he had heard about. As he reached the third landing where his room was, he ran into Raul. "I will be heading back down to go to class in a few."

"What's your hurry? You may find out more away from those lectures." He told him that if he went down to the hall on the first floor and turned to the far left, he would notice that there was a space with a two-floor library that had several books that weren't popular among readers anymore and if he wanted to be shown it, he could find a host of old newspaper and journal articles on microfiche and he might start understanding how severe the problem with some of the internet companies restricting information had become. "Those are major newspapers. They will go with a story a few days and backtrack it to a half-baked lie for a few weeks and then settle the matter for themselves by not going with the original one unless it doesn't involve remaking the economy or a threat to unregulated neoliberalism. I wish people like you would go away and do something about it."

"No one who doesn't want to be destroyed attempts to lead a people like that. Every politician who tries to do the same thing mainstream American media journalists do and mislead the American people gains supporters these days. Every so-called progressive Democrat that made it to the top of the polls the past year participates in misleading Americans according to the documents," said Travis as he paged through the documents.

"It's also WikiLeaks, Travis. Their candidates are wealthy and will back off the progressive movement apart from moving the platform a step further to the left with raising the minimum wage each time. You cannot introduce ideas like those for the public's benefit and back off them and not leave lifelong Democrats alienated. It may not have been a bad idea for them to run. However, the Democratic Party swallows up money from independent parties. The best thing you can do is cut off your money supply to those candidates and give to the independent left unity ticket to get it through its court proceedings with the Democrats. It is sad that way, but if an issue is unpopular with the special interests, it gets reflected in polling and is underreported in the mainstream American media. The trifecta there in corrupt DC with the American television networks, their favored politicians, and their preference for weekly American religious devotion, what has been dubbed the opiate of the masses, has every American hurtling off a cliff. The older people, many baby boomers who are in steep debt, are driving us there because they do not want to take on Wall Street and the inflated Pentagon budget, and everyone else is going along with them for the collision. It's true, Travis. You should put ideas like that up on social media using social language and see if they get any traction. Or you could write and make art. That is much better for helping people develop a survival mentality than going to counseling or to a symbolic bloodletting ceremony every Sunday."

"No one would pay it attention. Would it have been a popular remark to say in most college classrooms? That's about what I was thinking. You wouldn't have any luck with that being accepted by most college graduates without them working on a graduate degree, and then sometimes it might still be rejected collectively by airheads. It would definitely be that in an undergraduate classroom of fifty people or the most political social media outlets, like Facebook and Twitter, rather than being considered to be food for thought. Most people could end up unemployed and severely indebted and still not have enough sense to stop trying to outcompete one another to act the best puppet for the billionaire class. I would have loved to have had a better option than a seminary for my graduate degree than what I had that was affordable. I hate that my parents and my brother encourage me to act like I am less intelligent than I am, like they raised me to stay a part of the middle class as a science-denying, teetotaling fundamentalist moron who doesn't know how the wealthy are in private or how to enjoy the same things they do. I have a malicious brother who has been hostile to me for being well-rounded and showing manners while not remaining at least outwardly religious. He and my parents behaved so creepy the last time I saw them all together at Thanksgiving. They threatened to spread lies about me, and when that did not go anywhere, they started threatening me with blackmail. How can families like that think that will help them remain intact?

"People everywhere do not believe the entirety of the message they are trying to deliver to people. Many of them have been nice to those people for an exceptionally long time, and they have misperceived it somehow as an openness to the gospel. My family replaced the gospel of love with the gospel of hate. They were the first to hurl insults over the former then to do it when I decided that there was not a lot of substance to their Christianity. They would act as saboteurs openly if I moved to join the socialists. Their entire religious community would do it with them and cover for them. They really think that they can keep someone in the church and under their nose by gathering information to use for blackmail—as if the better choice is to be a science-ignoring, capitalist, fundamentalist, blackmailing Christian. No, thanks! How would someone in their right mind who knows how fundamentalist Christians are want to keep a shred of Bible dogma? How would they have a high opinion of their decaying way of life and, as you put it, the parties of War and Wall Street? They really are the scum of the earth rather than the salt."

"That was an immature remark to tack on at the end."

"I thought it was more original than douchebag or scumbag."

"If you stayed here now that you have got this far away from them and continued behaving like this, that would be wonderful. You are going to run into Christians with a privileged position in the organization profit or not-for-profit wherever else you go, except the entertainment industry, and be met with hostility from them. They are convinced they have a monopoly on the culture. It will speed things along for people to realize there is no influence for people when they pivot to religious authorities," Raul said. "I will show you how to look up old newspaper and journal articles on microfiche, and you can miss the first half of the lecture on egregores you had been scheduled to attend."

"That's awesome."

Travis and Raul went through a few microfiches together so Travis could see how to operate the reader, and then he showed him how to look up periodicals and books the old-fashioned way on index cards at a department file cabinet. "And if they do not have what you are looking for, they can even get it on loan from a neighboring library."

"Thank you, Raul. I am also heading back out so I do actually see the lecture. I am definitely coming back here and looking through all this history."

"It does help to know what you are searching for."

"I actually did attend a class today that was intriguing."

"You won't find anything in there on the mischievous Annunaki and benevolent Pleiadeans, the same as you won't on egregores."

The guy who had the after-dinner lecture had a defeatist attitude. Reina was there on the stage nodding along with an open mind and available to lead the audience of seventeen people in a round of applause. Travis noticed that it was her doing it the loudest and not very many others were joining in. The theory this person had was as anti-humanist as what he had seen from the devoutly religious regular attendees among most monotheist practitioners in the nation. Apparently, we all needed to understand that our negative attitudes developed a consciousness of their own and were there to reinforce our old destructive patterns and there was no sign of them breaking anytime soon. That guy probably had seen what Raul was talking about with the sanctimonious airs that Christians gave toward New Agers and other religious minorities outside of these circles.

He still had a negative outlook on recovery for the earth and animals, with the Americans being a global presence and apparently all the major political parties being corrupt. The speaker said that the American economy would continue its military presence regardless of promises being made to them by people pivoting to be their next great political savior; that, in effect, meant that there was not a solution to the sixth mass extinction our planet was facing. The greediest humans were going to use up the earth, as a few nations planned to hoard a few finite resources for themselves rather than part with serious money. He really emphasized his pessimism toward every one of the companies capitalized by the big tech billionaires whom these hippies were the most irritated with and who seemed to be viewed favorably by Americans, even though their combined wealth was worth more than the entire German economy.

"The people with the most influence who are spoken of the most favorably in California as well as New York really do not care at all about the struggles of the world's poorest. The world's poorest would do themselves a tremendous favor by not giving them any money. As bad as that would make a global depression, it would result in a better global deal being forced on the world's wealthiest because the last thing they want is a world without currency and lending and an end to property ownership. They probably threaten other millionaires with ostracization and blacklisting if they do not also try to keep debt creation controlled by the current banking cartel and neoliberal hack appointees at the Fed that they depend on to create everything that would normally have required a redistribution of wealth and not extremely high debt that could become unpayable. What are all those billionaires doing capitalizing all those stock exchanges that heavily to try to sell people goods they don't need instead of having paid a relatively small amount in taxes to deliver the public goods that would expand the social safety net and bring in revenue to pay down the debt? They are going to have to hand over more money in the end than they otherwise would have had to do— money that was not even collected by them morally in the first place.

"I bet that many of them have watched that money pass on into their bank accounts thinking it is theirs to decide how to invest as they saw fit and have watched it move on back out, sometimes much more out than in, and felt no need to worry about it leading to an abrupt end in capitalism. The more they fight a shift in the socioeconomic mode, the more money they will lose for themselves and their families. Those egregores must hate the billionaires who created them."

Reina asked him if those were his closing remarks. The audience and Reina gave him a round of applause for his dystopian, new age speech.

Travis was glad that the speaker had left the stage. He sneaked off to the library to see what all he could find about these agents against humanity, but they were not there on any index cards or microfiche. So he left the library for the night, took a hot shower, and then went off to bed.

In the morning after breakfast, he headed out to walk to Nature's Hospital, a labyrinth of flowering plants, ferns, and trees with some mycorrhizal and saprophytic fungi fruiting rubbery mushrooms along the path that had not been plucked up that were obviously planted on top of mycelium compost to make a peaceful setting for an inconspicuous apothecary.

"Hello!" said Olivia as he walked up for the class. "We have here an apothecary. You only need to correctly identify the plant or mushroom if you didn't plant it yourself. I see you got here early. Have you ever used a natural cure before?"

"I took one this morning. It's a cognitive stimulant, about as powerful as the white-collar drug Modafinil. It is a natural cure from the kingdom Protista."

"Ah yes, that is pure brown seaweed extract, particularly good for the immune system as well as a long productive life, like the Japanese. That is kelp. It used to be referred to as algae. It is not, however, in the same kingdom as algae."

"Ich heiße Travis. Es freut mich, sie kennen zu lernen. Ich spreche ein bisschen Deutsche. I am conversational in French and Dutch as well as speaking English fluently."

"An excellent idea. Today's class is going to be on natural healing for veterinary care. I will have one again on Thursday. I am covering alternatives to pesticides and the future of antibiotic development. It is true mycelium helps us detoxify from the carcinogens in our surroundings. After the Chernobyl meltdown, the mushroom and truffle industry of Eastern Europe and Italy went into decline. Do you know why? It is because they voluntarily carry all the mercury, lead, arsenic, cesium, cadmium, and all the other toxic metals that are produced by radioactive waste, munitions, and nerve gas. You should store radioactive waste above ground, of course, especially once it can be kept to a minimum. Then you can go around picking up dangerous mushrooms that fruit around such sites that can be placed there for mycoremediation, including smelting centers, and cart those off to be stored away from people and wildlife."

"You mentioned that it is the future of antibiotic development."

"Well, that is where antibiotics started. It is not where they are focusing on developing new antibiotics right now. The big thing rendering them useless is big agribusiness and confined animal operations. Those people use them like they don't even do anything. It is the same for medical doctors except for a very few expensive and hard-to-supply ones. They have even used cultures grown from the bowels of other people to produce new expensive antibiotics to shove down people's throats when they go into a hospital for an extended stay. They have been in use there the past few years already. I am more inclined to put my faith in bacteriophage therapy or good old-fashioned mushroom antibiotic development."

"I have not had to go to a hospital in a while. The last time I went I was out the next day. I have had to visit urgent care centers before when there was pollen in the air for a steroid shot, and I have needed them to set stitches when I was trying new outdoor activities, and they prescribed doxycycline that I did not need, a lot of it, but I have not had to visit one in over a year with better foot care hiking and with natural cure supplements. Even gardening with pollen and spores in the air, I have not needed to see a doctor. I like these ideas more than that other stuff."

"Do you practice safe sex as a polyamorous person?"

"I like that you automatically presumed I was polyamorous as a natural healer. The Christians down South had me at the point where I didn't care about their standards of indecency by the end of my time living there. Of course, I know that poly people usually get regular testing. I use a condom. I don't want HIV, and I don't want children."

"That was a polite response to an intrusive question, I guess, in hindsight."

Raul arrived. "You can also use mushrooms to create mycopesticides as well as use mycofiltration to farm and not pollute watersheds or clean them up. It also comes in handy for mycoforestry and keeping a garden from dying off in climate change-induced blights. You might wonder how can something that creates carbon dioxide reduce climate change impacts. You would be experiencing a dumb thought. There are greater contributors to climate change, and mycelium protect the natural ecosystem from invading insects, plants, mycelium, and bacteria and keep the native insects, plants, mycelium, and bacteria thriving." He was a very extroverted New Ager; he was by far the best person to start and carry a conversation.

Raul continued, "Did you know that dentistry wanted fluoridation practices for healthy teeth, so they enlisted the health trade associations along with the USDA to give approval to fluoride in medicine and in the water supply to make it so that people would decide that there was no going back and just accept the increase in toxins in our water and air? We will be lucky to preserve 30 percent of our water supply and public lands as pristine and free of environmental degradation by 2030."

"I am like the egregore guy, and I don't think anybody cares here. I would like to go to Europe next, but I would also be content going to Quebec first. I would have a head start on my French," responded Travis.

Raul ranted, "We are the only nation that cares this badly about using up the earth and moving on right now. It is even our own resources on our own public lands we are depleting and our own water supply we are limiting now. Many other countries who benefitted from the exportation of jobs when we started moving to a postindustrial capitalist society have already created for themselves a situation where the median income is higher than in our country. If the United States, which had the equivalent of half the world's economic output in the postwar years, did not deliver the details of its economic planning to third-world countries, then that has been a weapon of American industry for producing cheaper goods since around that time. Bringing in multinationals is the only way that their governments have been shown to pay off the debts with wage slaves. They have a particularly onerous burden with weakened labor safeguards," Raul continued.

"The social degradation has been a thing since the Pilgrims stopped having Thanksgiving with Native Americans," Travis interrupted. "This is a country whose largest population is urbanizing and whose interior its young people are leaving to live the way they would prefer—not living trapped in a theocratic hellscape. In coastal cities, except the Southern cities where there is a high population of privileged White baby boomers in a self-perpetuating hierarchy with influence over the educated White youth, the people do have a degree of freedom. They have a major problem with Republican governors who engage in doublespeak, and those cities are in decline. We are witnessing a swath of repugnant older rural hicks determining how to select two bad interchangeable candidates brought to them by the parties of War and Wall Street for the young to choose from. They really do not believe young able-bodied workers will leave those states when they turn them into theocratic regimes, or they believe that they can force them back. Some of the old-timers are pretty full of themselves.

"Well, I knew people were peeling from the Democrats back in 2016 in the South. I knew some who voted Green. I knew I needed to remain there when I was voting in the 2020 primaries, and I am glad I voted for a financially plausible candidate before deciding to also join the Greens who would take this nation to its logical conclusion if the Democratic establishment, journalists, and religious administrators wouldn't stop hijacking the progressive movement and intentionally misinforming people who do not know how White people—in particular, how nominally Christian White people think," said Travis.

"Another American Revolution," replied Raul. "That is something many of them would try to end. I am surprised to hear you going along with it, Travis. You look like you have medium skin. Have they not already gone all out to try to keep you in your place? Do you not know better by now than to go off the reservation?"

"I am half Indian and half German, but my family would like for me to be a part of the privileged White Christian theocracy that affluent White Southern Christian baby boomers are envisioning for a better American future. My brother has gone along with it ever since South Carolina elected an affluent half-Indian and half-European Christian baby boomer to be another Republican governor for theocracy. I watched the Democrats nominate a Democrat for war, Wall Street, and theocracy and said, "Hell no, not having any of it myself."

"It does certainly look as though they do some election rigging and voter suppression themselves," Raul offered. "We need more done now than ever. The time for halfway attempts at protecting the consumer base and therefore the money-market system is over. Anything done by executive order can be undone, as you pointed out has happened, and taxes can be rolled back. With the environmental degradation of water and the newly added public lands being decimated that easily after electing a Democrat who did nothing fiscally responsible his entire administration, it is obvious that getting his VP as our next president will keep us on a collision course at fifty-five miles per hour versus seventy-five miles per hour."

Travis responded, "The Independent Left Unity ticket is one of two minor political parties that gets a lot of votes each time. The Libertarian Party is the other one, but they are comic relief in the political system if you needed to know. Their party platform guarantees civil liberties, it used to guarantee the right to choose, but most so-called Libertarian pundits are pro-life walking inconsistencies that support the Republocrat cartel, and you cannot get anything done to protect civil liberties without restoring a moral economy through an economic bill of rights in a Green New Deal that can be paid off such as the Europeans have."

"There are problems with corruption in socialist parties too if you did not know, so watch out for manipulative and presumptive foolishness the same as you would a fundamentalist or a neo-Nazi-led organization," answered Raul.

"I may be like you about it from now on, Raul. There are too many people out there who have inflated egos swimming in shark-infested waters and who haven't realized it yet."

CHAPTER 6

"So, CLASS, TODAY I THOUGHT IT MIGHT BE FUN to talk about the benefits of medicinal mushroom growing. We can still discuss antibiotic alternatives found in the natural environment for homesteading and veterinary medicine. Maybe Travis can check out the energy healers before he leaves and arrange for past life regressions later via a directory. I thought since he is so open-minded about everything, why not?"

Travis had a blast during his natural healing class at Nature's Hospital and went indoors to his Kundalini yoga class feeling excited. He was very anxious to see if he would experience samadhi.

"Good morning, class. Let's start by chanting along to a mantra. If you do not know the words, just make some noise and you'll pick it up quickly."

"OOONG NAMOO GURU DEEEV NAMOO" deep breath

"OOONG NAMOO GURU DEEEV NAMOO" deep breath

"OOONG NAMOO GURU DEEEV NAMOO" deep breath

"OOONG NAMOO GURU DEEEV NAMOO" deep breath

"AAD GURAY NAMEH JUGAD GURAY NAMEH SAT GURAY NAMEH SIRI GUROO DAYVAY NAMEH" deep breath

"AAD GURAY NAMEH JUGAD GURAY NAMEH SAT GURAY NAMEH SIRI GUROO DAYVAY NAMEH" deep breath

"AAD GURAY NAMEH JUGAD GURAY NAMEH SAT GURAY NAMEH SIRI GUROO DAYVAY NAMEH" deep breath

"AAD GURAY NAMEH JUGAD GURAY NAMEH SAT GURAY NAMEH SIRI GUROO DAYVAY NAMEH" deep breath

"That was pleasant. Before we move along any further, I wanted to take a moment to say that what makes Kundalini yoga so different from what most Westerners prefer is its emphasis on breath manipulation and extending the length of repetitions—such as frogs. Let's do 108 of those now."

Travis looked around the class and saw people moving up and down, but the guru just sat on her white platform with a brass gong behind her, talking about the benefits of manipulating breath and using postures to expand and heighten the body's energy field and push the self into a higher plane of consciousness than the physical by the end of the session. It was the real deal in other words.

"If you get to sixty and need to take a break, it is better to slow down. It is so important to not stop doing the correct breathing for that blissful moment of ecstasy—when you realize that the world you wake up in is a transitory illusion."

Frogs woke Travis up. He was a bundle of explosive energy.

"I need you all to come down onto your stomachs. You may have tried this in a Western yoga class before. I want for you to lie on your stomachs and grab your ankles and lift them away from your legs and get up off the floor, really lengthen the muscles on the front of your body. We will continue doing that movement for the same number of repetitions with regular breathing." She just sat back and let it go on for seven minutes. "I now need for us all to come to a sitting position. In Kundalini, it matters how you position your fingers with Sat Kriya. Now I need for you to position your fingers just so. Guys usually do this with the right thumb on top of the left, and girls usually do this with the left thumb on top of the right. Now do not drop your arms. Breath with me SAT NAM SAT NAM SAT NAM SAT NAM and so on to 108."

They went through a few more of those until she said that they would be fine to let their arms and upper body have a rest with the palms open in their lap. "I want to teach you an old chant to use with your fingers to connect to the Deva within us. Saa Taa Naa Maa Saa Taa Naa Maa Saa Taa Naa Maa Saa Taa Naa Maa Saa Taa Naa Maa Saa Taa Naa Maa."

Travis had a moment's empty thought; it lasted for about two minutes. He lost his awareness of sound and feeling and could just see red in his eyelids. He came to when she started the Saa Taa Naa Maas once more and wanted to be back in the zone of ultimate reality without useless human language.

Travis went away from his two classes feeling like he was on top of the world. They were having a cookout that night. They were serving vegan hot dogs. He enjoyed the taste. "They don't even try to resemble pork."

"Hooray!" said an older man. "When you have not had animal meat, other than perhaps seafood for a while, you can appreciate that it does not resemble pork and has its own distinct spices sizzling in hot juices within a sausage-like wrapper full of ground lentils."

"I don't think I could ever talk like that."

"It's a better way to talk than to do a political rant," said Valerie. "You seem more reserved now than you did that first night. I bet if you have a few more drinks, you may find you have the gift of gab.

"How many people live in your state?"

"It may be around nine million. They don't know about this type of life in those communities in those states, and most people there don't talk right about living free on purpose and misinstruct their youth. I didn't see an awful lot of that in Portland. If you could do it in a way Oregonians like, it may fly in flyover America with younger people," said Travis.

"Drinks, anyone?"

"Oh, is that bitter tea? Is that ayahuasca?"

"It is, honey, with chacruna as well. I smuggled some in with me. I know how to get the good cured variety."

"I would like to try some."

"Here, have a glass, and trip balls while you are sitting down though."

"So you just do it without a shamanic ritual preceding the ayahuasca eucharist?"

"Pretty much. It's like quick Kundalini. You don't need a blank mind though. You just don't care about what you see or hear. It may be prophetic, or it may be adult entertainment."

"Well, hang on, it may be important!" said the older guy there with her.

"You don't have to make it that. If a messenger visits, they may not have anything smart to say. Learn to recognize the difference between an intelligent spirit and a dumb one. Not everything you experience in life is fundamentally relevant. Just lie back and enjoy the show.

"It's also easier to do than lucid dreaming if that is an art you decide not to master."

Travis sat there with them sipping the ayahuasca eucharist after the vegan cookout. He heard Mother Earth talk to him. He heard Father Sky answer back. He saw wars, thousands of them, hundreds of thousands of them; the further back he went in time, the less variation there was in the phenotypic exterior expressions of the warriors and the simpler were their implements of war. He saw stones levitating and blue angelic beings with elongated skulls who had taught people a technology to levitate stones in an ancient civilization long gone. He saw that those people painted their faces blue thousands of years later as they stopped visiting as regularly because the people would not stop sacrificing prisoners for a good harvest. He saw ruling queens as well as priestesses get sex from whomever they pleased among the peasantry for a good harvest or to get revenge on a woman competitor they saw as a bitch. He saw genetic hybrids of humans and animals that the extradimensional beings were working on before they took their technology and left earth. He saw the sun set. Everything turned into a dark indigo. He lifted his head up off a recliner three hours later with the sky a bright indigo. His mouth was closed.

"Your mouth was closed the entire time, but your face was awestruck. It must have been amazing."

"It was an amazing trip I just took."

It was a clear night with a bright moon. "You have been out for only a few hours. You can still get to bed on time. Now that you have seen whatever it is they wanted you to see, you can watch *The Green Mile* with the rest of us."

"The Annunaki and Pleiadean medium will be here tomorrow, won't she? I am not sure what to make of ayahuasca if everything I see is just like a movie. Let's just watch this movie instead."

After Travis had seen the movie with his new companions, he walked up to his room on the third floor, showered, and climbed into bed. He woke the next morning feeling a lot less irritable after a dreamless sleep, went downstairs, and had a mango/pineapple juice blend and a bagel with strawberry cream cheese; and Valerie showed up with Raul. "I am less cranky now than I was last night. I never want to drink tea again. It stains your teeth."

"I didn't notice you acting cranky. A lot of people are like that on alcohol. You do the opposite. You are a very laid-back person when you are tipsy."

"Then when it wears off, you can go back to dancing. You can also walk to the bus stop and get a bus back to your flat."

"What type of alcoholic drink do you want us to serve you at our next cookout?"

"Beer and hard lemonade, probably. It's usually better without a sour overtone. Most dry wines have high acidity, and I think it is the acidity that will sometimes spoil them for me. I know beer has been around since people were dwelling in caves in Europe, and it's easier to cultivate than wine in a lot of European countries. Wine is my preferred alcoholic beverage, but you don't need it at a cookout. Some of the liquors are fine, but they usually involve a hangover. You can make liquors from just about anything too, so if you want to try a new liquor, just have a little of it and move on to the next one."

"Oh, if that's where you are, then that's where I am.

"That will probably be good enough before Wednesday classes. If they don't want alcohol, we can have mineral water available at luncheons and cookouts, don't you think? I like for the fun people to drink at a party and not the obnoxious ones," proffered up Valerie. "Are you going to the second workshop on expanding consciousness that Druid sorceress is offering?"

"I am."

"Good. She has the best ideas for us right now."

"Good morning, students. We are going to begin the class by starting a meditation to reach into the eighth dimension to contact the divine source, the goddess of the dimension of light. It is all right if you do not hear from her your first time. You can hear from her on ayahuasca tea. I will show you a trick to hear her speak to you with summoning. I have at my house altars facing each of the four directions of the universe. If you would do the same and regularly petition her, you could hear the will of the goddess. I will be a medium for her to you. I will teach you how to enter that realm of expanded consciousness when you are ready to leave here and head out into the world. You can always reach out to the good mother of us all. Then we will work on leaving that and studying the aspects of the sixth to the ninth dimensions."

Travis heard from her all the ideas for reaching into the higher planes of existence—how one could place meaningful objects upon altars and they would look inconspicuous and offer prayers to the goddess of light in the eighth dimension who held up the first seven and the god of time in the ninth dimension who held up the eight visible dimensions. "We should think of the ninth dimension as a plane where time has no real meaning. We should think of it as an everlasting knot. We should think of the seventh dimension as a dimension of sound, and we should think of the sixth dimension as a space where Sirians take form. Any dimensions beyond nine may be beyond this universe—a place of infinite freedom and even possibly the ability to move between universes."

"Have your guides given you an idea of what the tenth and eleventh dimensions are?" asked Valerie.

"No, not yet."

"I don't know about your thing. I got on my mobile phone and did some searching. Strings can have both left and right charges, which makes them compatible with a four-dimensional universe. You have to account for warping, whereas physicists who stick with a four-dimensional model do not."

"Why are you even here? You should do *my* thing."

When the class ended and they had gone off into the field for a luncheon, Travis began talking with his group about what was a good afternoon class to attend. "That's a no-brainer. You cannot leave without hearing Randy Griffin talk about the problems we have had with the USDA and the AMA in our country. Then you can go to the library and do research tonight and tomorrow before you leave Friday."

When they had been seated for about ten minutes, Randy Griffin had decided to not do a PowerPoint presentation and just play the video that he was going to use to get his discussion started. It detailed the same history of abuses the military economy, which relied upon sales of technology developed by the military, forced through the USDA and AMA, that the American Dental Association used to use toxic mercury in dental amalgamations, and that if you'd ask a dentist whether or not there was any truth to that, they could not answer it directly because their trade association would revoke their license. He talked about how vaccinations would get people sick and that if one was released too soon without moving through each of the phases of testing in clinical studies before offering a widespread distribution among the population, then people could become sick.

"There is a profit incentive driving the capitalization of Big Pharma in the United States and then proceeding on as a neoliberal tool to undo social safety nets around the globe by treating every health issue as a chronic condition. Very few new vaccinations are universal accounting for antigenic drift. The world's wealthiest continuously create health problems to profiteer because they do not want to invest in a universal vaccine for something that isn't generally maiming and life wrecking when contracted by an infant, as opposed to simply thinning the herd every fall and winter."

Then he started his discussion about how the military under George Bush senior poisoned the fertile crescent for what could be considered the duration of human habitation in the area. "The armed forces are probably not going to be repurposed for humanitarian relief. That has been done once before, and after several coups and regime change wars, they have lost their market dominance on world policing. Sooner or later, everyone will know it even if they don't talk about it and expect us to do the same. The troops given pyridostigmine bromide and sent there to suffer the effects of toxic chemical compounds being inhaled from munitions and nerve gas they had been ordered to drop that have filled the air and water had gone away and came back home never being the same physically and mentally.

"They initially called it Gulf War syndrome, and then George W. Bush went into office hell-bent on justifying his father's provocations in the Middle East. His excuse for getting the military economy firing on all cylinders again was that the dot-com bubble burst and the American economy did not need to suffer the same shockwaves from it as other economies with tech producing stock exchanges. Even the war in Afghanistan could have been done in a more surgical manner that did not drain American finance the same way the Afghan mujahideen had drained the finances of the expanding Soviet Socialist Republics. That triggered an economic collapse from their inability to produce goods sustainably as a warring modern empire. Also, George W. Bush had had his wife, Laura, go before the nation and tell the American people we should engage immediately for the sake of the Afghan women when everyone was suspecting that the reason was to bail the American economy out of a recession with another full-on American military economic production mode that they will never pull away from even when they have a Democrat in office. Their idea was to head toward a wreck at fifty-five miles per hour versus doing it at seventy-five miles per hour. They could have solved it by being less militaristic and redistributing wealth, but what was clear to only a few West Coast and New England radicals at the start of the century is apparent to everyone else who has turned out to vote Democrat since then. They are a disastrous idea without a peaceful endgame and bad financiers if they are tackling climate change without a demilitarized Green New Deal and continuous deficit spending. No one would be surprised if they kept repeating the same bad ideas for three more terms the same way they did when FDR was president, and we never pulled out of the last economic recession of late capitalism.

"The Bushes got twelve years collectively, and even if the Democrats get back in the White House in January, they will enable twelve more years of fascist groups on the rise and a full economic collapse attributable to both parties by 2032 unless they can plan a world war to ignite the economy again. That one would be significantly worse than the war that followed the Great Depression because it could end in nuclear annihilation. Instead of planning to disarm nuclear warheads, we are building up our nuclear arsenal. The Great Depression would have ended earlier if we had taken on Wall Street. And for the cost of World War II, we could have built housing for all the world's population and delivered universal health care and secondary education a generation ago. Instead, we planned to build the economy around being the world's police and selling armaments to other nations. We took it way too far and for way too long. The last time they had a president in office, he pledged to make a difference on ecology and social justice and left with his best accomplishment being his Supreme Court picks. They do a halfway attempt at everything.

"The White middle class has been disenfranchised by undemocratic processes starting after FDR left office. The middle class may have become bigger temporarily because of them, but they were large enough to engage in suppression of the Eugene Debs ticket that got one million votes in 1917. That was during a war that everybody knew was meaningless in hindsight, and nations like Switzerland with the Swiss Guard knew to not engage. Other people mostly know that they are saboteurs now unless they are an old worker holding on to a job they are probably doing badly while ignoring science and attending a dry church in a miserably hot area. They are going to end up on the streets protesting as well by the end of this all unless they vote in socialism. Continually making bad investments in their future, whether it be in their pension or their borrowing capacity, will not do anything to make things turn out differently from what you would normally expect when people choose not to show any agency. They will either support socialism or their creditors will demand that they return all they have borrowed. Those people are going to persistently cause trouble for young people in the interior of the country the next twelve years until socialism gets into the economy via a complete systemic overhaul of the antiquated lending mechanisms.

"I know it might sound insane to someone from abroad when they observe some of America's greatest exports, but if you head into the interior of the nation where the middle-class decay is obvious and the least populous segment of the population is in decline, you can start seeing a resemblance to some other science-denying, theocratic countries such as Turkey. Places that engage in doublespeak for their own self-preservation, at least for the immediate future, turn away a highly educated workforce of consumers. It is basically the case that the menace we have in office now has undone every environmental protection the last president tried to roll out by executive order. We will need a more robust Department for Environmental Protection than a simple regulatory agency whose protections may be rolled back, but at least we are not going to be getting sick from Big Business. They all look absurd participating the way they are in letting a mass extinction of possibly 50 percent of our native species die off as if they have no role that is beneficial to human communities in the ecosystem. It is going to be chaos in the 2020s if sweeping changes are not made by 2025 compared with the first years of the Great Depression. Both the Republicans and Democrats would go to war to bail out special interests rather than the two stock exchanges taking a hit from less consumption.

"On a different note, if you go back to the 1950s, you will see that the wealthiest Americans and the wealthiest Europeans were fighting against the Green Revolution that their liberal parties were trying to start with their farmers with subsidies and no guidance by investing in Big Agribusiness concepts. It should never have been the case that the go-big-or-go-away market pressures of capitalism would have put small farming operations out of business. Confined animal operations, fast-food franchises, the development of MSG to make junk food seem more filling, diet alternatives that included a chemical called aspartame along with many other artificial sweeteners before that all should not have ever become so prevalent in our food markets. It has led to an epidemic in America of childhood obesity. With the USDA whoring itself out to the wealthiest Americans, the use of chemical pesticides became commonplace, and then the use of plants genetically modified to withstand these pesticides became accepted. I wish I had the footage in that video so that you could see that during that decade you could see advertisements for big tobacco where you literally had a physician lighting up a cigarette and saying that this was the preferred cigarette by doctors. It is not only American Big Ag companies that have participated in getting people sick these ways. The American Medical Association has been whoring themselves out to the wealthiest in America since the end of World War II. And it is, simply put, a set of worthless new health commodities that they are trying to sell to people. 'Here, public! Pick your poison and go deal with bad health, hopefully starting directly before retirement. Just continue living and overconsuming and borrowing more than you can ever pay off for what you are told is good for you and your family.'

"The health care and agribusiness sector of the nation's GDP is bloated so far above what it should be. They are treating problems other postindustrial nations avoid, and if they are not reigned in with crippling sanctions that force some businesses to go under and new industries to emerge to replace those displaced workers' jobs in the energy and food chain worker sectors, then they will want to export those problems to impoverished nations that have no idea what these companies do to workers. Those are two goliaths of wrongdoing, and most people here find representatives of those sectors trustworthy. American cultural dominance has replaced that of Europe after World War II, and much of our entertainment industry as the big representative for the disastrous new American way has already suffered the consequences of the American lynch mob mentality. Neoliberal imperialism has already come to an end. There will inevitably be markets crashing without consumers, and your average American has not awakened to the reality of diminished American influence globally over the past twenty years."

"The older people in the interior of the country are like North Koreans in the head. They want us to have ten hairstyles to choose from. It is capitalist North Korea in the interior," said Valerie.

"You are awesome!" said Travis.

"You sound like you are from one of those states."

"I am from rural North Carolina. People still farm tobacco, and I have no idea why."

"One out of three White men from the South uses tobacco."

"Well, okay, I thought if it was ever necessary to have a PAC to get airtime, it might not be a big deal to fund it with money from big tobacco and the gun manufacturers who do not make weapons more lethal like military-grade weapons. People there are still resistant to a serious attempt to remake the economy even though we obviously need it, and abortion is also a big deal to Southerners. They would not like having abortion and contraception paid for by Medicare for All, but they do take it too far attempting to ban it. If the doctors were available affordably and their education was available affordably, a young woman could dispel a clump of cells from her womb affordably. The safest, most effective way to do it is the morning-after pill. I took a girl to a doctor who I think may have given her relief from an unwanted pregnancy before."

"Was it yours?"

"Of course, it was mine if she was telling the truth. I was seventeen and going to college, and she was eighteen and almost six weeks late. She said she wanted to make sure she was not in trouble and was going to see a woman's doctor. It took forever for the trip to the hospital to end, but if she had an unconscious clump of cells in her womb, nobody noticed it again after that. The only people who are that pro-life down South are people you cannot have a rational conversation with. They are older, they go to church every Sunday whereas I stopped going five months ago and they still think I care, somehow, and they have not stopped counting me among them even though everyone else knows all the reasons why I stopped paying them attention long ago. I have never seen people go about trying to destroy other people any dumber honestly. 'Son, if you want to get ahead in life, act like a professional. You are not doing the best you can unless you are getting more indebted!' 'No, thanks, Pa! I do not have a lot of debt now. I could work three days a week, as a shirtless bartender if that would make you angry, and I would have all I need. If I still cannot pay the rent, then I will make sure to have shacked up with someone just as irreligious and as irreverent in your eyes as I have become the more I have seen you people persistently try to intimidate me into a church pew. I do not want to spend eternity with you. You are incapable of getting me to want to spend eternity with you. Do everyone a favor and stop trying it,'" Travis ended his rant.

"Your family is pathetic. You should be a Buddhist and be concerned with the Ashurans and not dabble too much in New Age material. You can possibly try Tibetan Buddhism for more compatibility with what New Agers and Wiccans like. They cast spells while people pray to the Devas. I could see you doing that. You would think like a warlock by the time you are a full-grown man. I know a warlock when I see one. We still do souls even if they are temporary ones. That and karma help. They are nowhere near being enlightened. It is obvious that they will look different when they are enlightened. No one here expects you to care about your family there. Do not go back and see them," said Raul.

"Oh, if only it were that easy."

"Why not? Do you have grandparents or other family in the country?"

"No grandparents. I have some German cousins and some Indian cousins here and in Canada. None of us really call one another brothers and sisters like they still do in Asia. I have some family in British Columbia nearby. It is a simple process getting a visa that way. They wouldn't want me to stay forever though."

"You can stay here on the West Coast."

Travis frowned. "I do not think that is necessary. Maybe the social decay of the nuclear family has to become visibly precipitated by the failures of patriarchal fundamentalist families in order for it to remain intact despite attempts at sabotage, blackmail, and intimidation for things to change. They will form a lynch mob by the end of it. They have a history. I think I know what those people are about. They hate city life and are convinced that rural values will undo the fable of urbanization rather than educated young people giving up on staying and dealing with all that bullcrap that long."

"That is a bad world for you to live in with the family you have now. If young people like you don't work on them before you leave and we go bankrupt, no one will ever care again about throwing those grannies off a cliff as we all once saw in ads. People will travel from other countries to American cities to see the culture and leave those rural areas alone that do not have enough beauty to get a national park. If only because others can see the state departments of other countries advising them not to travel into the interior of our country because of uneducated, deeply religious, and overweight hillbillies behind disappearances and robberies committed against foreigners and minorities. It will be worse than traveling to Latin America on your own when you are not a native Spanish speaker."

Travis knew that was entirely possible and walked away from the meeting feeling a small amount of melancholy. On one hand, living in the rural South surrounded by some of the most two-faced, cowardly people you would find on the entire globe, he knew it didn't resemble the Hallmark Channel at all and knew they deserved to suffer a much more terrible fate than American city dwellers. On the other hand, he did not know how to get other people to see that our financial institutions were so weakened by all the outstanding derivatives that after all the recent deficit spending, we probably did only have twelve years before there'd be a tremendous financial melt-down that people were gleefully heading toward.

He headed off to the library after he and Raul had verbalized their musings about the apocalypse to pull out an index card. He had several out on a table related to the USDA, and they told him where to look in the library for articles or periodicals that covered what had become government cover-ups as opposed to what they would do in a library with internet normally. He headed to the department that had old newspapers on microfiche. He had cards on two topics that the speaker had not covered relating to the passage of food irradiation and raw milk with inspections and the stigma associated with the hippie stance through the decisions of the USDA, DHHS, WHO, and CDC without hearing any testimony from concerned citizens. They, of course, heard plenty from concerned scientists—scientists concerned with making enormous profits. The agenda of businesses growing or going away was neoliberal Republocrat orthodoxy, and they had been complicit in using the tool of pasteurization and the unnecessary process of food irradiation to remove small farms from the agricultural sector and slowly unravel rural communities. It did not mention whether or not the Annunaki were behind it or if the billionaire class was aware that once they had stolen all the money from the labor pool, they had to be prepared to kill off any stragglers too late in joining the wealthy and powerful circles in brutal massacres before there were no longer working-class people to produce value-containing goods for them and then demand to be treated decently in billionaire's utopia once everything had been properly automated.

He decided not to look for any tags on secret Pentagon science initiatives. Maybe some other trip someplace and there would be documentation of the Philadelphia Experiment, telekinetic warriors, and telepathic gifts. Who knew? All the downed Soviet aircraft might even be aliens who could not already visit us telepathically coming to visit us. Those Annunaki/egregores/jinni/Ashurans were obviously not sympathetic to people who would not show any human agency and finally fix their problems for themselves. "If the Annunaki were not behind this, then the people who have knowingly done all this still need to be prosecuted for white-collar crimes. It is wrong that the poor are filling the jails."

"I guarantee you that there is a cabal of wealthy people deciding how to keep capitalism going: Bilderberg," said Raul. He had been in the library the whole time, and obviously, he and Travis were sharing the same inner conversation earlier.

"What was it you decided to look at on the microfiche reader?"

"Oh, that would be pasteurization of raw milk and food irradiation for long-term storage and food transport since the 1980s." Travis was perplexed but got over it quick enough. "That has been a bad idea. It is not an industry where the business is too big to fail. Food deserts could be a thing the next time we have a pandemic, and we are overdue for one. I honestly do not believe that big banks and automobile companies qualify as that. Maybe if we had another economic crash, we could not give bailouts to companies like the auto manufacturers in Detroit and the travel industry. They can decide to become progressives and vote for someone as liberal as Senator Buffet after four years of misery versus twelve," said Raul.

"If you condensed it briefly, you would say the American dollar is only still stronger now because our level of income inequality compared to Europe is so vast."

"That has enough of a semblance to the truth, but economics is a complicated matter, and people here cannot acknowledge that they have reached the end of their economic mode."

"That, remaking the economy, is about what Senator Buffet was open to in New England. That other senator from New England who didn't continue picking up votes once again after Super Tuesday did not detail how he was going to pay for everything. It was horrible for him at that point. I do not know why he entered in again anyway and stayed after they asked him to explain how he was going to tax and spend again to the American people differently. Anyway, he has finally left, and I am glad because he was attracting people who were showing up just because they had a lot of feelings but could not make a clever argument."

"He was a man of principle, was he not?"

"I didn't actually know him. I do know that in 2016 he promised that there would be a progressive plan for free college and in 2020 he promised that there would be a progressive plan for criminal justice, and there is not anything like that that will be at this fall's debates this year either. I think the Democrats make him do it. What a horrible situation to be in. It must not be bad being a senator and having a net worth of $10 million."

"Why not choose to be an entertainer and make $20 million, Travis? If the whole thing is rigged by Annunaki/egregores/jinni/Ashurans, just be an entertainer.

"You can stay on the West Coast?"

"This is the most embarrassing political contest that has ever been conducted in the history of our country. There is literally no alternative to the pain caused by the Republican Party other than to drag it out with the Democratic establishment. It's pathetic of the Democratic establishment and the mainstream media that they make it that. You could also lop into that mix that group of posers I have seen trying to hijack socialism as simply economical justice with lip service paid to ecology, direct democracy, non-hierarchy, and peace."

"Travis, try to not do that. That first one has been the only big motivator for populist appeal and voter turnout since the Bolsheviks overthrew the Russian monarchy."

"That is so insane. The big thing the Communists cared about was eliminating capital, and they used their military to ensure that they had access to the raw materials needed to continue keeping their economic mode running until the mujahideen bled them dry before they were ready to move on to doing that to the USA. War is the number 1 pollution mechanism, and our military is by far the worst of them all to continue wreaking havoc on the environment. The Bible-thumping, fundamentalist, devout, overconsuming American middle class of old is the only constituency that does not want global peace and that wants to continue the sixth mass extinction event our planet is facing. The Nazis promised economical justice and, after nationalizing a few industries, never did anything else other than a widespread eugenics program based around their Aryan race mystical form of nationalism until Germany used their money from the Marshall Plan to participate in reconstructing Europe in a more tolerant fashion than what had been sweeping across their region since the economic crashes at the end of the 1910s and 1920s. It was a reaction to the inflammatory gestures of the Communists and artistic communities and nineteenth-century Protestant liberalism in their universities. Racism directed at Black and Brown people is a problem everywhere still, and religious conformity is the hallmark of cultural hybridity in Europe still, and many governments pay artists to be the soothing balm needed for the masses to keep calm and give up without a fight.

"Do you want marijuana legalized? Do you want to decriminalize drugs? Do you want safe needle exchange sites? Do you want community control over the police to finalize your progressive stance on criminal justice reform? Then you would be where you need to be until there is an end to the nuclear arms race and peace with a Global Green New Deal. If you go back to the 1920s in Europe, all they cared about was economical justice. Now there is much more support for ending the sixth great mass extinction our planet has faced there than there is over here. We still have not seen an end to capitalism with all those people being left out of the mix and not seen as important people to not kill off in order to protect the number of finite resources that wealthy people are predicted to overconsume the next century."

"Do you want to bring all the Muslim world in at the same time?"

"Sure."

"Well, it was nice talking to you, Travis. If it helps you out, you can probably leave the country for Europe and do well, and rest assured that those old people who should have known better would be obnoxious on a prolonged stay elsewhere."

"Good night, Raul."

"Good night, Travis."

Travis went upstairs to go to bed. He was not feeling great. Somebody had told him that Africa had formed its own free trade bloc now. About twenty countries there were having tremendous problems found nowhere in the Americas. It also looked like populated India and China might suffer along with Muslim Asia, but not Muslim Australasia as bad, which meant to him that living conditions in the majority of the world were improving quicker than they had before. It made him sad seeing few people in the developing world open to changing their traditions. He could see that the Annunaki/egregores/jinni/Ashurans had pushed the world to a breaking point. Now the rest of the world was ready to ditch them if they could not start acting like they, too, wanted to survive the next century.

Travis woke from his sleep in the night after a dream where blue aliens had abducted him and left him lying in bed before he needed to be up the next day. He remembered a blue-skinned guy. He guessed it was an alien avatar. He took him onto a spaceship that looked like a train and told him that all his former lives were gathered in all the passenger cars but to not go too far back because if he did then he might get some surprises.

"Animals? Dinosaurs? Prophets? War generals? You could have been that one there recently." He looked across the compartment to find famous author Agatha Christie sitting across from him at his table suddenly. He was giggling in his sleep. He had to be mistaken. That could not possibly be it. Ms. Christie told the Indian guy to make sure he was explaining that he was in fact a South Asian Indian.

Travis said to her, "I heard that!"

"That guy is a manic prick," said Agatha Christie.

"Are you sure I am not a crocodile?"

"What is he talking about?"

"I will let you know."

"My heavens, that all looks disgusting. I have never been as surprised in my entire life to find that all out about guys." She had a grin on her face. "You're not going to do that to him, are you? That's a setback. That is not even what those people are about."

"You always wanted to write something scandalous. Why not help that guy out?"

"The Big Blue Aliens will be watching."

"They are now," said a deep bass voice.

Travis woke up. Then he drifted off to sleep. It was early in the morning, so he had no reason to worry; not even Annunaki could work that fast. Unless his consciousness was so powerful that he just engaged in interstellar travel for the first time. He fell back off to sleep and slept until eight thirty. He got himself together quick enough. He did not have his class on natural healing for veterinary care until nine thirty.

On his way down the stairs, he noticed that everything looked the same as it had the day before, so he was still in the same universe. He went over to the snack bar and grabbed an apple, a glass of raw milk, and a roll; he decided to just open a single-use spreadable butter packet and spread it in the roll. He headed on out to Nature's Hospital when he was finished.

"So, Travis, how have you been since Tuesday night?" asked Olivia.

"I have been doing well. Do you live here in the area?"

"I do. I have a homestead near the educational resort. I participated in a regenerative agriculture program, and I have a licensure from the state to inspect raw milk at the grocer."

"Like what the kitchens here have in stock."

"That could be mine. I do the inspection here as well. They also take fruit from my orchard, even the ugly ones the supermarket doesn't want. There is a lot of food waste that happens over ugly fruits and vegetables, and mine don't even carry disease because of how I have grown them."

"Does the state feel that way about the raw milk you produce from your cows?"

"I don't normally have to disclose the way I handle the animals from calf to heifer, dear. I have never been dragged into court for getting someone sick. That could happen anyway because of antibiotic resistance, and I guarantee you that farmers are not carefully reading *The New England Journal of Medicine* to find out which antibiotics are better for fighting disease. I have brochures here that I have printed off on how to tell if a plant has any antibiotic properties or whether you are better going with something cultivated from mycelium. Now you can always go roaming off into the forest to try to find plants that have these characteristics or be dumb enough to try experimenting yourself first with mushrooms without reading first. I suggest you buy a book telling you what seedlings and spores have been known to grow into malevolent microbe exterminating natural remedy aides. Then you can order what you would like to try growing and get started. I was going to show you a few plants and fungi that I have found beneficial to my health. I have colleagues who agree with me. They do the business of printing books and selling things known to grow up into disease curing medicine woman or medicine man fixes."

"Have you ever run into trouble with the law?"

"Why would I? If anyone wanted to know about the orders you were placing to a company, they could check them out. It is more pleasant than your phone having a record of all the forest locations you have ventured into foraging for plants and mushrooms to experiment with. Be grateful for the hippies that came before you."

"What if a neighbor gossiped?"

"Talk like that around them and they won't want to anymore."

"What if they mutter under their breath so low that you cannot hear but know it was a snarky remark?"

"Don't think of them as a neighbor. It is the same as living in a big city. Stay in Portland. You'll love it there!"

Travis had a good time in that class. He had Kundalini yoga again before he left for Portland the next day. They were beginning the class with the same set of mantras and got into the deep breathing and repetitions, but instead of taking off again at warp speed with the Kundalini energy already pulsating through them, they lay down on their backs and the guru turned away from them to bang the gong. It sounded like an ayahuasca trip. It sounded like something he would like to do for a living if he wasn't going to be an entertainer. He saw himself hurtling through space with stars passing him by. He saw a golden temple in India. He didn't want to see it, but it wouldn't leave his field of vision. He was approaching a place where time slowed down and moved where there was a lack of stars; the stars around him moved slower. On one side of him was blackness, and on the other, the stars were slowly removed from his view until he was surrounded in blackness. He could hear the gong eternal. He could hear extradimensional beings talking to him. They made him aware of the red light coming through his eyelids and showed him a world of greenery with a blue sea nearby with him in the blue sky somewhere up above it in the clouds. "Go there next! That world needs a savior badly."

"Will I ever see you again?"

"You don't need this that badly."

"We're only a universe away!"

The gong had ended. Then they brought their palms together and sang a blessing to one another. "May the longtime sun shine upon you. All love surround you. And the pure light within you. Guide your way on. Guide your way on."

"Thank you. Sat Nam."

Travis felt like he was having a winner's day. He wasn't sure about the god where time got funny. That god was a silent one. He also wasn't certain the Annunaki and Pleiadean visitors weren't trying to get his attention. He did know there was something to natural healing and being on a vegetarian, certified organic—when possible—diet and avoiding eating fast food. He knew that nutrition and physiology experts had replicable scientific studies conducted to substantiate the values that the New Agers held on holistic health. He also knew that he had a better psychological massage from Kundalini yoga class than he had ever had after hearing a Jewish or Christian sermon, although it didn't produce the same enlivening visions as ayahuasca tea or marijuana. Even as the sound of the universe contained within the gong of bliss tended to produce extrasensory perception, he could find cured green a lot cheaper than he could a five-foot-tall brass gong. That throbbing eternal sound would show up in odd places. It would show up when you'd be stoned on just about any hallucinogen; it would show up when you'd be traveling across the earth in an OBE (out-of-body experience).

He knew he would miss Kundalini vibes when he went back home. He also was open to extradimensional beings visiting him as opposed to that horrible egregore teaching. Unless, of course, it was other RPJIHD (random people jettisoned in his direction) while he was having OBEs. He had enough of those where he was going next to deal with—people who mistook his politeness for a desire to stay in the South when he was not Christian in the slightest. He was just not ready to commit to mischievous Annunaki/egregore/jinni/Ashuran extradimensional beings bothering him about (impersonal) god knows what next. It seemed like it had the potential to mess with a lot of the more ancient teachings to which he was still attached—even if it was only bits of them here and there.

He joined the group on the lawn for an afternoon of cricket. He did not know the rules. He knew that it used to be America's sport before baseball took over America in the 1960s. The games tended to last awhile because they traditionally took a break for tea in the middle.

"Are we breaking for tea?"

"I don't see the need."

"Okay."

That went on with people stepping in and having a go at it and then getting out when they realized they did not understand the rules as well as longtime players and fans of America's favorite pastime. Valerie sat in a lawn chair and played umpire. At five thirty, they went off to have dinner.

"We have a mango-banana smoothie offering tonight along with mineral water. There is also a Mexican potluck-styled dinner with vegetarian options that has been prepared by the kitchens. Some of it does include meat, even if it is just fish, crab, and squid. There are people here getting off meat, and it is usually easier for them to do vegetarian as a pescatarian first. There are plenty of fruits and veggies that have been run through a dicer. There is also heirloom corn, which does not resemble the variety English-speaking Americans prefer to be grown and sold at stores. That one is genetically modified by Sanmonto, which put many small farming operations out of business. Bon appétit."

Travis filled up a plate with corn and Spanish rice and diced peppers, mostly mild chilis, on a flour tortilla. He had a lentil dish available but put refried beans, shredded lettuce, and diced tomatoes on his plate along with a bit of guacamole to mix around; he put a salad of pineapples, grapes, and oranges in a bowl next to him to satisfy his sweet tooth.

Raul was on his right side, and Valerie was in front of him. Olivia was on his left, and Don was at the end of the table.

"If you drive over the border to Baja California, Tijuana, you would have more variety as a pescatarian. They sell squid cooked in marijuana oil. You would probably like that indulgence for yourself. It is a healthy cooking oil," Valerie told him.

"I went to a North African-style restaurant earlier this year. It was different from what I expected it to be like. They had vegetarian options. It billed itself as a nightclub and stayed open on Christmas Day. It was about like going to a nightclub in Sweden where you are expected to wear a suit and less like a Bollywood music video, but the performances were not done for a White audience. There were a lot of upturned White noses on Christmas Eve. There was a much different crowd in on Christmas Day. I would like to go to Charleston again to do my volunteer work as a museum docent. That city may have a visible wealth divide that is ugly the same as any other in the country now, but it is also jam-packed with colorful characters the same as New Orleans. It is not the same in Florida, Georgia, Alabama, and Mississippi. It doesn't make a difference that Florida, Georgia, and Alabama are wealthier states. It is the most backward part of the country apart from Atlanta and Miami."

"I guess that is the Deep South?" Raul asked.

"Yes, the people, in general, are presumptive on top of being ignorant. It probably has not changed a lot since the days of slavery in that respect. They can get an idea in their heads that they would not have seen in print or on the news that would not occur to a rational person anywhere else and collectively act on it like it is a normal pattern of thinking. They used to form lynch mobs. I could see them doing it again."

"I have been trying to talk Travis into staying here now that he is here and not leaving under any circumstances, but he wants to go back and live with his parents awhile longer."

"You may learn to appreciate family later—even if they do not listen to you when you are trying to explain to them that your political and religious views have changed and are now different from theirs."

"They have probably been trying to cover for you and their religious community acting like you are unwell and stupid and not them the past five months."

"My family is not like that. They would not become backstabbers just because I make the choice to adapt when I recognize their worldview as falsified."

Raul looked horrified. "When people move to a vegetarian diet, they often find eggplant filling. You might consider eating more of that when you commit to a vegan lifestyle."

"Having Mediterranean vegetables that you know are filling also makes it easier to travel without doing culinary research into your options before you head off on a passport for adventure." Olivia continued, "There is not much discussion about veganism or vegetarianism in Italy and Greece, and there are still many noteworthy places to visit other than churches."

"Thank you, Olivia. I was already aware that there were many vegan restaurateurs in New York and Amsterdam and that it was fairly easy to travel as a vegan in the low countries and Paris. I did not think it was that common in Germanist cultures or Scandinavia to have vegetarian food at a restaurant apart from ordering many side dishes or vegetable stews. I will have to look it up to see what travelers there have discovered works for the culinary exploration when you head over to that part of Europe on an adventure. They probably have vegan or vegetarian options. The frugal five has done some of the best scientific work in sustainability. That is true for Denmark even as they export a high amount of pork."

After they had eaten and finished their dinner conversation, they left the dining hall and went to the resort's rec room. Travis brought his mineral water with him and sat by Olivia and Raul as they tried to get a puzzle of the Eiffel Tower started, while Valerie played against Don on the Sony PlayStation. They had about two hundred of the 750-piece puzzle together. He joined in with them, and they had it in place very quickly. Raul must have done it before a long time ago because he got Olivia and him off to a great start where they had it completed by nine twenty. That could stay there and be lacquered now and framed while all the puzzle pieces were in good condition. "Does anyone want to watch a movie?" asked Olivia.

"Which one?" asked Don

"How about *Forrest Gump*?"

"I like that before bed," said Don.

"I think it's a good one too," Travis said.

He had fun watching that movie with them. When it was over, he got a group photo of them taken on his camera as well and then headed up to his room to change out of his clothes, shower, and go off to sleep. He awoke the next morning earlier, had his last meal there, packed up everything he had in his room after combing it over, said his farewells, and then left in his car to head back to Portland at about ten thirty Friday morning. He was leaving from somewhere verdant above Fresno, so he thought he would drive to the East and see the Kings Canyon loop as well as the Sequoia trees, having already seen Yosemite. He drove through a Sequoia tree. Then he headed Northwest toward Portland. It was as beautiful as he had been told it would be in the spring with waterfalls flowing.

It was a long drive to Portland; he arrived two nights later having skipped a night's sleep before he had to board a later flight. He ate at a Waffle House when he arrived in Portland. Then he checked in and hit the hay. The next morning, he was able to leave his hotel room quicker. He did not have a free breakfast, and he did not have to put a lot back in his car. He had packed up his luggage and basically worked with his carry-on bag at the hotel that night, so he was ready to return the rental car and board his flight and head back to the South for two months.

CHAPTER 7

Travis showed up at church for Sunday evening services for the first time in five months.

Hey, you sexy beast, thought the divorced Baptist lady.

Hey, you slutty blonde lady, Travis thought.

Looked at anything dirty recently?

Why are you asking?

Always inquisitive myself.

I did order some trunks with mesh all the way around the top but with a white drawstring. They were black. It will look great on me. I still have lighter skin even though I got to have brown eyes and black hair. It is almost a Grecian thing that I have going on.

Oh, that's hot. You have pecs now as well.

That's not all. I am starting to get those muscles on the lower back. The type that arrives from many leg lifts on top of squats. I am going to have a muscular back from the dimpled muscles above my behind to the dimpled muscles beneath my neck. I still have work to do on the abs and obliques to get the most important side looking like it should. People still appreciate a nice muscular blacksmith type. The type of a marble sculpture. Why not show as much of it off as you can at the beach? Three-second rule.

What's the three-second rule?

You can look for three seconds at that eye candy, and then you look at another. If someone creepy does any more than that, tell them to go screw themselves.

Is that underwear, or is it for the beach?

It can be both on a North American beach that is not clothing optional. I'm going to wear that at the beach when I have the results for it. I have my muscles, my beard, and the money to get waxed and get a haircut frequently again in June. I just spent a bit going to a New Age retreat in California.

Have fun!

That guy is such an a-hole now, thought Dr. Freemoney.

There is nothing wrong with an a-hole.

You are a trashy dog! There is no need for that much variety in the boudoir, thought Dr. Freemoney.

If a girl like Ophelia ever let me know my advances were unwanted, I would stop caring about drawing the line on premarital sex immediately. None of us guys can really follow that rule anyway. You, Ophelia, I would like to see with your pants off. Even though it is not an economic right, humankind has libidinal rights. I would like to meet yours and have you meet mine someday. If you say no and you are the type of girl my parents would prefer me to be with, I can't say that I would care anymore to be with a partner my parents liked.

I am with her. We should never have admitted you into that seminary. He isn't even planning on returning next year. He interviewed for a job at a joke shop, the type that sells edible panties. He also drank rum recently. Who is supposed to eat the edible panties, Travis? You, Ophelia, or an old friend of hers she calls up when she is in town for a ménage à trois.

Don't ever come here again if you, too, have been that way all along. It ruins everything. He told us he was going to get a part-time job at an independent bookseller. Then he takes work at a joke shop like one of those crass mall gift stores and takes work as a bartender at a nightclub so that he can tell a bunch of horny guys when they have had too much to drink and toss anyone out who slips something in someone's drink or is otherwise inappropriate. When is he going to learn? Do not drink and dance. We have been trying to tell you that you can't do that since you were a kid. Get that right first, and the rest will follow. He cannot be allowed to move to Oregon at the end of the summer. We must do everything in our power and outside of it to stop him from doing it. There is no way it wouldn't be intimidating if we all do it together. Who the hell does he think he is? Has he never heard our battle cry: "I'm in the Lord's army!"? You had better be afraid, Travis. Just because we are ignorant doesn't mean we aren't a real threat.

I also have a trip to Charleston coming up soon. I have some people in that area I was close to back in the day before you all got confused and thought it was only about you.

You will never be welcome to live here again after you do that, and we want you to spend eternity with us. Try that, thought Mrs. Blossom.

Amazingly enough, I don't give a rat's rear. I have waited long enough to have my freedom. I am not going to have to deal with BS from my parents or the people they bring over for their social gatherings where they don't drink and they don't dance anymore. Where is the fun in that? I'd rather kill myself than live like that. I can understand why somebody who was a problem drinker may want to cut it out entirely, but who wants to live in the town from Footloose *where they call you names if you need dope beats to dance to and only a few passages from a sixty-six-book collection of fables make sense to you? I was like that in the third grade when they got into the meat of the Bible and were telling me to take it at face value. I convinced my parents I had better things to do than go to Sunday school, and I got away from a private Christian school so that I could get taught evolution in a public school the year they start explaining that part of the science curriculum.*

But you're enrolled in a private Christian school now.

I'm not enrolled again this fall.

Then there's hope.

You cannot be that crazy! I stopped resembling my family when I left high school, and my family was rotten to me then. I will not start doing that like a high schooler with religious nuts for family who can be easily intimidated at my age. What a waste of your time.

Then we must plot.

It will not work. I guarantee you it will not work. I will smash it all to pieces if it's the last thing I ever do. I think I will skip along merrily somewhere else.

Skipping along to Sodom and Gomorrah instead of heading down to the front pew to repent. You couldn't be more of an a-hole about it. We thought we mattered more to you. You cannot be allowed to make it look like we do not. We will refuse you that opportunity. Plus you are nice in person. It would make all the difference if for once you would stop being nice to us.

You people are presumptive and highly oblivious. There are two types of people in the world. There are good people, and there are bad people. You people are bad Christians.

We're the only Christians.

Right on, sister.

That is nonsense. However, the least you can do is pay people to watch them have fantastic sex. You should not be getting it for free each time.

You bastard. What makes you think we would do that?

See, he threatens us right back. He just does it with his mouth as if that was mightier than the sword, thought Morgen Blossom. *I am looking right at his mother now and thinking of all the ways I can help her with the child of hers we all have the biggest problem with.*

You bitch! You said you would never look. We are going to get back at you for doing that, thought someone from the Methodist church down the street.

I needed to. It wasn't right of you to do that then. Travis is not a big problem even if he is still not keeping scripture, and it is not simply a new thing. He requires an all-hands-on-deck approach.

I am with the men on that one for now because I am also with you on that old stuff with scripture needing to be followed. We can shag many ways later, Travis. We just can't right now, thought Ophelia.

My main problem is with fundamentalists. People raised by you do not give to your churches, nor do they attend. Find something better to do. Who told you that a religion or, I guess, now a scientific philosophy of life had to follow the same trajectory as your awful idea with your cult that behaves like an exclusive club? I have better things to do with my time. It is difficult enough having to deal with reincarnation. I have more difficulty believing I should want to spend eternity with a group of people who continuously spread lies about me. You have a whole lot more dross caked onto your religious enterprise than anyone else and a much worse history of starting wars. Everyone else thinks that Christians are the biggest group of religious posers on the planet. The ones helping you out are few enough in number that you call them heretics. I think it's better to take a step back and not associate with you anymore. It is probably great to avoid using your terminology. Once we started using your terminology, we have immediately begun losing the battle against the warmongering Christians. They have dysfunctional family units. They set up kinky households full of violence even if they never resort to wife and child beating. People end up so screwed up in the head until they unlearn all the lies they teach them at church. They would all be better off being polyamorous and child-free by choice. They have that settled so that it is difficult for polyamorous people to raise children anytime soon, and humans have definitely shown that they have no self-control when it comes to having children with that being the least rewarding of human endeavors.

What an awful thing to say, thought Mrs. Blossom.

Having children is riskier than polyamory. If you have a child, you never know what you're going to get at the end of it. Communities raise children and not families. If you are out of sync with the community and society at large, you are having children for one reason only, and that's to help you burn up bad karma. If they are working in a hellscape temporarily and less violent toward the people everywhere else on the planet than the others from their background—

God, you have no clue how to talk anymore. Everything before that made sense without exceptions. Just don't have kids for the community or society to screw up. I would expel it from my womb if it had to be born here now, thought Ophelia.

Ophelia, that was like the big thing I thought I could start with the Baptist lady, and you just ruined it, thought Morgen Blossom.

I don't care. If I was pregnant now with people acting the way they do, I would be getting rid of that clump of cells, no exceptions. I could order some witch hazel and do it—even if they make it illegal.

That entire lot of intolerant neo-Nazis does not really have anything to offer the world. They exist to keep socialism out of the economy and force people to accrue wealth or else starve and die of thirst before midcentury. No one cares about the church. No one. The bride of Christ has turned into a megabitch. You won't win souls for Christ unless you learn to stop threatening them with harm. Have you lost all your sense? ranted Travis telepathically.

You can't really do that and win at life. Called it. You need to walk that back a little. You just took on all Christians, thought Dr. Freemoney.

I don't think it matters when they have to put a spin on my words and invert the truth. The bride of Christ is a megaliar out of desperation.

Walk it back further.

She needs to reform her stance on official dogma.

That was good. You were talking about the bride of Christ like she was an actual person. That is a stupid thing to do. Christ never married, and that blasphemy has been done before. You would do well to avoid sacrilege even when we are pushing you to give us that.

Since when did I say it was blasphemous?

It doesn't matter. We will do that for you. If you come back in a week, we will teach you more, thought Dr. Freemoney.

Travis, I did not know you were polyamorous. I support you in your decision to come out, thought the divorced Baptist lady.

I am not going there yet publicly. I am not old enough to have the privilege to do that where I would be accepted. That is also a major reason why I did not commit to labeling myself as socialist or New Ager.

Well, when you are ready to join the poly community, I will support you. I want to be able to say I have a poly friend to others. When you are ready, you have at least until the woman you were shacked up with decides to act on her ticking biological clock and start a family, and then the game is over.

What if I deny her the fatherhood of her children?

It will end badly.

Custody arrangements favor the mother everywhere. That is a legal hurdle you would run into if you decide to be a father as a poly person.

More than anything, it is the stigma associated with being a drifter that is worse if you are not already rich.

You could look up the definition of a drifter and avoid it. You could have a family together. At least that is how I think Christian polyamory will be, thought Ophelia.

Probably, thought the Baptist lady.

That's not how others do it, and I think we outnumber you. We could make a go at getting polyamory going and alternative legal contracts going when a woman decides to bear a child. It is less costly than divorce to start off deciding how to manage multiple residential properties as a long-term item in and out of love.

Good luck with that. The church is everywhere. You cannot ignore the stigmas we want associated with you. Your kids will hate you, thought Mrs. Blossom.

When you say the church, what do you mean?

In that context, I mean Christians who profess Jesus as their savior globally, thought Mrs. Blossom.

Oh my god! Cultlike sect. Called it. I was told how it was, and now I have seen it with my own eyes. Cult! Cult! Cult! thought the Baptist lady.

It's like you said, Travis. It may be better for survival to not be a Christian when you need to pick a label for your philosophy of life, thought a Methodist from across the street.

That woman is likeable. I don't care if her church thinks I am going to hell or even if she does. These people at this church here are so screwed up.

Oh my god, he also checked out Islam the past few months. I went back and looked at his memories, thought Dr. Freemoney.

That makes Travis a jackass if only for a brief moment. Those Muslims will mirror us and do what we tell them to do even to their own detriment. These Western ones are so gullible, thought Mrs. Blossom.

What an unpopular choice to make saying that out loud though. I think I'll pass, thought Travis.

Just go ahead and tell everyone you sold your soul to Satan. Make it easy on us, pleaded Morgen Blossom. *I don't know how to handle the other. I beg of you, give us that, and then we can go away and not bother you again.*

How do I do that and get into Ophelia's pants?

She obviously isn't for you. In her eyes, you chose fornication over the American military and its church.

Your daughter wants to get laid. It is going to be the downfall of her conservatism, thought the Baptist lady.

I forgot how concisely you word everything, divorced Baptist lady, thought Travis.

You're welcome.

"I will just say this one thing," Ms. Blossom said as she walked out of the auditorium to Travis. "Have you given any thought as to what people are going to make of you being back here again? They are not going to know whether you still care about the Lord's church or not. It isn't fair to tempt people to talk about you like they know anything about you at all by living near them. You know how we are. Therefore, you are partly to blame for embarrassing us like this. That is a cruel thing to do to us when all we ever wanted to do was for our input about how you lived your life to not go ignored."

"You do horrible things to try to get what you want that other more mainstream groups know not to do."

"I guarantee you other people are going to presume the same things as we have about you that you have never said out loud or in electronic correspondence. Nobody likes being called presumptive even if they are. What are you going to do about that?"

"Oh my god, lady, that is not a normal way to talk. As long as you are continuing to do that, I think other people will listen to my side of the story and suspect you for a liar."

Well then, we'll make it that. We'll get you in the end. It seems like a worthwhile crusade to me.

Only an a-hole wouldn't let us have stupid, oblivious douchebag, thought Dr. Freemoney.

Doesn't he know how we are? Why can't he see he's better off with us? thought Mrs. Blossom.

And who is encouraging that again? Who needs this solved this way this time, for the stakes could not be higher? Who is getting you to act erratically like a cornered snake?

I am, said the rumbling bass voice that belonged to the Big Blue Guy.

I guess we are going to intervene, or we need to. That way you will know to back off these charades at the very end and you won't have to fry, she followed up in her head voice.

You are a stupid woman. You cannot outwit me.

We'll see about that.

I hate to break it to you, but I am leaving soon. I just wanted to tie up loose ends with my family and not be forced to sever ties there before I am damn well ready to do that. I won't get the best outcome over the course of my entire life in that one. I sensed that earlier.

You can't leave this community. We have nobody else your age who hasn't done that already if they were going to do that. People are going to presume you want to stay. You used to talk like that. Just because you stopped doesn't mean we won't run with it for your sake. What were you expecting? We are looking out for your interest as well as ours, so try trusting us. If you don't know how to do our thing the way we want our thing done, then you will be a douchebag here until you do. If we say that, you could wind up dead leaving here, then you need to know we can arrange that.

Damn. Those people. Killing me. They won't do that. Fine, threaten me with violence after invading my privacy. I won't show up at church again. I think that solves it for everyone. Unlike you, I know who I am.

I like your take on it, thought the divorced Baptist Lady. *Also, remember to watch out for your mother. She may talk sweet to you, and you may not think she will join in, but if she engages in name-calling toward you and if she is partial to conservatives in the family, she will try to submarine you at the end. Beware of your mother. She has a broken conscience.*

You would've won with that last trip had you not just arrived back here like your parents had something to offer you that they do not have, thought Mrs. Blossom.

Mom is right. You need to fear God while at the same time talk like that about sex in your head and not out loud, thought Ophelia.

Not at church he doesn't. The sermon was on loving your neighbor. Did either of you two hear that, or were you listening to those sex-obsessed, problem Christians in the balcony? thought Dr. Freemoney.

I am ready for him to leave the Bible college. It is really messing with my mind that he is getting a religious education from one of our schools and doesn't officially designate himself as part of the Restoration Church. In fact, I think it's a license to take it elsewhere that he is a problematic person and to put up a proper defense of ourselves as not being a cult, thought Ophelia.

I just want for you to come back to the balcony with less of those thoughts in church and stay focused on the sermon. It will go better for you, thought the Baptist lady.

Of all of them, you got me spot on before that. It will be a while before I care again. Most people instinctively want to leave a group that engages in coercive and manipulative acts.

Travis got up and left the service, glad he was only in town for eight weeks.

"The Nicene Creed should be destroyed," said Travis as he got in his car and turned on National Public Radio on his drive home. "The culture is going downhill when fundamentalist Christians will lie, cheat, and steal to cover their tracks, and not a single one of those people can see that more than any other religious adherents. They're a bunch of walking inconsistencies. They just want endless purchasing power. I wonder how they will be when the recession finally hits them."

Like companies that misinform and do not promote competitive markets? asked the Big Blue Guy.

"That sounds about right."

He remembered the Big Blue Being with the pimp's cane at the art exhibition by Zeer Goede. *That does not need to get started,* thought Travis. *Too much history there.*

On his way home from church, Travis stopped at the convenience store to buy a quartet of Mike's hard lemonade in glass bottles. After he had driven home and put it in his fridge at his parents' house, he poured a bottle into a glass from a whiskey decanter set he had got for himself as a gift. The rest would go in a cooler with him on the drive to Charleston. He had to travel four and a half hours out of town tomorrow to receive training to guide people through an exhibition on Dada and Surrealists from Annette at the museum of art. It had got old doing it one day at a time, so he thought he would ask Oliver Gupta if he could stay at his place again. He also said that he would be fine watching a Bollywood movie on Wednesday night.

He did not oversleep and was able to pack up what he needed to stay in town a few days at Oliver's house. Travis would be fine to do this again for a week like he had before he moved out of the city and back to his hometown to go to a Bible college.

He headed directly for the Charleston museum of contemporary art. He had his orange checkered dress shirt unbuttoned to show some chest hair and had on mushroom leather black dress shoes and gray socks with an orange top lining, heel and toes, and blue lightning bolts in the gray. He pulled out a wooden comb and ran it through his neck-length black hair and prepared to replace his Southern accent with his Continental accent. It was much harder to do nonstop in a room full of Southerners.

After locking up his car that had a can of mace in it along with a pocketknife to substitute for a gun because all the kung fu in the world wouldn't save you from a stray bullet, he tucked his car keys into his pocket and went to talk to Annette, the volunteer coordinator. He walked up the steps and opened the door, flashed the devil's best grin at the receptionist, and then walked on past the doors to the gallery floors. Annette was talking with museum staff the same as she usually did, so he walked on over to the museum's largest gallery floor where the Zeer Goede exhibition had been at the beginning of the year and took a look around.

They had three Magritte paintings on loan. He recognized *Thunderstruck* the moment he saw it leading off the visitors' promenade through the museum. It was a painting that depicted a nude White woman arriving with the clouds—like the goddess bringing her children on home. He walked over to a second space and saw Magritte's painting *Golconde*, which appeared to depict every single

European Calvinist on his way into the heavens. They had another painting of his that had a gentleman coming home from work to make out with his lady-in-waiting at home, having difficulty because both of their heads were covered in cling film.

The next wall held four Diego Rivera paintings. The first painting was of him coming home to his Frida to clasp her hand and look into her eyes adoringly. The second painting was of a man working the field during the spring with a farmhand, tilling the soil manually and breaking a sweat. A third painting showed a woman cutting white flowers and handing them to their children to carry away and possibly place in baskets on a truck to carry to a flower shop. The man of the family had a large basket full of calla lilies he was carrying on his back in a fourth painting. There was a beautifully surreal painting of a fantastic world of colorful mushrooms on a green background the color of an aurora. A second one appeared to sexualize a factory assembly machine.

The next series of paintings was done by an artist named Arshile Gorky. The last painting showed the woman at the homestead at the end of the day after gardening with a book in her hand and a smile on her face, glad she had this moment for introversion and escapism. He was ready to go peek at what lay beyond the wall in the second space.

When he walked around to the other side, he saw that they had an infamous photograph of Man Ray on loan sandwiched between two sculptures of his placed-on tables. At that moment, Annette walked over to him.

"I wish you had not brought Man Ray into the exhibition. He had a reputation as a chauvinist."

"That was most guys then regardless of how progressive they were. The Surrealist artists in the second and third spaces mostly sought to challenge that. There were some famous ones who sympathized with capitalism and the church like Salvador Dalí. I do not have him at this exhibit. That would be beneath me. If you want to answer questions about chauvinist attitudes in favor of female submission in the development of BDSM, then this is the wall where you can field them."

"I figured that might be it then for most of the gallery viewers. Why is this in an exhibition for everyone young and old to see? You should lead people through this exhibition and not me. I cannot explain the world of kink to people. I have not been active in their community before."

"They may not mind if you do as long as you are not judgmental. Tell them to buy a book about it or attend Kink University. Tell them you should never try anything without paying for proper instruction in a book or video format. Tell them do not play with people who do not know what they are doing and are not competent to give you a good time. What was it you asked me to do on Thursday? Go to a séance with you and Oliver?"

"Yes, I had saved up for that."

"Duke and Walt will go to the séance if I tell them to."

Travis said, "I find your version of this more intriguing than Oliver's. Are the two of you never going to have a relationship with a partner who is a challenge and more of an equal again?"

"I could care less about having one of those. I get along great with women and men my own age, but I don't like dating men my age," Annette replied. "And I have kept friendships with other men and women my age longer than I have ever remained married."

"I guess if you're faithful to your freedom and you keep your physique and invest your time and money responsibly, you get to have sexual partners on reserve that are not a challenge."

"You get away with a lot more than others when you are old, even when your partners your own age have said stop taking risks. Who needs to be challenged by a partner like that? I have my career and more than enough to get my desires met." Annette was maintaining her professional demeanor. She was not even commenting upon Travis's overall increase in muscle mass.

"What you can say to people when you arrive at the Man Ray wall is 'While most of them were chauvinistic and homophobic like everyone else in their day, the Surrealists despised the teachings in mainstream Christianity (at the time and probably for its duration) that sex should fill a primarily procreative role. When they looked at a backside, they, like most people who take charge in the home, saw the potential for a sexual act that is gratuitous and serves no procreative role and is a direct attack on church teaching on the supposedly splendid economic arrangement the church gives women who allow themselves permanent enslavement in matrimony.'"

More!

That was odd, Travis thought.

"Man Ray took a photograph of a bare-naked woman on her knees with her keeping her hands behind her back to block the photographer's view. The photograph was called *Prayer*. He knows what I know, what my young men who dominate eventually know, which is that you cannot get a good girl who has a kinky mind. You often get a floozy who still expects economic support. It's often better when practitioners of kink who are often poly anyway keep a good emotional distance between themselves and their partners. Most poly people find that it works well to have only one long-term partner to live with. They call them their primary. It's a rotten deal for two young people to try kinky monogamy together. You could get a partner who has a kinky mind and let her have her freedom and listen to her and make sure she feels understood and meet other needs and possibly not end up losing out on a relationship with a partner who has the same interests as you, but you need to know that they can be volatile and not be cruel to them in response."

"I see why you still have sexual partners here in Charleston," Travis noted.

"None of mine are going to stick around. I do not expect them too. I have plenty of people my age I am friends with. It isn't too great not having a secure retirement available for everyone here, but I have planned well, and my closest friends have as well, so I know I will be all right when I am older. I'd rather just move to a retirement community and be amorous the way many of the old folks in those places are since I have the money. Some people live like this. I am surprised you came back for this exhibit. You know how being a museum docent goes. You do not have to volunteer to walk them through the exhibit here and discuss it with them if it makes you uncomfortable."

"I can volunteer for this week before I head back up to North Carolina. I am going to go over to see Oliver. I am staying at his place again."

He walked up the steps with his duffel bag in his hand, his umbrella in the other, and his backpack on his back, with a set of his keys in his pocket. He moved through the foyer into the hallway and down to the first bedroom on the right. He could hear Mr. Gupta in his bedroom.

Travis dropped his duffel bag and went into the kitchen. He grabbed a carton of eggs out of the refrigerator and set it on the table. He got out a skillet and sprayed it with butter so that the eggs would not stick. He turned the eye of the stove on. He cracked an egg on the counter and broke it over the skillet. He repeated this two times. He grabbed a handful of shiitake mushrooms and washed them off and dried them in a paper towel. He tossed that in the skillet. Toward the end while the eggs were cooked on the bottom, he put in chipotle seasoning. By the time his omelet was cooked and he placed it on his plate, Oliver was walking in. "You look nice now. You are really succeeding with your workout regimen. You're bringing in that waistline. Work on that and a six-pack once you have the pecs and the guns."

"I may not care if that never happens if I am in better shape than you now and stay that way when I am your age. I may get my haircut. I'd be keeping the old ways alive."

Oliver asked Travis how his trip was.

"Portland was nice. I had a great trip. I found out some things about the way Americans try to do Hinduism in California. I do not know how much of it was practical. I liked a lot of it. I may borrow quite a bit of it and do it in private, keeping an open belief in God even if it is an impersonal one along with reincarnation. It is not just a séance I have arranged. I am getting a Roma lady to lead me through past life regressions tomorrow."

"Then you're kind of doing Hinduism without the caste system, which is the big thing unifying all the variety there. You might do Buddhism and have a philosophy of life you are more consistent following. There are not a lot of differences between Hinduism and

Buddhism. The big one is their concept of the self. In Hinduism, it is permanent. In Buddhism, it is not," Oliver said.

"Anyway, they talked a lot about messengers or extradimensional beings. I was not sure at the end of the trip whether that was really going to catch on. There is something there influencing the thoughts of people. I do not think angels and demons clarify it either. I have seen how those people behave following orthodox dogma, and I do not want a bit of their thoughts influencing me. That holds true whether it is Annunaki/egregores/jinni/or Ashurans that are the extradimensional beings directing them to fling strange people in my direction saying odd things out loud that are not tied to anything. I could do without many of the strange things like the goddess and clairvoyance. I did like the way they were encouraging vegetarianism, natural healing, and esoteric energy field manipulation. I may receive proper training in Kundalini yoga, maybe even Reiki and leading people through past life regressions. I think people who do badly at martial arts are probably ignorant because I think the key to breaking a pile of cinder blocks lies in that Kundalini/chi field. Once when someone agitated got near me, I used a block from Tai Chi, and it propelled him all the way across the room. That person was a condom and had a pretty messed up energy field or else that would not have happened. That energy field works in my favor every time I reach out for it. Other than that energy field and reincarnation, there isn't a lot of that unscientific esoteric stuff worth keeping. I may be open to some type of extradimensional beings messing with people who are not as informed as they could be. I see that going on with ignorant and presumptive people all the time."

"You should do Tibetan Buddhism. It is that simple. They wouldn't care if you don't care about hallucinogenic use and human sexuality if it transcends desire. A lot of Buddhists mimic the Jews and Christians on forbidding sexual indulgences. If you are not lusting, then others wouldn't care. That is why that one is not popular in the West. If you do not lie, cheat, steal and do not murder and are not mean and selfish with your money and time, then you are practicing that one. They have a good ancient concept with their Wheel of Life so that you could follow that, and the extradimensional beings and their messages do not get out of hand. I think that the Christians who believe they are getting messages from the saints believe everything they are told at this point, and that is what is making them act like dangerous, mentally unstable people."

"I don't think it's that bad here with them yet. When it is, I would have moved already. I don't want to do Buddhism in New England. I think it is more glamorous to do the New Age movement on the West Coast. The Buddhists I have met would drop humanism in a heartbeat like they were not even attached to it even if they were not prone to messianic ideologies like Judaism, Christianity, Islam, and some new age cults. I would never stop being a humanist."

"Why not be a Buddhist? You can pretty much do it on your own. They do have temples here in the country and members who call themselves bodhisattvas. It differs from an arhat. The arhats do not do reincarnation. Bodhisattvas will do that. The Dalai Lama does it from time to time according to them, but you don't have to be the Dalai Lama."

"What does the Dalai Lama do?"

"He gets reincarnated to lead the people of Tibet."

"Anyway, the séance is on Thursday. Somebody at the resort said I could find out for myself whether I believed in reincarnation and extradimensional beings by doing past life regressions, and I decided to arrange a séance with the same psychic. Do you still want to watch a Bollywood movie on Wednesday night?"

"That is the only night of the week I am available for a Bollywood movie."

"Okay."

"You should plan on arriving back late Tuesday and Thursday nights."

"Oh. That's fine. As long as I don't have to pay for a hotel."

"I am going to let you eat and go to bed. I did get your text that you were going to be here in an hour. Make sure to do that tomorrow night and Thursday night as well."

"That works." Travis placed the omelet in a hot dog bun since that was the only bread they had until he went to the store and put mayo on it. After he ate, he went to his room at Oliver's and crawled up in bed and went off to sleep.

He woke up with a clean face. Mr. Gupta had still been great to him since he was young. He got up in the morning, got dressed, headed over to the museum to do his work as a museum docent on the Dada and the Surrealists exhibition, and drove out of the cultural district to the city's Black and Latino neighborhood to get the groceries. He drove back to Mr. Gupta's house and had a peanut-butter-and-jelly sandwich on wheat bread. He had his appointment for past life regressions today. Then he was going out to a pool hall with Demarcus, his White friend from high school with a Black name. He had plans for Tuesday and Wednesday as well. He was meeting a friend of his from college who was now a Communist for lunch tomorrow and getting a Thai yoga massage at a wellness center; that was supposed to be like someone else doing your yoga for you. Then he was heading over to Fort Sumter and the Charleston Market at some point before going back to Oliver's home to watch a three-hour Bollywood movie. He had not planned out Wednesday or Friday before he left to make it to his piano and voice lessons. There was a whole lot to do in Charleston if you didn't mind going into the poorer districts as well as the colorful French quarter.

When Travis arrived at Rita's Psychic Parlor, he was greeted by a friendly woman in her fifties who had her hair pulled back into an indigo scrunchie and had kohl on her eyes and wore purple lipstick and an ultramarine tunic over black pants, black hose, and black slippers. A gray-and-white female tabby cat stepped out of her business with her.

"Who might you be?"

"I am Travis Marx. I am here for my past life regressions. I have an appointment for this today and a séance Thursday."

"Oh, you're good for all that. I already have everything ready for that first one. Come inside?"

Travis walked into the parlor. In the front room, she had a lizard in a terrarium from the neighborhood's reptile store. That seemed like something he could check out later. The business was full of the smell of orange essential oils, and she had a fountain going, and she had women's clothing from Southeast Asia, possibly monsoon coverings, for sale on racks at the front of the shop. There was a large brass statue of Rama as well as a large brass statue of a Buddha lined up against the far wall and a selection of chalk paints for Holi festival as well as candles and lanterns for Vesak Day. She was carrying a collection of items—paraphernalia, if you like—for people who follow the path of dharma.

"So you sort of blend the path of dharma with the New Age movement."

"Since 1992. Have you ever had a past life regression before?" Rita asked him.

"No."

"Well, I will have to help you summon an animal guide. I have something you need to take once your shoes are off and you are sitting down."

"Is it a hallucinogen?"

"It's a tea."

After a fifteen-minute conversation, he heard a whooshing sound and Nintendo music, and he saw a monkey riding an elephant traveling in the air as it beat two palm branches like bird wings.

The monkey said in an exceedingly high girl's voice, *We volunteer to show you how things used to be for you.* The monkey and the elephant both winked at the same time.

"You should begin to lie back and let me find a guide for you."

"I actually have one, maybe two, already."

"You do! Oh, that's convenient. Has it spoken to you yet?"

"She did."

"You don't have to tell me a thing she tells you. I will warn you, if I did not grab her for you, I cannot guarantee you that anything she tells you is true. That's how you need to be at the séance with whatever thoughts you are experiencing."

"That's fine."

It is, the elephant interjected in a bossy yet playful voice. *First things first,* she said as she somersaulted three times, *you need to make certain to get somebody's past life memories in their first six years of life. If they say something about a past life then, it is probably true. It is much more difficult to get to them later. Hmm. It looks like you have mentioned two past lives to other people. I looked back over your memories from those years in case you were wondering.* She and the monkey flew behind his head, and he felt his neck tingling, like feathers made of icicles were licking him.

Well, let's see what else there is here. It looks like you were a Brown man in your past life or possibly Gene Kelly. No, you were definitely a Brown man, and you lived in China as an ethnic minority. You died protesting against the Communist government in 1989.

"So I stayed around for five years and then became me?

Who knows? Let's go back further. Before that, you were a Black woman, originally from the South. It looks like you hop genders every third life but not while you are an animal. It also looks like you stop believing in a personal God and praying by the time you are thirty in every life. I will leave it up to you to decide whether you have chosen the path of dharma openly as a bodhisattva in any of them. Also, there is this!

Surprise! said the female monkey. *You have been an activist for vast social reform in backward communities in the past two. What are you going to do in this one?*

Travis couldn't think clearly. It was all new to him. He didn't think thought was even necessary most of the time.

The elephant interjected with *I will leave that up to him to decide. If you ever get tired of that, you can always go to Nepal for your next life. You can be a woman there and not have to be in the order with the men if you must be reborn and want out. That is probably a good thing to do to yourself if being a bodhisattva never works out. You'd do well there as a nun not meeting your libidinous rights.*

Travis asked, "Have you gone back any further?"

Well, I could, but it's more of the same. You choose to be born where the community is backward and challenge them to revolt. When they do not, you do not always leave. Sometimes you do and lose touch with them not doing their thing. You have just not done it anywhere where people have accomplished actual reforms that meant anything. It sounds anti-humanist though it may just be your particular world. I will spare you the details, but both the past two individuals were good players in ongoing resistance movements late into their lives before their time came to an end. They made a good choice with the families they picked to be born into. They encouraged them to be inquisitive even if it sometimes backfired. That has often been the extent of it. Families could go, and it would fix a lot, but don't make that a thing. There were just too many problems in backward places due to their willful ignorance and collective panic when things do not work out the way they dreamed them for you not to manifest yourself again here or there. Too many new things you had not experienced firsthand, you were ready to experience. I think I'll human again!

"So I was not liked."

But you don't seem to care! How annoying! What an awful way to be about it all.

The monkey clanged a gong. *You got around. Yes, Travis have information will travel.*

Rita interrupted, "You have passed ten minutes with the animal guides. Have you asked them all you would like to know, or do you need more tea? I bill by tea mostly with past life regressions."

"I can still ask more? Am I anywhere near my past families and progeny?"

Did that sound like a stupid question to you too?

...

Bye. Interview's over.

Travis got up and followed Rita to the cash register and gave her fifty dollars in cash. "Thank you, Rita. I don't know how you do it, but that stuff works like magic. I will be back Thursday."

"See you then."

Travis got in his car and turned on the AC. He gave Demarcus a call on his phone to see when he was going to be available to meet up.

"Hey, Travis, I just got off the first shift. I am going to head home and take a nap. I am still planning on catching up with you tonight."

Travis headed to an independent bookstore there in Charleston. The business had bought up a local record store and a local toy store in the neighborhood during the past two years, built a new building with a café with *en terrasse* dining, and located it near a bus and trolley stop. It had been getting beaucoup business. He ordered a lemonade and perused a coffee-table book on Paris, and a White chick came up to him to start a conversation fifteen minutes into his reading.

"Do you not drink caffeine?"

"I don't."

"Is it for religious reasons?"

"No."

"Then I guess it's all right."

Travis was irritated. "You presume an awful lot."

"I am just making normal conversation."

"Go away."

"Fine. Nobody likes your type anyway. Do you see any 7-Elevens around here? Think you could open up a business around here?"

"That child there is poor White trash, honey. I wouldn't normally intrude on someone else's conversation unless it was abnormal. She doesn't have a dime to her name she isn't borrowing from Wall Street. Look at her go inverting everything. It's like she was born into a traveling circus family."

"I didn't want that. You are kind of doing it too. Somebody someplace may have been born into a traveling circus. I am heading someplace else." For the first time that day, Travis was genuinely pissed off. He tossed his lemonade into the trash receptacle and headed out the door and joined the first trolley tour available. He was sitting directly across from a couple of older people speaking what was probably a Chinese language. The seats were wooden, and if his memory served him correctly, his back would ache from moving over the pebbled street of Charleston in this vehicle well into the next day after this, but at least he didn't have to deal with trying to make conversation with random Southerners.

Is that not just what Demarcus has planned for you tonight at the pool hall? said that rumbling bass voice that sounded like the Big Blue Guy.

"Demarcus is like me and doesn't have to talk nonstop. The worst part about it is that you are either playing pool or smoking. I don't smoke, and I haven't played pool in a while. He will probably play one hour and then want to go grab a bite to eat before China King closes at ten and then get home so he can work tomorrow."

Charleston is full of more history than you can see in the Old Quarter alone. You can take a ferry to Fort Sumter and see where the Civil War got started, or you can get off at the next stop and tour the town's market. You could shop around for the best deal on a sweetgrass basket.

"I'll get off here," Travis said to the trolley driver.

Travis walked into the market at about five thirty, when it had cooled down substantially. He saw many vendors selling several different crafts. There was a vendor selling chess sets who spoke to him in a German accent. "I have the best chess sets from all over Europe for sale here, sir. Are you interested?"

"Not today."

"This one is from Germany. It is made of linden wood. It weighs little, but isn't it beautiful?"

"I said not today." Travis said that brusquely.

He made his way to the second hall and found a little old Gullah lady with a relative there with her selling sweetgrass baskets and sweetgrass roses.

"Those are gorgeous!"

She didn't give a response.

Talking to the younger of the two, he said, "I am interested in the bundle of sweetgrass roses that you have there for sale. How much are you selling it for?"

"You can get that amount there for $180."

"I am all right with that. This is something people come here to get. I know that."

"Are you from here?"

"I have lived in the Carolinas since I was ten. I think that is a nice bouquet. You probably know it is worth $180 too."

"Buy it then, though you can get a basket with it for $150 more."

"Maybe some other time."

Travis walked away with woven sweetgrass roses, backtracked to the independent bookstore, grabbed another lemonade, and hopped in his car glad to not at all be concerned about starting a spending spree. He had never had one before. He even drove back in the direction of Rita's Psychic Parlor to check out the reptile shop that was in her neighborhood. He saw a Russian tortoise that was priced for $150. The store care sheet said that some tortoises could outlive their owners. He walked out, having decided not to go through with a major decision like that today. You did not usually get buyer's remorse when the purchase was under $300. At least that was how it was when you were a trust fund baby who had the privilege to either be a free spirit or a mean, narcissistic jerk. He would still probably feel buyer's remorse if he purchased something that might have been alive for fifteen years already and thinking he would be able to keep it around 85 more years. It had always been a good idea before to give decisions like that some time so he could think out how practical it would be to have a legacy tortoise by his side.

He drove clear across town to see where the ferry station for the Fort Sumter excursion was located for tomorrow as well as to buy two bean burritos at Taco Bell, one of the creature comforts of home, which he was really starting to believe needed to be the West Coast next.

Going back to eating fast food all the time will destroy your figure, said the rumbling bass voice of the Big Blue Guy.

"What if I want to have kids and live in the suburbs?" Travis retorted.

It's better to not have kids and keep your figure.

"Hmm. That makes sense. It's getting late now. I am ready to get this over with."

Now, Travis, you do not know how random Southerners at a Southern pool hall are going to be. You have not been to one since the last time you had a serious girlfriend.

"Shut up. You're not even the Blue Guy.

That is so sick. Well, I may be another one like him engaging in interstellar travel.

"I can grab my own train of thought, you jackass Annunaki/Egregore/Jinni/Ashuran. It is not the type of place an introvert like me kills time."

Are you having social anxiety?

"Because I won't call you a demon? NO! Demarcus shaved his head two months ago, and I can see that being a place frequented by White people or tokenized mixed people who are kind of trashy. Demarcus was in the gifted program with me at school, when we still had one. He is one of only a handful of the people I could stand in that town where I went to high school still living in the area whom those fascist, self-appointed dogma police have not managed to get addicted to one drug or another and end up in jail at some point. I want everyone to know how bad they are, and he acts like I should do their thing too!"

You've been to one before. They have loud music. It will drown out whatever conversation gets made at the pool table. You won't want to dance, and no one will ask you too. Indian guys dance better than White guys. That's how fights get started.

"In which future are you planning this secret project, Blue Guy?" Travis asked jokingly.

In the one we are hurtling to, of course. Blackmail shouldn't be a thing for family. It especially should not be a thing for honest people.

Travis sort of gulped down that lemonade in his car. It wasn't a hard gulp, and it certainly wasn't unusual, like the rest of his day. He felt confident. Something awesome could happen. The voice was deep enough. Travis got in his car and headed a bit further away from Charleston.

Demarcus made his introductions for him well. They both kept it brief. He said something about wishing he would stay in the South and not move to Portland. Travis expected an awkward silence. He finally said, "I like it there. I know that jobs are available here, but the people there are more like me."

"Is there a large Indian community there?" said a guy named Bryce as the night passed on.

"No, they are just more libertine. They respect other people's right to behave irreverently. I thought I would call it like it is again. Not that that applies to anyone but religious leaders. You have no business lopping me in with them."

"You should ask Jesus into your heart. That is in case you have never done it before. Trust me. It fixes a lot for those presumptive people you mentioned."

"Douche!" said Demarcus.

Bryce looked in his direction, looking a bit uncomfortable himself.

"Portland it is for Travis. He has the money to move there and has apparently found two part-time jobs."

The music had stopped playing as a track ended but quickly resumed, and no one cared anymore. He was still glad when they left, and he had gone with Demarcus to China King across the other side of that neighborhood for dinner.

"I know you're not as hungry as I am, but it is just $10 for as many plates as you need and a soda, and this is the only meal I have been able to fit in today," said Demarcus.

"That's cool. I can get a bowl of vegetable lo mein. You can pay $10 for something like that in a big city. I would not normally be eating out then."

"What would you like to drink?" the waitress asked him.

"I'll have water," said Travis.

"Sprite," said Demarcus.

"So *you're* not going anywhere anytime soon?" Travis asked as he sat back down.

"I am not like you in that respect, Travis. I do not think things are going to get ugly here too quick. I just got this job, and I still have a renter's contract for almost the next six months."

"That was a good one. I think you may like the West Coast. If you start talking back at the religious nuts here, you may want to head over there. There are fewer of them there."

"There are fewer in Massachusetts on up through Canada and over to the UK who speak my language. Attendance and devotion aren't that high in Catholic areas. You only need the Eucharist three times a year, so it's safe to throw in Quebec and Ireland. You could head up there."

"A-hole!" a fat old White woman muttered. "Of course, they are still bad there and getting away with it."

"Most everybody like us who has stayed put has either left or is in jail for drug possession. I figured there must be a good reason keeping you here still. I have had difficulty getting connected since we left high school. It was awesome back then. Colleges in the South favor a nominally Christian culture, and then my parents made attempts to submarine me—my Indian mom as well even though there's less money in her family."

"Was she not an orphan?"

"She had cousins and called them brothers and sisters. It goes on in Asia. I am not sure how much it goes on in India, but she has always said she was from an Adivasi background. She has been bringing them all over via chain migration if she can get them married off. I wonder if that is going to start again after the election."

"The elites don't do anything. The median income is still going down, and the wealth gap is increasing."

"The current president says he is going to stop bringing in immigrants and continues doing everything the others have done with the warming climate exacerbated by developed economies to make them arrive wanting into the country."

"God. I was hoping for something different," said the fat old White man sitting next to the fat old White woman.

"Like some sense on the part of the Indian," said his fat old White wife. "Why should people be arriving from other countries during an ongoing recession? They'll just go to the West Coast and take your job before you."

"You pathetic substitute for a human," Demarcus said to the fat old White woman.

"We are getting up and leaving," said the fat old White wife as she slowly raised up and walked away with her husband arm in arm, as if it was supposed to make a point.

"Premises are under surveillance. Every time you talk like that, there is a record of it. Just because you are full of self-righteous indignation doesn't mean you look better with the electronic trail you are leaving," said the maître d' of China King.

"I bet billionaires like us better," said the obnoxious chunky old man. "That was all I had in the end, but I know for a fact it was good enough."

"I don't care if they don't come back," said the Asian lady behind the desk. "They paid on credit." There was a 91 A score over her shoulder.

"It is the best one in town," said Demarcus.

"Are you going to try to switch to a different shift as soon as it is available?"

"I like working first shift."

"Oh. So this is not a thing normally—binge eating at China King at 9:00 p.m.," Travis asked sarcastically.

Remember what you told Raul about these people being highly presumptive. Try not doing that yourself.

Travis and Demarcus parted ways after that, and Travis drove back to Oliver's place, saddened seeing his friend staying stuck in a community he obviously would do better to leave ASAP. What on earth could he be keeping from everyone about his personal life, and how would he prefer to handle his own life in a worst-case scenario? He did not think he would see him again for a while. He was basically doing well enough when you spoke to him, and you could get a coherent response. It seemed a lot better compared with other people down here. He walked into Mr. Gupta's house, went to his bedroom, and got ready for bed.

Travis awakened feeling very rested Wednesday morning. Oliver had gone off to work, if he had even come home last night. He left a note that said, "To Travis, I am still all right with Bollywood tonight and seeing the witch on Thursday." He poured a glass of orange juice and spread peanut butter on two slices of toast. After he had eaten and got dressed, he drove on over to the museum of contemporary art to lead a walk-through of the exhibit. He was looking forward to going to the wellness center for a Thai yoga massage, but he was looking forward to seeing his Communist friend from college even more. He wrapped up the exhibit that day, his next to last day in town with no one commenting on the *Monument to D. A. F. Sade.*

If anything, the residents of Charleston wondered why something so risqué had been dropped off at their art museum for a long stay.

He stopped at a convenience store for a sugary sports drink. This one had yogurt and a banana, and he thought after meeting Demarcus that one of them would be putting weight on from their diet and not the other. He headed over to the local college he and his closet Communist friend Jack had attended where Jack was now working as a teacher's assistant in graduate school, convinced that he could decolonize academia better than anyone unaware that Communism was the real deal for Socialism and that it would take a White Southern man to get it started. They had a lively discussion about the state of art and health care in Cuba under the Communists there.

"You still picked a better school to go to than I did for your next degree," Travis told him.

"Don't get down on yourself, Travis. We all make mistakes."

"Oh, I don't know that it is a mistake to get a degree in counseling so that your parents and family do not expect you to ever see a counselor again. You probably save a lot of money over the course of your life. I just meant you picked a better school to go to than I did for your next degree. I have never seen a group of people so twisted as at a Christian school. They tell you they will let you handle your own life matters, and then they go on and interfere and try to handle them for you. Spread rumors like you cannot even imagine."

"Would it make a difference to get your degree and then go back to normal?"

"I would like for my credits to transfer, but I do not see a way for that to happen. I can head into the house even with a mild alcoholic beverage and my parents do not get irritated, but if I spoke against their church, all hell would break loose. It would be the same if I brought a relationship partner I was living with home to them for them to meet. They would want it to end and that not be the person I married. They made that clear when I was seventeen. I would have thought I would have been all right staying if I took a break from what they considered sexual misconduct while I was working on my degree. I don't care anymore. I wish they would let bygones be bygones. I don't have any positive memories or feelings that involve either, so it would be nice to see them allow distance to have its effect.

"I would have thought I could go to a New Age retreat in California and nobody find out, but from the looks everyone was giving me at church on Sunday night, you know it had got around. Oliver says I would be better going with Tibetan Buddhism than being a New Ager. When they are ready to talk about it out loud, there is no telling how badly they will pervert it to turn it into a pernicious lie designed to intimidate me. Once again, I am left wondering how they don't know that these acts look like malevolence directed from them to me without any provocation in the eyes of everyone else and why they do not see a need to stop. How long have you known me again? Hank and Viviane Marx confirmed that? That's what everyone else does the rest of my life for me, and the pathetic cult devotees do not see that they are at fault. They think they are helping themselves out."

"You are right on the mark. They are incredibly dense if they think they hold any worth as a supportive family for you after all the backstabbing they have participated in as well. Are you all right if you never have to be near them again in close physical proximity?"

"How do I arrange that?"

"Stay. Get your documentation for your proof of citizenship and identity plus proof that you are eligible for social security benefits and never go to them for help again. They don't even provide what you really need, the dirty liars."

"Are you still sure you don't want to go to the séance with me?"

"I would love to go to the séance with you."

"That's great. I will let you go back to work. I am going to check out Fort Sumter today. I heard some a-hole on talk radio spouting off at the mouth about how the South would secede if there was ever going to be a Green New Deal. I don't want another Fort Sumter to happen, but I also don't see the need to stop them if they try to exit. Looking at how Brexit was done, if there is a peaceful exit, they get the worse deal. Where are their financial institutions, transport vehicle producers, audiovisual technology producers, and communications infrastructure businesses located? I hope they call it Sexit in the media when they threaten a Southern exit. Mock them for the rest of time if they go through on it. Make sure to provide a guaranteed income above poverty to all their offspring when they reach the age of sixteen so that they can head up North if they want to leave."

"Their businesses will move to the South because our taxes are lower," said a White guy with a drawl, and then he spit some of that old North Carolina tobacco into a used-up water bottle.

"Their businesses won't close the doors for good if there was an economic crash just like that hillbilly says," said his Communist friend. "Have fun at Fort Sumter. You can come back and see me anytime."

Travis had to wait in line at the noon hour for about an hour before he had his ticket and had boarded the ferry. He went to Fort Sumter with just the sound of the open sea splashing up against the boat and parents hushing up children growing restless on the thirty-five-minute ferry to the island the fort was on. Nobody was holding a conversation the entire trip. He had a camera app on his phone named after a prominent installation at forts such as these. He was ready to take impressive photos that would leave out any light elements he might want deemphasized at the time of day he managed to get here. They then docked, and everybody started up talking again as they spread out over the island for an hour of conversation and social media selfie pics. He was by himself for this one. None of his friends really cared to see historical sites or natural wonders the same as he did. It was something his parents made a point of doing when they went on family vacations when he was younger that he continued to make a point of doing even though he kept all the vacation memories compartmentalized now that his family was increasingly hostile toward him. One person giggled at him. He did have to get back on the boat with them, so he told them to mind their own business. He did not leave feeling ashamed, but he also felt dirtied by the experience. *What is wrong with White America?* he thought to himself.

"Look at the funny European visitor taking travel photos of Fort Sumter," said an obnoxious and presumptive eight-year-old White kid. His family was possibly from a fundamentalist background or otherwise thought they were important enough to talk out loud to themselves about their most recent presumptions. At least his parents weren't the type to strap a bomb to his chest and send him off to kill soldiers against his will. Even if they started training them to hate that young, they still hadn't resorted to sending their kids off with bombs strapped to their chests, these "soldiers of Christ" as their creepy song foretold they would become.

He headed on back to Oliver's house for their Wednesday-night three-hour Bollywood movie experience. It was obvious to Travis now that there were better ways of spending your Wednesday nights than at a Bible study or a gossip circle, as some of them were the last time he checked in on one. "I have buttered popcorn and beer," Oliver offered.

"That's great, Oliver. I will have a beer. Why did you leave the former Mrs. Gupta again?"

"She cheated on me to let me know it was over officially, so I cheated back on her. She wasn't expecting that. I was good in her eyes and her family's eyes before she did that. Well, we did that and ended it that way. No-fault divorce is awesome when you don't have kids. Don't talk about bad times from the past."

Travis's eyes twinkled.

"That's odd. For a moment, I saw your eyes twinkle red."

Mr. Gupta knows how it is to be human and reckless, the Big Blue Guy told Travis. *You don't have to join him just because you are condoning his behavior.*

"I have never seen a Brown man's brown eyes twinkle red before. It is like an alien experiencing earth for the first time is in there."

"Maybe beer puts extra kindness in my eyes. It also makes me warmer without feeling an absurd need to cuddle. Oliver, I would never become a swinger. Even with a time limit. To each his own though," Travis offered.

"Then we will just watch the movie."

When the Bollywood movie had ended, it was ten thirty, and they went to their own bedrooms. Travis dropped off to sleep and stayed asleep until the morning arrived. They had breakfast and then headed off to the séance with Annette and her two subs and his Communist friend.

When they arrived at Ms. Rita's, she took them into the room she used for séances, to the room with the chairs and the table and buffet with a tea set laid out. She had a tablecloth set out on top of the table that had writing in Gothic script written on it. It appeared to be knit.

"It is in a language derived from Old Gallo-Roman. It is Alsatian. I was living there before I moved here. That was ages ago. I am going to check and see if the guests are arriving—just so that they know it is legit. I remember how you were on Tuesday."

Travis went to the door, and Jack had made it. Annette needed to get here with Duke and Walt soon. This séance was $100 and scheduled in advance. Annette made it fifteen minutes late, and one of her men parked her pink Cadillac in front as the other, a clean-shaven taller but muscular guy in his early twenties dressed in black and blue, helped her out of the car as the other yet-to-be-introduced man drove around back to park the car in the narrow parking lot. He showed up and looked the exact same as the other until he took his blue sunglasses off and tucked them away. They were both blonds with hazel eyes, but they did not appear related. They both had on a pouty bored model's expression on their face.

"In here, boys." Annette called to Travis, "Are we on time?"

"You arrived in the nick of time."

"Which one of you is Duke, and which one is Walt?"

"Okay, Walt, walk over to the table with Rama and one of the Buddha's and bend over."

Walt did as he was told.

"Now, Duke, spank him."

Travis laughed. He had not had as much fun as this since the last time he was on vacation. "Hey, do either of you have any inquiries for the psychic?"

"Does it require personal information?"

"What doesn't these days?" said Rita as she walked back out to greet the party.

"I won't. I will just watch."

"Well, Duke and Walt, there will be no forced bi at this séance. It was a time slot booking. I still have enough information to fill up a forty-five-minute appointment. Sometimes people show up to these and get more prophetic revelations than they wanted. Many people are, however, required at the table."

"Annette thought you both might have fun doing this for a change, and I agree. I will keep it going along with Oliver and Jack."

Rita directed them all through the shop to the very back room where the séance table was set up.

"There is a window in here. Do we need to shut it?" Walt asked.

She looked irritated for a moment and then brought them into the parlor and turned on an oil lamp and cut off the lights.

"Now I want for you all to know that the nature of a séance is discretion. It is also a strict matter of being clairvoyant and not abusing it. I do not require crystal balls, a tarot deck, or the *I Ching*."

"BS!" said Oliver.

"I figured that one would be the most reluctant to show up here at this séance. He is the one bottling up emotions the most until they spill over in unassertive reactivity and insults. If you only knew what he thinks when he isn't talking. That is a lustful, dirty old man."

"So you have telepathy."

"Well, sort of. I hear your thoughts before you do."

"What are you talking about?"

"It is simple. Thought as part of mind is not a permanent part of our nature. Much of it originates from the beyond."

"So are you going around guarding your mind against useless thoughts all the time?" asked Travis.

"All *my* thoughts are awesome," Rita said. "Dumb thoughts from a dumb mind do not appeal to me. They do almost everyone else. When they get started, they take on a life of their own and are hard to kill, but really, they are arriving from nowhere."

Everyone in the room felt uncomfortable. They were trying to figure out how to help Travis get his money back, or they were recording the séance on their phone under the table.

"I actually don't think anyone has their phone under the table recording the séance."

"That's what I was thinking!" said Oliver and Travis at the same time.

"There you have it. You two need to be more open-minded like those four over there. Neither one of you is going with the teachings of your ancestors anyway!" she said, and her voice boomed temporarily.

"Oh, that was creepy," said Duke and Walt at the same time.

"I know. It's hard to be me, but there is a reason this shop has been around forever."

"Travis," Rita said ominously, "I want you to know that I have looked into your future and have seen a high probability of you splitting the universe in two by the mere force of your will. I know that is a very sordid foretelling. All the extradimensional beings confirm that you are a world weaver."

"That is BS," snorted Duke dismissively.

Undeterred, Rita continued, "People are doing that all the time. It is useless to stop it. The worlds are woven together in a great ever-expanding pattern diverging into other planes all the time with Brahma/Allah/Yahweh at the vortex. It is impossible to see a way out of the third dimension when you are trapped in mind." Rita sat back, waiting to see Travis's reaction.

Startled, Travis exclaimed, "What a horrible deal. You mean there is somebody like me in another parallel universe, problems they have caused in a perpendicular universe with people who are not even represented in ours?"

"Well, some people are not represented in our universe. Just because those individuals look like you doesn't mean that they are you. You are the choices you make. If you ever met yourself in another universe, that individual may be morally bankrupt. Why would you claim that person as you?"

"If that is true, Travis, this whole thing today was not awesome," said Jack. "Spare us moments like these from now on. I do not want Space Buddhism to become a scientifically provable phenomenon. The implications are truly horrifying."

"Is that really possible, Rita?"

"It depends on what your purpose is you are here to achieve."

"She is talking like a bad witch. I knew this about her. People talk about people like this even in Charleston. What happens when another individual thwarts something you want to have happen most of the time? Do most people transcend desire? No, they try to destroy their enemies completely. What if you decided not to transcend that moment in a parallel universe? What if you perpendicularly wove your way into another? She is telling you something horrible about your purpose here in a veiled way. She's probably been doing candomblé the past two hundred years and not dharma. I wish there was a way I could have her arrested. Does this have anything to do with transcending desire and getting out of mind?" Oliver asked, hoping to spare him and Travis any more Space Buddhism nonsense.

"If you could transcend desire, you could go back to having a single reality. Ultimate reality, Brahma, whatever you want to call it, you can head there and cavort with the other arhats/Buddhas. Whatever world you would like to weave, you may. Just do not become attached to it. When you get thoughts from nowhere, they are deep in the future sometimes apparently. You're like me," answered Rita.

"It does not have to be that far into it when you could split the universe," Rita interjected. "You are going to have to learn to shut out all thoughts that are useless. The big thing is to leave dumb thoughts in a dumb mind and to only have awesome thoughts. As long as you do that, then that means you are in the same universe until your life ends."

"I do not like you as a person," Travis said to Rita.

"There is nothing you can do about it. I may weave my way out of town. You will find a different building where my shop is, and my name will disappear from all telephone directories."

"That woman is a nut," said Annette.

"She's just a space witch," said Oliver. "Don't dwell on it too long. We can go now."

"Here is your $100. Leave town on it."

Oliver had a grimace on his face as he watched Travis do this. He wondered why nothing really mattered to him. He also sensed that they might very well be in for a horrible reality in this universe if the realm of Ashurans and humans was getting this blurred. That was looking true regardless of whichever world Travis was supposedly weaving.

"I don't think any of that matters, Annette, Duke, Walt, and Jack."

"I think everybody else in that universe is just going to weave their own selves back out of it. You shouldn't try to get another séance, Travis. That one was funny like you thought it would be," said Walt as he climbed in the car to drive Annette and Duke away.

"It was kind of like that—a foretelling instead."

Jack and Oliver had not left yet.

"No, in this one, I definitely think everything is recalled properly. Someone starts Judgment Day, and I am not certain who. I was certain that was not a thing the way I was taught, but I am sensing that it may be one in this world soon, and only the most mentally fit will survive," Travis said to Oliver and Jack as they left one another's company.

CHAPTER 8

WHEN HE ARRIVED BACK IN TOWN, HE HAD TO do some intensives
with Viola. He had a good Bollywood song and dance number prepared, but he had busted his opportunity to properly perform "Clair
de lune" by Claude Debussy while he was traveling in fast company.
He did have his Meals on Wheels route to drive for a week on rota-
tion every five weeks, and he also had enough time to do that once
more before leaving to go to Portland. He spent his time trying to
perfect "Clair de lune" and walking in the park and building his
workout regimen up at home. He also spent time on the beach in
the trunks and received proper attention for his new muscular definition. The only downside to it was that these people thought he was
accessible to them for getting his haircut and getting in shape, and
he had every intention of leaving the area to never reside there again.

He was glad that he had a beach nearby and could lie out on a
beach towel and soak up the sun. He had beer in his iced bucket that
he brought to the beach, along with some of the roadhouse White
trash from the area. They had the fun remarks out loud, the occasional territorial fight, and he had giggles he had to muffle. He had
a better wit when he wasn't on the alcohol. Sometimes it made him
sleepy, and he did not want a sunburn on the beach. It was great
staying put with these people and not living on the road during these

periods without wanderlust. He handled himself well among the roadhouse White trash mostly because they didn't consider him to be very different from themselves. It didn't matter that he wouldn't make a pass at a drunk chick and that he wouldn't pick a fight when he was tipsy. He was enough of a jackass to blend in. People were not likely to go dancing in this town, and this was an area where the town folk considered to be the crassest by people like his family headed for their drinks and marijuana when the police were not around for the sake of the tourists.

He decided he was fine with his choice of swimwear but wanted to see if young Europeans in good shape still wore speedos to the beach before he died. He wanted to travel to Europe. He was thinking like he was drunk. He wanted to head out to a nude beach now that he was properly fit for it. None of these were thoughts he shared out loud. He did giggle a bit as he thought them and went back to sipping on his drink with rum in it.

"This is a good digestive for after eating a meal," he said to his bleach blonde and overweight White female friend Lucinda, who was peering at him a bit too knowingly.

"I come from a long line of alcoholics, and none of them drink like that."

"I am glad I live near enough to walk home."

"That's it. When are you going to leave and head back to Portland?"

"In two months. I am not in any rush. I paid a lot of money to do voice work and to learn to play classical music on the piano. I also thought about singing in a choir for a while. I want to show it off, then I am going to go away for a while. My family does not like me right now."

"At some point, you need to learn to make your own."

"That sounds dumb."

"It doesn't to most people who already know the family you have now is pretentious. Don't think like an Asian if your mother no longer does it. Not about some idea as meaningless as the patriarchy. You are continuing the cycle."

"Is that not what you do when you only date Southern White boys?"

She looked at him and belched, "We don't belong together. Don't be dumb about that. Always wait until a White girl flirts with you to make a pass at her."

"That's what I thought it was."

Travis went on with Lucinda to a guy named Cody's house for a party a few weeks later. Cody was a guy Lucinda was interested in sleeping with. Cody appeared pretty laid-back. He threw parties on the weekend and provided alcohol and let good conversation happen and stopped bad conversation immediately. He was not one to stop the flow of alcohol. If anyone was prone to making bad conversation on the alcohol, eventually they would be asked to keep their preppy selves away from Cody's place the next time he held a party. One of the guys he had got the lease on this house with had rock music from the nineties playing in the background. Travis had a discussion with Lucinda and another girl he had kissed about how soft his lips were when most guys had bad skin on their lips. She asked if he used lip gloss or kohl like an androgynous Indian guy might do when not on a Bollywood film set. He said that he did not, and they thanked him for the kisses.

He struck up a conversation with an art school student about animal rights and reminded her that they were going to use lab rats for testing in pharmaceutical laboratories and had not been investing in alternatives to animal testing. She cut him off and said that a vegan commitment to removing the use of animal products and by-products needed to be a part of his environmentalism or else he was not doing it the way it was being done elsewhere and, for the record, they used beagles too.

He said he was already a vegetarian and was not spending a lot of money to become vegan again. "It is bad enough that renewables have not come down in price, and that is something we are all going to need to start using immediately. I can wait twenty years before committing to the vegan lifestyle."

"That was a bad deflection, douchebag," she said to her girl-friend she was holding the conversation with before he interrupted.

"I would like to get laid by someone as liberal as me my own age, but they annoy me when I see them learning how to do it right so slowly."

"And why do you think I don't know what works for me?"

"It's not what any of us want. I think I'm going to have a starter marriage to have my kids, get divorced, and then find an older and mature academic type to be a stepdad."

"Are you going to be okay with him chasing after younger women, or does it need to be challenging women like us?" one of her friends asked.

"Travis, do you like older women?" the art school student inquired of Travis.

"I do."

"If you are like that, then you can have fun awhile and settle down when you are older."

Lucinda was coming back over to Travis after getting a drink. This time it was mineral water. He then violated the student code of conduct. He followed her to a bedroom and had sex with her— twice. The first time was quick, and he forgot to announce when he was ready; the second was long and at a slow, steady pace at her request. He hated it. He just wanted to go fast and back off to slow and steady before picking it up again, like they did in porn. He cried for the first time since he was twenty-three. Not a sad cry. A happy one although the sex was bad for him. He got up, and they headed out at the same time. Travis had trips on alcohol and ayahuasca in seminary; he had violated the student code of conduct with a White chick from his hometown. Someone who probably had gone to a school not too far from his own in the consolidated city system and who could find out anything and everything about him from now on and rat him out to the religious people in town as a person who genuinely didn't belong in a Bible college. Amazingly enough, Travis did not care. Lucinda was a good girl. He didn't see her getting on well with Cody anymore. He was a happy guy.

The party had wound down, and Travis had headed home. Viviane and Hank were full of anger toward him. "Did you forget about your recitals today? Did we pay all that money for music instruction to help you appear more well-rounded for nothing? I guess you are just going to be an a-hole your whole life. We were hoping you could put on a good show. How are you going to do that when you are sleep-deprived?"

Travis went to his room and slept a little bit. Then he popped some of his pure brown seaweed extract supplement. He got to the piano recital. "Clair de lune" was a disaster. It was as if he had taken the ACTs in the morning and attempted to do well at playing a complicated Debussy piece. He also had a break for a snack in his car before he had his voice recital. His parents showed up to that. He sang his piece and then did his Bollywood song and dance number with the other South Asian girl from Viola's music studio. It received a mixed response. When he sang "The Music of the Night" from *The Phantom of the Opera,* it was more of the same. It just didn't suit the audience, expecting better from a local Bible college kid. His parents went to the recital and then over to a Mexican restaurant in town. They complimented him on the resonance of his lower register but advised him to be a musical comedy actor and not be a villain or utilize sex appeal and be sacrilegious.

"It's a gimmick, hon, and everyone sees through it. It isn't who you are. Not that you are not a foxy guy."

"Don't talk like that."

"I guess that's all right to not compliment you on your looks. The end point I was trying to make is that I need you to not be brazenly sexual, and I need you to not be blasphemous. If anything ever happened to you, it would be difficult to throw you a good funeral. Just saying. When do you have Meals on Wheels again next?"

"My *god*, I completely forgot about that. It isn't important to me. Half the time the recipients are not at the doors."

"Oh, you don't really mean that."

"No, I do. I don't see myself sticking with volunteer work forever. It is the same for continuing education. I am ready to move on. I have a flight booked for Thursday. I guess I could do it Monday through Wednesday."

"Well, are you not going back to school? If you are not, then this is the first I have heard of it."

"I think you are a madman, Travis. We are your parents. You would have told us about all that a lot earlier than now unless you weren't well," said Hank.

Travis was thinking *Damn you! Damn you! Damn you!* at Hank, but he could not actually say it out loud there at the restaurant. It had turned out that he was a douchebag more than anything else for arriving back in town after the arguments that they had this fall. He honestly had no idea how to escape this situation.

"Don't talk to me like that again, Hank. I have not held a deep, meaningful conversation with you in years."

"I don't blame him," said a Black woman seated nearby. "You two are missing all the important bits. Have fun with your kid now because he probably isn't going to see you again for a while."

CHAPTER 9

TRAVIS HAD JUST DROPPED OFF THE MEALS HE WAS delivering as a volunteer. He headed out to his car and hopped in, turned on the ignition, and opened a bottle of mineral water with fruit punch powder mixed into it. He drove out of the parking lot and onto the access road, yielded to a driver at a stop sign, turned right onto it, and eventually came to an intersection where the road opened up on the other side after crossing the main boulevard into the town. He waited for all the cars to stop and the light to turn green, and then he put his foot on the pedal. He was moving across the six-lane boulevard at a slow clip at the front of the line; and before he had crossed the entire breadth of the road, the car gave a lurch to the left, knocked off an oncoming vehicle, and spun back in the direction it had been driving. In doing so, it made a complete 180-degree turn, as it came to its complete stop facing the wrong direction. His remaining arm on the steering wheel caught the weight of the airbag, and cool red water went flying all over him.

"Damn it!" he exclaimed. "This cannot have just happened! There goes my whole summer healing another broken bone, and I have no idea when I will be able to replace the car that is obviously totaled." He took a deep breath and looked to his left and saw what looked like Ophelia driving a car with a guy in the passenger seat.

She had her hand over her mouth, but it was clear she was muttering "Please be okay. Please be okay."

"Are you okay?" said a woman.

"No, I am not!" said Travis. "I am mad as hell about it."

"Is that blood?"

"No. It is water with fruit punch powder mixed into it."

"Then you need to get out of the car because it is smoking."

"I have to get the seat belt off, and my arm is broken—shattered is more like it." He pushed his left arm down his chest and onto his lap and unbuckled the seat belt with his right hand and, while biting his lip, opened the car door with his right hand and then climbed out of it while his arm, bent up like Abbey Road, dangled on his left side.

"Your arm is broken."

"That's obvious! I want to know who did it."

"Is he okay after the wreck?"

"I do not know right now."

"I am heading into shock. Get an ambulance!"

"You need to get him and take him out of the road. Help him call his family," said another witness.

He walked over to a curb with her and then began to get his phone out for her to make a call.

"Honey, can you tell me your dad's number?"

"Who the hell do you think you are taking my phone from me? At least call a damn ambulance."

"I'm done. That guy's a douche. He was cussing like a sailor, and that is not even something we do here."

"Do I need her helping me? She may be insane. Call an ambulance and I will be fine." He was feeling pain in his arm. Travis put his phone in his pocket with his right hand and focused on not blacking out. When he noticed himself tilting to his left side over the evil arm, he would kick his right leg out to bring himself back to full consciousness. When he heard ambulatory alarms arriving, he knew to be more attentive to his surroundings. The ambulance went past him and had stopped before entering the wrong parking lot.

"No, stop, he's right over here!"

"Where?" asked a woman as she flung open the back doors.

Travis hopped to his feet from his strong abdominal wall, like bouncing back after a kung fu opponent knocked him down. *Do not listen to her. I am right here. That woman is the devil in disguise.* His left arm was dangling bent at an angle where the bone was shattered and at a different one where the wrist was off a few degrees as some tendons had become detached.

"Get morphine ready."

"Is it a compound fracture?"

Travis was skipping toward the ambulance.

"No, you need to slow down."

"I need morphine!"

Travis slowed down and walked briskly toward the ambulance. "I will be getting in and going to the hospital with you. Do it good. I do not want another ambulance ride. Where do I sit?"

"Up on the gurney."

"Okay." Travis situated himself down on it.

She asked him questions, he fielded them, she asked too many, he asked where the morphine was, she grabbed his arm to set it in place, and he slapped her hands away. A cop climbed in the ambulance. "I would like your statement."

"While I am on morphine? Someone hit me in my car, and now my arm is broken."

"Do you need us to call anyone?"

"You could call my dad, Hank Marx."

"What is your name?"

"Travis Marx."

"May I have your phone?"

"Yes!"

"I can't find anything on it."

"Don't try to blackmail me. I will remember that until the day I die. I guarantee you we will defund the police and bring you under community control."

"You and what army?"

"The angry workers of America. People who want socialism more than an invasion of privacy. What was it you were looking for again? Something funny in the search history."

"I needed that like I needed a shot to the head. I was hoping there was going to be a string of curse words and blatant disrespect of law enforcement to nail this guy to the wall. Take him to the hospital but hold on to his phone awhile. I want his mental breakdown to be bad. I will take anything as reason not to prosecute the other people at the scene. These liberal, socialist dirtbags need to know that law enforcement officers don't have their back and never will."

"I wish you wouldn't make me do things like that, officer. I am just an innocent bystander."

"We'll get in touch with your dad."

"Fine. See if he cares. Then see if I care. I won't. I am the only shameless Marx in town. The pretentious architect Hank Marx is full of himself, and even his own son won't have anything to do with him."

The suspicious cop left his ambulance feeling disappointed, and then he was taken in the ambulance to the hospital.

Travis was certain that he did not have anything he needed to do other than stay awake until surgery. He would just stay in the present moment without thinking and be so thrilled he did not have a small inner voice to chatter for him like some of those awful people he was going to have to deal with again once he had completed healing his arm.

This kid is so unfortunate. He is dead by the end of June, and it doesn't look like he gets to have a happy ending.

Go away, thought Travis.

"It is time to get him on into the emergency room."

"Do I get my phone back?"

"Well, no, not immediately. We don't like that for you now."

You heard the suspicious cop.

"And off we go."

The doors to the hospital flung open, and the ambulance crew delivered Travis into his hospital room on a flying gurney.

"The trick is getting me up off the gurney and onto that bed."

"You are right."

"ARGH. No. You should *never* do that. What an evil hospital."

"Look at how quick his recovery was."

"Adjust the pillows pronto!"

"You know what, I can at least help with that. Then I need to step outside a bit. You have someone waiting to see you."

Hank Marx walked into the hospital room and gasped at the gruesome sight. "Oh, that is a very bad arm injury. His mom needs to get here."

"Where does she work?"

"She is a librarian across the river."

"That shouldn't take too long."

"When am I heading into surgery?"

"It'll be any day now. Just kidding. Time will fly by. If your arm starts hurting, ask for more morphine. We'll do the rounds again eventually."

Hank stood there and looked at Travis. It might have been five minutes, and he had asked for morphine once more by the time his mom arrived.

"Hey, Hank!"

"Why did you take so long? I told you he had been taken to the hospital."

"I got here as quick as I could."

"His arm is very badly injured. The doctor thinks he is going to need surgery."

"Does he know anything even?"

"You could actually look."

"Oh god, that is sick. Yeah, he is going to need surgery. Hey, Travis, how are you feeling?"

"Crappy."

"Is your arm hurting or anything?"

"Not that I am aware of *now*. I still have some morphine, but when they move me, I feel the anguish of a thousand hells. Nobody has come in to check on me, Viviane. No doctors or nurses."

"Here is your phone," said the ambulance lady as she walked into the room.

"I'll take that," said Viviane Marx.

"Yay, you! There was a whole group of people I just had to deal with that were acting like America had just turned into the Christian Republic of America."

"Well, that's not all right. The dollar bill does say 'In God We Trust' though. Were you acting irreverent?"

"Yes!"

"Oh, I guess that one will take a while to live down then. That is a big deal."

"Hey! Nurse, you must get someone to talk to us soon. I need to know what type of surgery they are planning."

"They haven't even taken the x-rays yet, Mom! I want those over with. I also need more morphine."

"You need to get an x-ray technician up here. Pronto."

"I need more morphine. This is the same as going to the dentist and saying you need more funny gas. They need to get back here and raise my morphine levels."

"I haven't seen anybody come by who could do that."

"Trust me. I am going to need more morphine when that person wants to move my broken arm and partially detached wrist for x-rays."

Here came somebody to talk to his mom; he could not talk to her himself and could not pay attention closely to their conversation.

"No problem. I can get the x-rays very quick."

She was going in for the arm after getting set up with the lights off in what seemed like was a medieval dungeon from a prior life—a time when things got really sick. "You stupid bitch. I told you I needed more morphine before you did this. No. You should *never* do that."

"I know it may hurt, but I need the x-rays."

"Silly girl, just get the morphine. Do that first and then proceed."

"Look, it's really no big deal. I can probably get it done really quick." She went in for the arm.

"What the hell is wrong with you—are you deaf! Get me more morphine."

"Fine, have it your way. It won't be quick, but it will be painless."

"I am back in for the x-rays," she announced five minutes after the morphine had got in him. She went in for the arm.

He whimpered a bit, but he was polite. "You get to go to heaven."

"It *will* all be over with soon," said the nurse to Travis. "I was hoping I could get more than two angles, but I don't really care if you don't, Mrs. Marx. He needs to go to surgery soon."

"Of course, that needs to happen soon."

Travis could not tell who these people were anymore. He fell asleep and noticed a sensation of magic carpet flying as the technicians whisked him off to his hospital room. Shortly after, they took him away in the gurney; he was in the room he came to and did not notice the pain of living in the world.

"Take your clothes off and get in a gown. We have surgery for you next."

He stripped off his clothes like he was modeling for a class of artists despite his broken arm. He hated, however, that hospital gowns desexualized hot people immediately.

"When are they going to do the surgery?"

"Now if you are ready," said a doctor as he entered the room. "I am Dr. Hartford. I will be conducting your surgery very shortly. We will first need you anesthetized. They will be coming to take you into the surgical waiting area."

"When?"

"Now, as a matter of fact."

"Oh, that's a sad sight," said a tech bringing him out. "His arm may never be the same."

"The surgeon said it could go back to normal," said the other tech.

Travis was delivered on his flying gurney to the surgical area. The anticipation was driving him mad—or anxious even.

"Have you started the anesthesia yet?"

He didn't get a response.

"Hey, *you*, have you started the anesthesia? At some point, I am supposed to count backward from one hundred. No one has told me to start."

"You could start now."

Travis had got to eighty.

"I guess he isn't going to do it loud."

"You're a bitch."

At ten, he was still not drifting off to sleep. At nine, a strong desire to announce that he had reached nine and had not dropped off to sleep was burning so very strongly that after he counted to four, the next thing he knew was he had blacked out and had heard voices for what seemed about fifteen seconds getting louder to wake up to a gentle hospital assistant's voice telling him he had just awakened from surgery.

"Did it go well?"

"They did say it went well. You will have to wait to ask your surgeon any more questions."

"Okay. Thank you." He had his angel face on again.

Travis didn't have to wait long before the hospital techs had him flying back to his hospital room on the now noticeably noisy gurney.

Is it that noisy?

"Hey, Mom," Travis said to Viviane after he got settled into his room. When the hospital patient delivery personnel had left the room, Travis added, "I can't wait to get back to normal. How long is that going to take?"

"I don't know that I want that for you."

"What do you mean?"

"You should be more like your brother and stay competitive *in America* as a White Christian *unmarried* man against all the religious minorities and hopelessly depraved fornicators. I got to thinking about it and decided this is a good opportunity for us to settle a lot for you as your family. Hank Marx Jr. would never be as undignified as you in conducting his life. You would even get a part-time job or two working flexible shifts just so you can have independence from your family. You should let your brother get you a professional job while we can still cover for you. How do you not understand how this needs to work for you and for your salvation? You have to get a job with benefits if you are going to be a respectable person in America."

"What if I wanted to leave the country?"

Viviane looked at Travis over her reading glasses. "There aren't that many Christians outside of America. At least there are not that many with money. Even if you were not miserable, we would be, and that's enough to settle it for us. We are doing the right thing."

"Hank Marx Jr. can't get a job with benefits as a Marx in America."

"He did. He gets passed over for raises. It is only because he is a creationist and therefore denies climate scientists. He is doing the right thing by us."

"This is a nightmare I just woke up into."

"Amen," said an orderly carting a monitoring machine as they passed by.

"We have you under our control again, and that matters to us more than anything else we can think of."

"Like hell you do."

"Look at your arm. You will never get away with a stunt like that again. Look at me, Travis Marx. I flit here, and then I flit there, like a pagan butterfly trust fund baby."

"You cannot just do that to me after all these years. That money was almost gone anyway. I had enough from that to not have to work for three years while I was at Bible college. I still have plenty for leaving the area and traveling abroad."

"You haven't paid your own taxes yet. That's what we tell everyone. If you do that here first, then hopefully you will never again believe that a little socialism will fix our problems. Well, it looks like you get to pay into social security for forty years along with the billionaires even if it is just a little bit early for socialism to be a thing."

"That is only to keep social security solvent, you uninformed child slayer. You miserable old bitch. I wouldn't have come back to this town again without a security detail if I had known how wretched you are now. All these ideas of yours for helping me out will be the end of me."

"We are so competent in everyone else's eyes for how we are handling this. Get a clue already. The money goes to your brother, and if you ever wise up, you will try to be like him so that you might have a good life of your own someday—one that he will happily arrange for you."

"Hank Jr. has never been able to work the world out the same as my father did thirty years ago. That is not effective parenting to imagine that the way to accomplish survival in this country is the same as it was thirty years ago. You are setting us both up for failure. The only difference between us is that when everything he has been conditioned to try to attain for himself and to force upon everyone else proves to be unpopular with everyone meant to be his adherents and backfires on him, he still tries to cover for himself and his lies. I would have a better life with people around me who don't try to control me. I would have been happy not ever having to deal with this from you again. He is the person in the family who rages. He is a madman who needs help, and because you never can call him out on his wrongdoing, you have finally become as mad as he is. You don't have that problem with me. It is the same lie repeatedly that I am trying to do more than I actually can. I know what I am capable of, and if you are not going to be supportive, then you are no longer family to me."

"You threatened violence against your father once. We have that."

"I know what you think you have. I didn't ever do anything. You would not let me set up a bank account until I started showing up at your cult church. That is a fact. The two of you have restricted access to methods for gaining financial independence, and you have made ill-fated attempts at psychological abuse to try to make me into someone I never was and never will be. You are a monster. You have no conscience, and you have no moral compass."

"Have you become a Satanist? We watched you get baptized, and we remember how you were. We need that you are evil if you have fallen away, and you won't give us that." She bit her lip and smiled.

"Of all the stupid things to say. It really is not helping you, Mom, to not talk to different types of people. You are no longer communicating with other people effectively. You don't have to believe any of the irrational things you believe, and you don't have to resort to abuse to try to get the results you predicted you would get. I've known you my whole life. I never thought when it was your turn to go downhill that you would lash out at me and pull cruel stunts in a desperate attempt to get me to retreat from the world with you. You are miserable. It would have been much better if you had left me alone."

Travis had a miserable night, and the next day was unpleasant until he got the doctor to discharge him the next afternoon. He really didn't need to take the pain pills more than twice a day. He wouldn't take anything for insomnia in addition to a pain pill just in case he might start sleeping too much. He told his mother he was going to go to the school to withdraw from his courses that Wednesday, so when he was ready the next morning, they headed over to the seminary to get a WP in his courses. They told him he might want an extension, and his mother adamantly told him he would need that. He thought this was a good opportunity for him. He didn't care too much to put his foot down then and there. There was a time to be assertive like at the hospital yesterday, and then there were times to not respond to unimportant, brainwashed members of a cult and plot out the quickest path to safety. He was glad she agreed to make the payment the next semester. It meant he could announce his next and final flight away from home in a few months. So they left with him accomplishing nothing and then went through a fast-food restaurant drive-through to get a frozen treat even though he didn't want one. The whole thing was just horrible.

"You are making a show of mothering me now, and you are heartless when you decide it's preferable. I do not need it. I can see myself getting to the point where I do not even call you on Mother's Day when these three months are over."

"I don't see myself celebrating Mother's Day with any particular son any time soon. We just had it."

"Are you going to attempt to make my return trip home a five-year prison term?"

"That's up to you."

"I will be fine. I need the cast off and the pin out, but I can take care of my own physical therapy and recover by myself if this ever happens again. I will not stay here, and I will die trying to leave."

"How much do you have in savings?"

"I don't have to tell you that. I obviously can pull my own weight better without your bogus offers of assistance. You keep attaching weights to me."

"You wouldn't see it that way if you would just come back to church and start doing our new thing with us."

"Who cares? I still have enough that I can leave and never have to see you again."

Travis went home with Viviane. After she made him head to school and pick up his syllabi on Thursday from Dr. Strangeglove and from Dr. Freemoney, the head of the counseling program, and had got his shake, they headed home. He was feeling bitter, and he was convinced his mother was as much of a two-faced villain in the story of his life as his father and some other devious characters in this community they expected him to suck up to before it was all over.

Just then, Travis had a horrifying washing sensation in his brain. It was as if he had seen this exact moment before in a precognitive dream. "No!" he said out loud.

"Why did you say no all of a sudden?" Viviane said, chuckling.

Travis did not respond.

"I asked you a question. That was a bizarre thing to do. You should have an answer prepared for when you decide to do bizarre things."

"You took that turn too fast, and I had my arm set in a cast."

"Sorry."

When Travis got home, his chocolate shake had melted. He got rid of it without Viviane noticing and headed upstairs.

"Do you need another pain pill for your arm?"

"No, I do not. I am completely fine being off those within a week and then back on my treatment for insomnia." Travis headed upstairs to what was his new room accommodation at home. He mostly listened to music after running vocal scales and did citizen science. When he was ready to read, the local telepaths reached out to talk to him, like he was on a party line. This had been a thing recently. Some of them he recognized, and he told them he did not want to be bothered now and he wanted to get absorbed into one of the books in his collection.

I don't think that is necessary, thought Kevin to everyone; he had been a choir director at the Methodist church in town but now had left his choral directing position there to start a community choir in a neighboring town.

I will not be able to sing in choir this summer.

That is true, Travis. You can see us perform our choral showcase at the end of the summer. None of the chaos jettisoned in your direction here matters.

I agree, Travis, thought Viola. *You will not lose any progress you have made with your voice as long as you continue doing scales, and when your money situation changes, someone in Portland can help get you to where you can sing German opera well. I am happy we got to where you needed to be with the piano, and your voice recital was received well.*

It was received well? Matthew asked her.

He did all right in both. He chose more complicated work in his voice recital, a Bollywood dance number. I was thrilled that he made that call. It is always better to choose material that is challenging.

I guess she's right. You are a lyrical voice type and not a dramatic one. If you have a three-octave range, then you can sing music as dramatic as an opera piece. That is especially true when you can alternate between light and husky tones. She could have found something in popular music, but it is completely awesome if you choose to head in the operatic direction from Broadway and Bollywood, Matthew responded. *He sings the songs of the devil and he has the voice of an angel. It's disgusting.*

Travis responded, *That was Matthew, wasn't it? Tell him to go away.*

Okay, Travis. I may as well. The liberal clairvoyants in town flock together. You could try to do our thing.

Is it ever going to be okay to do Buddhism? Travis asked.

I would do faith and grace instead of finding another faith and works religion. You also do not have to deal with reincarnation. We don't think it is a thing. There are too many people around whom we do not remember being alive when we reach out like this. It must be the saved clairvoyants, Matthew added.

What happens to everyone else?

Total annihilation.

It's Mrs. Blossom, Travis. Get back to reading the books of prophecy and finish that course like your mother told you to do. You are not cut out for living anywhere but the South. We will fix this for you, but you must behave more like a Southerner. We can help you out in being perceived that way even if you have not been that yet. It will be miserable for you, but you will get to go to heaven with us and maybe even start liking us eventually once you realize we have you trapped here.

Or he can just commit suicide. You know that if you look at how your actions are intended to produce results, you are basically trying to get him to kill himself, Matthew added.

That is what they want me to do. It is the simplest way for them to say that person was never a Christian, and you do remember them gathering and asking if I was suicidal yet, Travis thought.

That hasn't happened yet, Mrs. Blossom chimed in.

That is wrong. We should not be allowing the soldiers of Christ to go around speaking like that. Is everyone else already that oblivious? added an unknown clairvoyant.

Why is that wrong? How does that not keep everything under control? added another unknown clairvoyant.

It makes it look like we don't have anything under control. We are obviously not supposed to talk like that.

The majority of the people like you who have not already lost their minds and can function in the real world are going to lose their marbles by the end of this decade, and I desperately need to be living far away from you then. No one will care if you are a two-faced bitch, Mrs. Blossom, if you are still living in that community and spending your time up to no good on social media and in private messaging, thought Travis.

Can you not just start becoming the person we presumed you were? Mrs. Blossom asked.

I could also destroy any delusion you might be experiencing there that I would bail you out after that long list of crimes you have committed. I would have a blast laying them all out for the world to see. You are the bastards who cannot handle the fact that our world is in a state of constant change. I am not here to help you feel safe and secure. Now that you are losing everything you thought you could keep, including your minds. I would like the whole world to see how you lash out at anything you perceive as a threat. You are like cornered and frightened animals. You lack the wit, the courage, and the nobility of spirit to take a more honorable path out of the wasteland you have become lost in, Travis fired back.

Are you really open to socialism, Ophelia? Travis added.

I basically am if you cut my mom a break, responded Ophelia.

Ophelia, you are not that dumb. That guy will never change. He wants to destroy everything we hold dear. He's been like that since high school, added an unknown clairvoyant.

Ophelia, remember what I told you at church. I would do anything to get with you someday. I would even convert religions and become a Christian again. That sect does have a problem with legalism and with making way too many things mandatory. If they do not adjust to the consensus that that is pharisaical, then their way of life is doomed to end, thought Travis.

That retort made sense. It may have been of Satanic origin, however, Travis, Ophelia warned.

Ophelia, you don't need to be like that. You know how I am. I am a fun guy. I may have been wayward recently, but I can be good, thought Travis.

Ophelia leaned in and gave Travis a kiss. *I think I know how most people are at church. There is still work to do. I heard you mention at some point that you were a Unitarian Universalist from the moment you set up your bank account. The first thing you need to work on is ditching a Unitarian position in favor of a Trinitarian one. If you follow the Nicene Creed, that makes it more likely that your faith will resemble ours and not that of other major world religions. Other people presume that you are doing something more mainstream. If you would do that, it would make it easier on you and them. It would probably be mostly them at this point, but at least they would not see an urgent need to force you to be someone you are not so that they do not look stupid for making fun of you as aloof when you kept your cool. You never did their thing and left when you had had enough of them.*

Done, thought Travis.

What? thought Ophelia.

Your lecture. When are you going to be back? thought Travis.

Tomorrow, thought Ophelia.

You are a pathetic a-hole, said the divorced Baptist lady.

I agree, thought Matthew. *I thought you were going to make all that a thing for Protestants. You are way out of the mainstream. I am done with you.*

Travis cut on internet radio until it was time to go to bed. He woke up peacefully.

CHAPTER 10

Hey, do you know who I am?

No.

That's fine. It's been a while since we have talked. I arrived early today before your testing.

Who is testing me?

I think you know who is testing you and why you need it. That is completely fine. If you let me guide you, I can help you repel the bad guys.

Travis walked downstairs and sat down in front of the news. The group of news anchors were lying again.

Oh, that is so wrong, said Doctor Strangeglove.

I would like for you to explain yourself to me, said a spirit who sounded very much like Dr. Freemoney. This professor had also taken to walking the astral planes during the day from the comfort of his office.

Travis, remember me and call on my name, and I will chase him away, said the friendly tenor 2 voice who spoke to him first this morning.

Is that a demon?

Of course, we are demonic, said Doctor Strangeglove. *We can go in and grab your memories, and we will get them for Mrs. Blossom. She is too good of a woman to commit theft herself.*

Run, Travis, run! cried Ophelia.

Travis got up and bolted out the door with Dr. Strangeglove and Dr. Freemoney following him. He ran down the street and took a turn to the right and went downhill and uphill in the sun. His feet were on fire from the scalding hot pavement. He shouted "That's hot!" and limped all the way back to the house like he was stepping over burning coals while trying to keep his arm level. He got back inside the house where Jesus was, and he said to Travis, *From now on, you can let me handle them. I delivered you once before. I am prepared to do it again. Go upstairs, Travis, quick!*

Travis hobbled upstairs on his burnt feet. He closed the door. The light suddenly darkened almost to nighttime light. He heard the giggling of gnomes and sensed that those must be real demons and not clairvoyants or extradimensional beings.

Quick, Travis, cast the spell I taught you!

Flee in the name of Jesus Christ!

The window had a circular rippling effect, and more giggling gnomes flung themselves into the room to march up toward Travis.

"I will say it again. Flee in the name of Jesus Christ!"

You silly boy! You only have the one chance to say it, and if you do not say it out loud the first time, it won't work.

Help me, Jesus!

Do you trust me?

Of course, I trust you. It's obviously you! Do your thing and close that tunnel to that other dimension.

You didn't really make that easy then. You are not supposed to order the Son of God around.

I am sorry, Jesus! I will let you do your magic.

That will help.

Are you doing your magic?

I am. I need for you to believe in me for the magic to work.

I believe in you, Jesus.

Then why is my magic not working?

Have I said anything I shouldn't have?

I do not know. Your biggest problem is doubt. If you had confidence my magic would work for you, then it would.

I have never doubted you, Jesus!

You liar! Six weeks ago, you were a Buddhist, and a week before that, you were cavorting with <u>New Agers!</u> I told you I was working magic, and five minutes later you said, "Are you doing your magic?" Oh, you of little faith, you are not worth it. I shall toss you from the palm of my hand. All of you demons may have him. He is yours from now on.

Travis watched the man of light disappear as hundreds of black crows flew in through the gaping hole in the universe that had manifested itself in his window. They flew into his mouth, neck, and chest; and terror flooded him to his inner core. Then he went back to sleep.

When Travis woke up, he was surrounded by a different set of telepaths traveling out of body from what he had seen before. Ophelia was there in the room, as was his former counselor, Karen Samedi. He had not seen Mrs. Blossom since last night. *I thought a lot about our talk last night and realized I needed to speak to a Democrat clairvoyant in the church. We need to consult the ones we still have in our denominations if this is going to ever work out well for us. My mom is going off the deep end. She is insisting that you have never asked Jesus into your heart and that therefore you cannot really be a Christian. What she got started then shows she is out of control. I went a bit further back than those two losers from that Bible college and found someone I thought could help me help you.*

That woman doesn't resist experience like you and your mom, Ophelia. She may not care to help me be a Christian for the two of us to be together if this persists. Is that something that you can handle? thought Travis.

Why, yes, of course. Trust me, Travis. I really want for you to remain a Christian. I know why you stopped seeing me, and it obviously is because I had inappropriate telepathic discourse to nudge you into being a better Christian. A much more feminine response than those jerks who were downstairs a few hours ago. One of them may not have been a jerk according to Ophelia, thought Dr. Samedi.

Oh, that one was definitely a jerk, thought Ophelia.

Then I agree with Ophelia. The Jesus-impersonating clairvoyant was a jerk, thought Karen. *If I were you, I would wait until tonight when they arrive back here again before siding with my girlfriend on everything. I have been around on this planet a lot longer than her, and I remember her mother when she was younger. It is the case that this situation may not be what it seems, and I hope that the three of us turn out to be more adaptable than either of the two of you have been since Travis got back home from the hospital.*

You can do whatever you want until you take your medicine tonight, thought Ophelia.

Okay. I'll see you two later.

Travis went about his evening about the same as the night before. He listened to internet radio and did citizen science. He read the newspaper on his internet browser. He also read a little in a German book. He let his mind wander. He had been wanting a strong redistribution of wealth for economical justice and restored democracy along with a Global Green New Deal and world peace and was fairly certain that in the West, it was fine to toss in a free sexuality and a lot less of the Cross and worship with all the people who knelt before it and to never sing songs about kneeling before it. These people were creating problems all over for what they perceived as perverted fornicators and people who wanted way too much personal freedom. Freedom from religion and freedom from family were never mentioned. Dumb people thought he cared about religion and malicious blood kin. Not just once had they proven they were a hindrance to all the other things that really mattered to Travis occurring. He knew that a free lifestyle they would consider to be hedonism would not be popular globally for an eco-socialist Global Green New Deal and world peace in a happier, better world; but those Christians claiming exclusive access to the truth really pissed him off the most by far. He was so over it with them and ready to make counseling a secular profession where human sexuality in its myriad expressions had a perfectly rational basis as a revolt against religious restrictiveness, and therefore breaking barriers in inhibition might serve a social role with positive effects on people.

He took his pain pill and turned out the light and crawled in bed. It wasn't long before the window began rippling again and gnomes started throwing themselves into his room again. He heard

Karen and Ophelia come back into his room and heard Karen telling Ophelia to be quiet and observe.

When are you going to trust me? said the spirit he had decided was probably Jesus earlier.

I am trying to go to bed. It is not the perfect time to talk to someone in case you didn't know.

If I was lost, like you, I would come back to my shepherd before I tried to go to sleep at night, "Jesus" said.

Then a much deeper rumbling bass voice filled the room. *So which one of us is it going to be, that one over there who refers to you like you are a sheep, or will it be me, the Father?*

I hate it when he does that, said the "Jesus" extradimensional.

You mean there are disagreements between you and the Father?

Duh! Did you not learn anything from your church history classes about theology? The Holy Spirit, which you do not hear, conveys messages between the two of us. I had no idea I was being sent to die on earth by that person referring to himself as everyone's Father. I thought I was going to have a kingdom then and there with spiritual subordinates flocking to me, and he tells me I have to get crucified that time and still hasn't told me I am going back again. I told everyone it would be soon. It is that bad for me after the last time he sent me here. I have been waiting for my earthly kingdom for two millennia.

They are not ready for you again. I told you to tell them that you did not come here for peace but to destroy and that you would turn a son against his father and a mother against her daughter. You handle it like a punk when you talk to Travis. Make sure they know what you were about, and then I will send you back in, the Father extradimensional said to the Jesus extradimensional.

You were supposed to stay in my flock, said the Jesus extradimensional.

Travis, if you have ever wanted to tell Jesus how you really feel, you need to do that now, thought Karen.

Stay the hell away from me!

You did the right thing, said the rumbling bass voice. *Just so you know, you will never be a good Christian.*

I agree with the first part of what that guy said, Ophelia thought toward him. *There still should have been a better way to field those two jerks. I do not like millennial theology working its way into the Lord's church. I wish we could keep them from finding him again.*

That may not be possible. I do know how to rectify problems they may cause remotely. Travis, close your eyes and count backward from ten.

Travis closed his eyes; he saw a giant pair of scissors and then a dashed line. The scissors spun 180 degrees to align itself with the dashed line about two hundred yards from him, and it started chomping away at the dashed line while heading toward him.

"Don't do it like that!" yelled Travis.

Sorry, did not mean to point the memory shears directly at you. Does this look better?

Travis had his eyes closed and could see a pair of shears slicing through the dashed line from the top of the unconscious sky all the way around, getting lower as it circled, lower and lower until it started reaching eye level. It did look better.

Does it not bother you when someone offers to take your memories? asked Ophelia.

Travis experienced a surge of the hormone adrenaline to cause him to be fearful.

"That doesn't belong in my mind. I will stop that nonsense for you right now."

It is obviously better to not remember and to resist experience than to survive with bad memories. That's how I have noticed old ladies responding to the crises of the world. You could stop your family, billionaires, and extradimensional beings from abusing you if you would let me pluck away some of your memories. I have been thinking that would help for a long time.

Travis fell asleep and woke up at about 6:30 a.m. *I cannot and will not worry about bad clairvoyants. I see no need to go into the hospital.* He made coffee, which did not help him do well with his pure brown seaweed extract supplement in the cognitive performance department. He didn't know why he was drinking coffee again after not being on it for a year. He then headed upstairs to read his Bible passages on the books of prophecy the exact way liberal theologians told him to, as if prophecy was a real thing; it just was the case that they were only fulfilled under certain requirements. He did not know why he would want to keep the prophetic books of the Old Testament, but the other interpretation seemed like a Christian version of Ms. Rita's witchcraft where individuals created new universes based on the way they responded to the constant change in the collective mind. There might be worlds where different Old Testament prophecies were fulfilled than the ones that had been fulfilled in our universe since the prophecies we had had handed down to us had been written; also, God might have sent or be sending other great reforming teachers to earth to correct oppressive regimes in whichever religion only had one God on those worlds that followed the Jesus we had documented in this world. He might be on another world teaching again and avoiding crucifixion so that they'd get his story right now for all we'd know.

You are so stupid. Why will you not just kill yourself so that we do not have to kill you for you! thought Mrs. Blossom.

Travis was frozen to his core with panic. He knew Mrs. Blossom hated him. He also knew she had been eavesdropping while Ophelia wasn't watching and hated her back right now.

Never fear her, Travis, not while I am here, thought Karen. *That woman is a Satanist if ever there was one, and you need to know that for a fact. She had to have sold her soul to Satan. There is no other explanation for all the words that come out of her mouth. She wouldn't be doing THAT religion THAT randomly and be THAT harsh to you if she had not given her soul to Satan.*

My mom goes to church with her.

Is your mom clairvoyant?

Well, no, she does not act like she has any extrasensory perception.

I am going to use MY magic.

That is not what anybody but Travis calls it.

"Stop! I do not want to be made fun of right now while she has something like that scissors thing in store for me."

Hush! When you talk, from now on do it in head voice. I actually hate that she has shared some of the things she has with you and do not need your mother coming upstairs.

MY GOD, she is forming a fireball in her hands!

A big blue dome burst forth around Travis from Karen to keep him from being incinerated by the fires of hell.

You cannot be allowing him to do this to us, Karen. How can you not see the ends justify the means?

She formed a fireball in her hands again and shot it out toward him. Karen got to it again.

WHAT IS WRONG WITH YOU, MOM? Ophelia thought.

Stay out of this. That heresy has no business making its way into our communities. He has to be incinerated.

And how is that okay? Thou shalt not murder.

That person is not innocent. That is how God saw it in Old Testament days. You could stay here and watch me and learn what I do. It's not murder.

Travis is going to need to be defended from these people until all has been accomplished, thought Karen.

People who want him burned out of this world for no good reason. I got it.

How did you learn that quickly? thought Travis.

I got a head start from that one over there.

She would be a good one to protect you when I am done, if you are too dumb to ever learn to do it yourself.

I know what to do. Mom cloaks her avatar. It is an alias. She normally ventures out onto the astral planes as herself every now and then she uses that character there.

OH GOD! That is hilarious!

I don't see what is so funny. Clara was a good character on The Andy Griffith Show. *A bit of a busybody, but that is basically what you are when you are traveling on the astral planes using an avatar for an alias.*

She couldn't be more obvious about being a Satanist. She picked that actress in a different role—the one from Rosemary's Baby. *She looks like she did in that one scene she was in at the end. The one where she said, "Hail Satan!"*

That's what I will do every time she drops by, Travis. No one will pay her attention.

Hail Satan! thought Mrs. Blossom.

I didn't want you to see her, but we all saw how she looked just then. I can't believe that my mom was secretly not a Christian since becoming a clairvoyant. Travis we need to get you someplace where you can be safe from violent members of the community. You are going to have to check yourself into the hospital.

I don't want to go to the hospital for my safety.

That's how you get in when they ask.

I am heading downstairs. I am going to have a miserable morning. Somebody is going to have to drive me with my arm being broken. My dad would not mind doing that, but Viviane will discourage him from it. I know it. It will take twice as long as it should to get packed up and down there and admitted.

You can eat breakfast.

Travis went downstairs and saw his dad already up. "I want to go into the hospital."

"Again? You just got out."

"I do not feel safe. Ms. Rita told me I was in danger of destroying the universe the way you people intended it to be, and when people find out, I think they may want to kill me."

"You should take a chill pill. Your brother and your cousin are coming in this weekend. Are you going to miss out on seeing him?"

"He is dead to me. I do not care to see him again."

"You are kind of manic. How can your own brother be dead to you?"

"He is a walking, breathing ghost as far as I am concerned."

"Your brother is your best representative, and he is also your savior in my book," said Viviane as she came down the stairs.

"Who talks like that, Viviane? You are an airhead."

"That needs to be you though. We are doing the Lord's work."

"You know I am not going to shout back at you when you phrase hostile sentences at me in a way to try and intimidate me. I know how things work. I also know how controlling you have been, and I will not let you continue to submarine me. I am heading to the hospital."

"No one cares to hear your take on political matters, and you were supposed to do *our* religion and not that New Age voodoo stuff you have got into. We will take you out if you ever try to make that a thing. You should let us. It is for your own good. One of these days, you will see things clearly and be grateful for how we engaged in sabotaging you with some of your ideas—like being an artist and not a lifelong museum docent. Then you won't mind it that we were controlling and restrictive of your freedom as heavily as we were and that we provided so little guidance to help you have independence and then thought we had pulled the wool over your eyes. You have to learn to want to spend eternity with us first."

"I really do not want you visiting me in the hospital. I do not want to see you again. You have given me no reason to expect anything different from you than foul play."

"You are a terrible son! What is wrong with us? You are the one with the problem. All our Christian friends will side with us. You have ensured that! You could escape punishment for talking back to us. Honor your father and mother."

"Trust me, I will not care if it's just you and your posse of science-denying, teetotaling racists whom I have to get the law involved with the rest of my life. No means no. You are going to have to stop trying to wreck my life. You do not share the facts. You share hearsay and expect to find that confirmed at the end of your reign of terror because you have a high number of members here in the states. At least the Amish allow a severance from the community at the end when their children want to part ways. Because you won't do that, you are going to run your cult into the ground. I have never seen a group of people as self-righteous and conceited as the likes of you."

"You are manic, Travis, or else you wouldn't talk like that. I will get you away from here for breakfast, and then maybe we can go back to normal."

"I don't want random American patriarchal cult to be my normal."

"Where do you want to eat?"

"Waffle House."

Hank and Travis got in the car and went to Waffle House. Before they got out of the car, Travis told Hank, "I still want to go the hospital."

Travis looked at the menu. He knew he wanted multiple breakfast drinks and no coffee.

Karen thought to him again, *Just order the two waffles. You can cut it in half and only eat one half.*

Is there a reason?

I think it will help you get someplace safe.

After Travis had lathered his waffles in butter and syrup, he proceeded to eat them slowly with his one good arm. He downed his cup of milk and his cup of orange juice and asked for a to-go box. The waiter looked at him like he was slow. He looked at the waiter like he was a dead man walking.

Just do it. Go to the hospital.

Hank had a frown on his face. He paid for the meal and left a tip, and they went back to the house. Travis got out of the car and told Viviane, "I am still going into the hospital. I'd like to get my possessions together that they will let me take."

"Fine, if you insist. Just so you know, you just started losing at life. You have not been to the hospital in forever. What is making you do it this time?"

"Ms. Rita's foretelling."

"And you won't tell me what that was."

"I also won't tell you about other things."

"Pack up your bags, Travis, and I will take you to the hospital", said Hank.

"You will have to be admitted through the ER. It will take forever," said Viviane.

"You can leave then," Travis said to Hank. He had noticed the gnome-like demons of the Christian hell following him around during the day. He had no idea how many there were waiting for him at the hospital. He didn't want to put his family in any more trouble than he apparently already had.

Hank drove Travis to the hospital. Travis got out and went into the hospital to check in. He had to do it through the emergency room. He signed his name and gave as his reason for visiting the emergency room "I have to save the universe." He sat down on a chair in the waiting room and noticed a gnome walk in with the next emergency room visitor before it disappeared.

"That is strange," Hank said. "I definitely saw something come in with that ER visitor."

"Did it look like a gnome?" Travis asked.

"It did, and then it went away."

They are surrounding the entire hospital. There will not be a moment the next week when they are not here waiting for you to die. More will continue arriving, said an alto voice.

Is it people who have clairvoyant capabilities who can see them?

Like your dad? Yes. More of us will drop by too. We know whether we are going to be able to help you out at this point. It would not help you to worry about what the demons and other people would say. They would say we are just making things up. Do not talk about us. There is so much people have wrong and so much that must be corrected. You could help us there though, Travis, couldn't you?

"Patient 50. Step over here. I need to know why you are here."

"I need to be safe."

"Are you suicidal?"

"No. Interstellar beings are going to hunt me down and kill me if I do not save the universe first."

"Are you sure they're not demons?"

"Who knows? I am still trying to comprehend how the Trinity is a thing."

"Is he a danger to anyone else, Hank?"

"Extradimensional beings are here to destroy me. I need to be kept safe from them."

"You may just need more medication. More medication fixes it usually," she said as she winked at Hank.

The last thing you need is medication, Travis, or to pray to God. God won't save you from religious nuts and family in the community who may want you dead. How do you expect to save yourself from those people and their attempts to ruin your life by taking your medication? Stop praying to God and start reclaiming your life again. You keep praying for God to save you from malicious character assassins and swallowing a handful of pills each night and you will end up here again, either catatonic or from an overdose. We can help you out. All you have to do is think like a crafty person and not a fool!

"He needs more medication, I think," said Hank.

"Do you want Hank to go back with you?"

"No, the gnomes will be a problem."

The first of many until everything is revealed, the alto announced serenely.

Travis paced back and forth in his waiting room. He gave blood so they could make sure he was not on anything. He told them enough but not too much, and they pushed him back to the behavioral health unit on a chair, carrying his belongings separately for them to sort through before assigning him one of the rooms he was currently passing to go back into. They pushed his chair into the pavilion where visitors in temporary residence were encouraged to spend their time in between sleep and group therapy exercises.

He saw the whiteboard that had the day's activities on the board and thought to himself, *Well, it isn't much of a life here, but at least I have not been destroyed. They do have it better here than people who have committed crimes.*

You are a douche! You want social pathology treated like mental health issues, and they will be bringing in incredibly disturbed people with behavioral health problems here to rehabilitate at facilities like this that, by the way, no one is ever going to construct. Do you see any of these people doing well with violent criminals in here to be coddled the way you nuts are? thought a shrill woman's voice.

Obviously, that went with the scissors of last night. If they need to be here, they need to be here. That means I need to get out at some point. I am not a paranoid person who cannot hold a conversation, and I am also not a sociopath who has unrealistic expectations for what they can do in the real world as a normal person.

A nurse walking up to him said, "We would just give them Ativan nonstop if they couldn't behave well with others. We do that all the time with people who are just heading to the detention center next anyway. That is rude to call them douches."

"Do you not also think it is douchey to give it away that you are Christian clairvoyant in a room full of people who may not be that?"

"Do you need Ativan?"

"I do not want or need Ativan. Stop harassing me."

"Whatever. Hold on a second while I call the psychiatrist on hours to see if I can go ahead and give you an Ativan. I really thought you could handle clairvoyance without being such a jerk about it."

"Did I just hear her say a rude word?" he heard the head nurse say. "Never ever do anything like that here at work. I will have to write you up." She went over to Travis. "What is your name?"

"Travis Marx."

"Well, Travis, I think it would go good for you to take an Ativan."

He took the Ativan and woke up again at 7:00 p.m. He had forgotten that when you were awake you'd notice that you were alive more.

That guy is awake again, thought an ugly voice of a woman with an ugly Southern drawl.

He is, Travis messaged toward her, but she warped his voice to be much higher and sounded like it was on helium.

You have to pay attention to which thoughts are your own and which thoughts of yours arrive from nowhere. You should block those, thought a smart Northern-sounding woman's voice.

What if I do not want to think and would simply like to be aware?

And how are you going to do that? thought another voice about like a little boy, only with the malicious mind of an adult.

I would not respond anymore.

Try that now.

Do you know what we just did? We have a direct link from your mind to a public broadcasting mechanism. Your thoughts will be going off around the city like a find-shelter warning siren if you have any thoughts.

Travis smiled and just looked blissful for about three hours.

This is all wrong! He should be going ballistic. How can you get him to act messed up if he is at peace all the time?

I am not a part of mind as bad as you. I can just check out and watch. None of you impress me. When you try to impress me, you fail!

Everybody in town heard that! You sound stupid when you talk. That is not what Christianity is supposed to look like. Any minute now, the Christians will be arriving to finish you off!

Oh! I am so scared. They are probably going to do horrible things some more if I am not impressed by their repugnant behavior until I am impressed enough by their repugnant behavior.

I don't want it, said a Christian clairvoyant listening in. *That is about how they are.*

God! That woman isn't even technically in the church. At least not the way it was conceived in the New Testament. We must go around and get more of us to knock him back in line. They shouldn't be showing up here just because they can.

How many of you are there?

Why, lots. It is a town of forty thousand, and for every forty thousand nonclairvoyants, you have one thousand clairvoyants.

Then call yourself Legion, for you are many.

You're an a-hole, said the voice of the malicious old Christian man disguised as a little boy.

Give me fifty reasons why I should care about New Testament Christians, and I will spare you.

We are everywhere, bro. You are baptized. We made sure you were baptized before we dropped by to destroy you. You cannot just escape us. We will beat you at this game, and even if you were a failure in life, you can be one of our slaves in heaven.

Those aren't acceptable reasons to care. Give me ten reasons to care, and I might possibly—

BS, I just gave you one.

You do not have to talk to them, Travis. Have you once heard an angel while you have believed in demons? thought the sensible Northern-sounding voice.

No.

How have you never heard an angel? They are everywhere. Even people who aren't telepathic hear angels.

170

Are they the ones talking to people and telling them that they are angels?

Why, Travis, you know how it is.

Oh, that makes sense. The messengers everyone else listens to and believes automatically are benevolent, angelic beings. I like how Rita just summed it up as dumb thoughts from dumb mind. I knew there were not any angels, and the people doing their bidding are acting anything but angelic.

But you believe that there are demons.

No! In fact, I do not see a difference between the wrongdoings of people and the wrongdoings of any other supernatural being who does not follow its dharma. These bad Christian clairvoyants have been acting foolishly, and they continue to do so, Travis replied.

I see. You make this difficult. If you kept it at Ashurans and ghosts, you could ignore ever having entered into the New Age as a clairvoyant and not have to participate in psychic warfare in this universe as it falls apart. The only ones doing it are Christians and New Agers. Everyone else calls it a dumb thought that is too dumb for their mind and moves on.

God! Is that a joke? Who does that with this extra form of entertainment? Who just ignores it? I am heading out of here and going to war, Travis responded.

That guy was probably never a Christian. Did he even say he was? I would take him at his word. As far back as you look the past year, he has never called out to God. Apparently, God visited him once and he went to sleep on him.

He doesn't even talk like he cares as much about us as we do him, and we were just trying to save his soul from hellfire.

Travis retorted, *Of course, I don't care as much about you as you do me. Do I even know your name? Will I even ever care to ask? Yay, me. You are completely irrelevant to me, and stop trying to ensnare my soul, you creepy fundamentalists.*

Oh, that is sick. He talks about us like he hates us.

I don't hate you. I just haven't seen any signs of you improving, and you have been known to lash out when people try to just ignore you, answered Travis.

He was kind then. Let's stick around. There may be more ahead. I am going to get even with you if it's the last thing I ever do! As long as you are nice to us, we have this long list of insults we have thrown at you that we would like to ask you to be.

Travis asked, *Is that how their mind thinks collectively?*

Of course, that is how they think. Try to get your memories back. They are dumb and forgetful. The best way Karen could think of to keep you and Ophelia together was to make you as forgetful as they are. They have a big sense of importance, and I am not sure how they get it. Looks like they just give it to themselves anyway. I would be doing everything I could to wreck that for them as long as I was alive if I was the old Travis.

Jesus, where are you when we need you? thought the belligerent and antagonistic Baptist-sounding man.

The woman who sounded convincing told Travis he needed to go to his room and see if he saw anything. He asked the tech where his room was. She told him he had the one with the camera to share with the other new guy, and they wanted them under observation. He went into it, opened the blinds, and looked outside and could see the orange glow of a streetlight.

Do you see gnomes? said a female extradimensional.

No.

Do you see crows?

No.

Do you really think that it is just the Ativan keeping you from seeing them or that they might reappear along with thought if you would hold a personal conversation with a close and caring God? Would you remain aware and not resist experience and finally accept this world the way it naturally is?

Can anybody be like that and not think about killing themselves?

Very hardy people. Adults who want to survive.

What makes them come back?

Dumb thoughts that belong in dumb mind and not enlightened individuals are there for you to observe. If all your thoughts are awesome, then you can win at the end. If you pray, however, you may be in for a long wait. Keep your prayers brief and don't focus on yourself too much.

Oh, God! That is everybody here doing it wrong. I cannot just not take whatever filth this is they are trying to shovel down my throat and practice mindfulness and remain all right. I must flee town—the country if necessary. There is so much going on here that isn't right and that needs to be fixed, said a frustrated Travis.

As Travis said these words, the gnome-like demons started popping into the night air in the shadows outside the window between this building and the next one.

Just so you know, those are hungry ghosts and not demons, said the Northern-sounding woman's voice as it morphed into the alto voice. *They may even be interstellar space travelers. Stop sending out dumb prayers!*

They sort of shivered with ecstasy when they sensed they were important.

Until you figure it out, do not talk in group therapy. Do not talk to a therapist or a doctor and tell them anything they do not absolutely need or otherwise lay a trap for yourself. Think like you want to be independent right now.

That is not the correct one to go with, though. I like extradimensional beings for Annunaki/egregores/jinni/angels and Ashurans/ghosts. I do not need attached dead people who look like gnomes to remind me to behave properly, thought Travis.

Those are the sweet ones. The ones that don't put dumb thoughts into an aware mind. They will leave here in the end.

About forty-five gnomes shivered with delight and turned their heads about ninety degrees to look at him. They had, of course, gleeful smiles on their faces. If they were leaving, then they were not dead.

The gnomes are sweet, I guess.

Demon worshipper! thought a Baptist-sounding voice.

You just keep making it harder for yourself not going with Christianity for your family's sake when you know they cannot handle it if you don't. This is the big thing they speak of as a problem they had with you when it became harder for them to explain your actions that anyone else in your home community would have flat-out called erratic had they been paying it attention. It is breaking their heart that they cannot control your behavior and that every disciplinary act they take only makes you more convinced you cannot speak with them again. How are you not better off if you are suddenly intimidated by them? Watch the gnomes never leave because we intimidate you back to Christianity and give your parents a nice, healthy family.

I don't care if the gnomes ever leave.

Fine, have a hundred thousand gnomes surrounding the hospital in a few days before you die, thought a high-pitched girl's voice.

Travis drifted off to sleep and slept blissfully. When he awakened the next morning, he had a smile on his face. He had a feeling this was going to be a better day than yesterday. He walked to the bathroom to take a leak and saw a face emerge out of the toilet pipe. It looked like Ophelia's face, and then it changed to Karen's face. Travis was reluctant to piss all over the constantly changing face.

If you are not willing to piss on her face, I can grab your father's face or your brother's face. You will have to piss on someone's face, or you can kill yourself to avoid the torment. You can't be good at another religion. TURN TO CHRIST!

Travis rolled his head back and pissed on the porcelain while providing the proper aiming protocol. He did not want to see whoever the extradimensional beings wanted him to see himself pissing upon.

He went back to his bed to pull out his Bible and read for the course he was taking. He could not remember the paragraph before the one he was starting and was ready to give up when a White man appeared. He needed this guy to go away.

I can show you how clairvoyants have sex on the astral planes.

He began running his tongue down Travis's back to his crack.

"Stop it!" Travis yelled angrily.

Okay, I will not make that a thing, thought the clairvoyant.

Stay away from me. I don't even know you. If you bother me again, I will destroy you.

But how?

I will find one of Mrs. Blossom's fireballs and burn you out of the clairvoyant realm.

BOYS WHO TEASE END UP ON THEIR KNEES! RANG A CHORUS OF MEN'S VOICES THROUGHOUT THE HALL. *BOYS WHO TEASE END UP ON THEIR KNEES!*

Travis was in the pavilion as four White clairvoyant men and a Latino clairvoyant man appeared around him. They urinated on him.

Don't worry, Travis, offered Karen, *They, as well as their urine, won't be visible when the plan has come to proper fruition even if they tell you that they are. We will pixelate everything.*

Well, that's good. I can still show my body off as well? Even when I am running water through it?

As long as you feel comfortable doing that. Exhibitionism is not a pathology.

That guy is rotten. Can you not do something to keep them away, Karen? Teach me the fireball maneuver to remove rogue, coercive Christian clairvoyants.

I will do something much better for you. I will allow you to take your new medicine tonight but with a bonus. I will make sure it is coated white with DMT. There is no need to wait anymore.

And what happens when you take DMT?

You will see the future. I hope you can handle it if it turns your world upside down. I need to know whether you are going to panic or not.

That is fine. I will do whatever I have to do to save the world.

That's what I thought you would say. You are kind of narcissistic, are you not?

No, I am not.

You are not ready to take on all the evil you must to undo that bad day in your life. The one when you were blessed with exceptional gifts for no particular reason. I would venture so far as to say that no one is ready to take on all this evil. I know for a fact that the extradimensional visitors want for us to abolish the government, and I want you to know that national positions of executive privilege must be brief appointments and extremely stressful without the reward of power. It must be a purely noble pursuit. You must have a thickened skin or else you will be too morally bankrupt to solve everyone's problems. You are a stupid person if you ask

175

for thick skin. Be careful what you ask for. I personally do not want to see any more presidents leading the country. The more I study the Bible, I decide that what will work best is a socioeconomic mode equivalent to anarchy. If you remember to promise not to ever try to save the world, you may be spared prolonged suffering, and your DMT-coated medicine you are given tonight may not reveal a future to you too horrible to handle.

Who is showing these people how to grab our old memories?

I will need for you to know that anyone you see the rest of the day is not me. Do not beg Christian clairvoyants to help you out. There is no reason to pay attention to any other clairvoyants except me and Ophelia, and you must certainly hope fervently that her subtle technique keeps her mother from entering the astral planes to attempt to rip you to shreds again. They are only messing with you or they are intent upon messing with you because you got in shape recently. You are supposed to do their thing or whatever the Big Blue Guy tells his minions to do, and you are not talking like you want to leave the planet with him. You must persevere against Christian clairvoyants, and you will be rewarded with a better future.

How do I get through the day?

You could do it more or less the same way you have been doing it so far—ignoring all your friends at church.

Who the hell are you? You are not Karen Samedi. You are new, and you just shared a bold-faced lie.

Yeah, but who heard it? It was only Christians who knew about this gift.

Do you never stop lying? New Agers never stop venturing out onto the astral planes in search of secret knowledge.

Oh, honey, there is no hope for you if you think that there is anything factual to be found in esoteric teachings of the church. Plus we got rid of the Gnostics a long time ago. We have been removing heretics from the equation since the inception of the faith. Sometimes the first person to inject a popular idea did not do it at the right time. This is why the church burned Jan Hus and Joan of Arc.

Not to mention that Jesus was crucified for saying that he came to earth to turn a son against his father and a daughter against her mother.

He was crucified for saying he was the Son of God.

But how much later did we have those texts?

We are certain that we hold some of the earliest documents of Paul.

Is it the Catholic/Orthodox communions who compiled them? If it was, then why did they decide to go with faith and works?

Why did they decide to create the Trinitarian and Christological formulas that they did at Nicaea and Chalcedon?

Oh, that is weird. Why would you be doing Karen's thing? It isn't mainstream like ours. You would be so much better if you would let us chase her away, and then you can go with one of our versions of the truth. Call them alternative facts if you like. We all get along better than those strange Restorationist groups, injected a local Christian clairvoyant into their discourse.

I really would rather do my own thing.

You are not saved, and you probably never were or else you would follow the rest of the preachers in the New Testament church. Get right with God. It matters more than you know. How can we get you to see it? Whatever it is we want to do next will be best for you. This is the beautiful truth of Christian fellowship. Those other churches do not get together for anything meaningful. They worship God and go out to eat afterward, or sometimes they take Sundays off. Is that something you can do in heaven?

The other voice doing Karen's voice was gone.

I don't know. If every day is Sunday in heaven, I don't want to go. I am tired of these collective bargaining classes on Wednesdays, and I am tired of Christian sadists attempting to control my every decision. Each and every last one of you has participated in taking this in the same direction as the International Church denomination.

We don't want to see you burn for all eternity, so we will help you burn off some of the bad karma if you will. We know you are secretly enamored of us. There must be a good reason why you do not go to church regularly.

When people ask me why I am not a regular attendee, I always felt pressured to give a church-conforming answer. I don't do it that great. Why would I be sleeping in on Sundays unless I did not see any need to go on a regular basis?

That is the most important thing in my life. For the life of me, I cannot see why it would not be that for someone like you.

No! God! Wherever you are, please help me get away from them when the time is right for me to never have to suffer these liars again! Keep me safe and thwart them at all their attempts to help me burn down karma. They cannot pass for normal by passing me off as abnormal in whatever way they choose to do next.

"Travis, it is time to take your medicine."

"I would like to know why the pill is white."

"They come in different varieties. Have you taken it? Open your mouth."

Travis did open his mouth.

The guy behind the desk grinned at Travis. "I don't know how you do it, but you continue to have brilliant white teeth."

Travis looked off elsewhere as he thought to himself that it was highly unethical to force hospital patients to participate in unregistered clinical observations rather than do anything to help them return to a normal life afterward. He took the pill laced with DMT, and he went off to bed. He heard the hospital staff refer to his grin in a vulgar way as well as name-calling him outside of his room, while his roommate tonight had not arrived in bed yet.

He heard them talking about how they wanted to discharge him to his family because he was not going to get better in the hospital and that he would have better luck learning not to be a prick about the position in his life that angry and resentful health-care professionals placed him in if he went home. The older people could not handle a lot of the ideas he saw working for him, and he was going to have to make peace with fundamentalism and hateful attacks against him by the world's most affluent and greedy.

If you do not get indebted to Wall Street, then you have no choice but to suffer the worst outcome. Then we have no choice but to fatten you up, force-feeding you Christian meat, and poison you on a plethora of drugs until you see Jesus as your personal savior. You'll lose your tech devices, warned a Christian telepath.

Not true. I will get to finish my schoolwork on those devices if it is the last thing I do, Travis replied.

Even if you cannot leave the hospital, more than anything else, what has people infuriated is whether you will insist upon a revolution. What will you do if you are kept from doing schoolwork for an antirevolution school? How will you get your message across that other people will have to suffer the consequences of their decision to be hostile to people like you the next decade until it breaks them on social media? What is it you are going to do to keep them continually dismayed at how little control they actually have over the situation again? said the Big Blue Guy.

I will be so ruthless that they lose hope in every one of their idols to deliver them from their impending doom. This is not what Christianity was supposed to look like. Every one of these militant churchgoers is a Pharisee and an Antichrist claiming to have authority that has not been bestowed upon them.

And that happens because they are prone to backstabbing. I know what I must do to keep you safe from prolonged suffering, said the Big Blue Guy, *by the way, Jesus was a Pharisee himself.*

Feeling safe in the hands of a notorious liar, Travis drifted off to sleep in bed. He woke up for vitals, and he heard Karen telling him that Ophelia would not be by to visit today. She found out that he was going to be a vehicle-less outlaw who had come to earth simply to mess everyone up, and she thought that he needed to understand that this placed them in a difficult position. He could not make sense out of the ranting extradimensional being he had heard last night on DMT.

CHAPTER 11

TRAVIS WENT THROUGH HIS DAY IN THE HOSPITAL FEELING better. He turned his parents away from visitation Monday and today on Wednesday; he told them that they did not need to arrive. He had sick, gut-wrenching feelings every single time he went to group therapy, and another hospital patient revealed too much in front of him. He had had to make up for lost time trying to figure out how to avert a catastrophe that could split the universe in two as well as potentially humiliate himself as well as everyone who had ever known him. He had been caught up in a wild-goose chase Monday and Tuesday and had ended up being forced to take his medicine last night. He had had no visitors today promising him that if he would look for the clues, he could find his way to safety. He did have some ugly behavior from many of the clairvoyants wanting him to stay in his room and not get out with the others. They had been augmenting the hospital experience and mocking these people and their problems. They could crack an evil joke and still be completely aghast as to how Jesus alone did not solve everything at this point. Now that it had got out of hand, what they were doing to these patients, he thought surely they would double back and ask forgiveness.

At the end of the day shift, they had dinner together, and they had the TV on until visiting time. They had a snack, and then they flipped on a movie. The doctor thought that Travis was improving, and he believed he might not need a medication change. That evening, a new group of extradimensional beings dropped by. They had Travis very confused. They had told him that he would die soon and that the police would allow it. They told him that they would have horrible things to say to him and that no one would ever understand why he did not trust the police. They told him that he would die outside this hospital here.

He remembered walking to his room with his pill and not taking it and spending the first hour of the night pacing up and down the hall until the hospital techs told him to head to his room to do what he needed to do. He paced the length of his room for two more hours until one thirty when the Big Blue Guy arrived.

You are doing this pathetically, said the rumbling bass voice.

Well, I don't need your help.

Just for that, I want you to have a bad trip. What monster will wake him up for an hour?

The Big Blue Guy grabbed an eight-legged crustacean-like beach monster from a planet Travis had never seen. It had pincers on its mandible, and it also had a whiplike sting. It was trying to lift its front legs onto Travis's shoulders and snap his neck with its mandibles, but he had formed a blue sphere to encase himself in for his protection. *You should have attempted to use the whiplike sting first.*

The crustacean hissed, and he felt a wet prickly sensation on the back of his neck. The beast had a tongue with suckers on it, and it was feeling around on his neck for blood to suck even though it had not decapitated him yet. Travis kept his blue sphere up and waited for the crab monster to give up and go away. He spent an hour standing in his room. He had left the planet. The wall where a window and a climate control unit had been had disappeared. There was a facility for pumping liquid energy or a factory in the background along with a series of spaceships docked near to the energy production factory. The air was cold and dry and almost nonexistent. It was no longer summer. He had no idea what lay on the other side of the door to the room, but he had just broken through to another level of consciousness in here and seen the center of the Big Blue Guy's home, Space Navy.

They are part of the Air Force here though. We used to hunt those crabs on the beach, and now we have imitation meat produced to taste like them. We produce it on board those. They don't take us everywhere we like to go at the same speed we can travel using the Inner Eye. That's when we travel in the dimension of mind. Interference with sinister forces is limited this way. Some people here are dabbling in it even though they don't know what it can lead to and that you can stay there indefinitely once you have been shown how to enter it. I do not like them for some of the mischief they are getting up to on the astral planes. Humankind should not start projecting themselves for others with intentional out-of-body experiences that casually. I will not let walking-around, alive people conduct themselves as such without retribution. If they started lucid dreaming and they could modify their own dreams as well as those of others, it would be as devastating as the invention of the atomic bomb. When you sleep, you can find the future you would like to continue being present in. Precognition happens when people sleep. I do not need these buffoons who are getting a faulty version of telepathy and walking into traps opening the treasure chest. I need them to panic soon. They are way too casual when they get it wrong for their gifts to progress, said the rumbling bass voice of the Big Blue Guy.

"Will they get to travel the old-fashioned way?" Travis asked.

They would if they had renewable liquid energy. It would take some time to create a fuel for high-speed travel, and people here are way too anxious to get into space to wait to develop the proper technology. None of us are worried though. There are plenty of monsters lurking in space, horrifying living and physical phenomenon that would remove your exploratory crews for you if you travel unprepared. You should work to care for your own and not lose biodiversity by restoring the earth first. You may have the secrets here that will help you out when you come across some of those.

Travis looked on his bed and saw a host of carnivorous animals that looked about like millipedes and beetles the size of dogs on his bedsheets.

And some of those.

Travis looked on the bedsheets and noticed spore-like remnants from the insect mammals had stayed on the bed and were quickly fruiting and growing into the carnivorous pups he had seen before. He waited awhile before he went to the nurse's station and asked for water. He then swallowed his pill and chased it down with water before he crawled in bed with the heat on. The smell of burning dust filled the air, and the sounds of a factory filled his mind as he drifted off to sleep.

He woke up to crows slamming into the window and a mental health worker on the other side of the door telling him it was time to eat. He went out of his room and walked down the hallway into the pavilion and saw spirits lined against the walls. They belonged to his Habitat for Humanity volunteer crew as well as Viola. They were smirking at him.

How does it feel knowing you are a day away from us murdering you? thought Kevin.

"I had no idea I was going to be murdered," a surprised Travis replied.

Where have you been, you forgetful loony tune? thought Viola.

"Did you find something out?"

Only that you are a despicable person in need of a reckoning, thought Kevin.

"How will it happen?" Travis asked anxiously.

There are a hundred thousand gnomes surrounding the hospital now who will show you, said the Big Blue Guy.

Oh, it's that demon. Forget about that, Travis. You get jumped your first night in jail and stabbed with contraband, said Kevin.

Travis finished his lunch and walked back to his room and noticed ripples in the windowpane. "I thought Kevin flip-flopped. They are already here. I wonder why the Big Blue Guy is letting this happen to me." One little gnome crawled up his bed and plopped into his side. Another little gnome came up behind him.

Watch out. They come up right behind you and do the same thing, thought Viola.

That one plopped into the back of Travis's neck. Travis was genuinely terrified now. A third gnome that had been clambering up his

183

bedsheets crawled all the way up to the front of his neck and plopped in. Travis made a resolution to spend time in the pavilion until nightfall and the time to take his meds. His parents were going to visit. He tried to play a game of chutes and ladders but was distracted by his impending death. The girl he was playing with made fun of his unkempt hair and said, "Well, at least you still look like a Backstreet Boy." He hated her from then on—not too much like enough to start wars, just enough that he left her out of his life story like she served no real purpose on earth. There were so many mentally ill people like that.

"You are right. I'd rather die than be you!" Travis shouted at her as he ended the game. Dinner came and was good.

"It's great to see you eating again, Travis," said one of the mental health workers.

"It's great to have food to eat." Travis smiled at her.

I hate this place. Everything about it seems wrong. I wish there was another way out and that I did not have to speak with my parents one last time. Travis called his parents once to say "I don't have to see you tonight" before turning around and calling them again and telling them to go ahead and come visit.

When they arrived, he was ecstatic. I guess perhaps believing in some collective consciousness made him believe they would be closer to him now than when he entered the hospital if he was going to die even though the Big Blue Guy had said nothing about that. They were anything but that. A lot of that was due to him asking his mother if she had consorted with Satanic spirits before she gave birth to him in a joking manner. "You see, everyone here believes that I am the Antichrist."

"I didn't think you would ever have the gall to speak to me like that."

He saw naked bodies engaging in orgies surrounding the room like wallpaper.

"I just thought there might come a time when you were pressured to call me the Antichrist, and I wondered what you would do if your whole religious community was doing it."

"Bless him, I think he gets it. He's dumb."

"Have you seen all the people fornicating around us? Because I can see them, and they let me know that things are not all right."

"Son, I am trying to follow you, but I cannot make sense out of you. I guess we just give the new meds time to work and let them fix it. Maybe you will stop having inappropriate outbursts."

After his mother and father left, Travis stayed around for a movie and a snack then headed off to bed.

CHAPTER 12

TRAVIS WAS LYING IN BED CERTAIN THAT THIS WOULD be the night that all his problems would be resolved as Ophelia and Karen had told him they had arranged for them to be. He was looking up at the fluorescent light in the ceiling of the hospital bed.

Man, this guy is stupid. He can't think right.

I am sleep-deprived, you stupid a-hole, thought Travis.

It is okay, Travis. This is about to be the worst twenty-four hours of your life. You need to be brave.

Travis answered back to his two trusted companions, *Who is this now?*

Pay close attention to those four ceiling panels above you as hard as you can.

Okay, I will do whatever I need to do, thought Travis.

Shh. Be quiet. It takes a while to go to sleep. Do you see the dots?

Which ones? There are many. Those ceiling panels are old and have flecks on them, thought Travis.

I guess it does not matter.

Why is that? thought Travis.

You do know we are doing this telepathically. You can have an empty mind at the end.

Shh. Do you see those dots? The ones moving from top to bottom? said the other voice.

Travis replied, *Yeah, I see one. Wait! There are two sets of two dots emerging repeatedly.*

Stay focused on that. And do as they said and be quiet.

As Travis waited in the hospital room, he tried to keep an empty mind. He felt a thrill running up his spine. *I just want this to be over,* he thought.

Do you understand that things will never go back to normal again?

I got that a long time ago. Which one of you is this anyway? answered Travis.

Trying as hard as he could to hear what the next horrific ordeal might be that the demons were planning, he still could not hear a thing. The two paths of dots turned into three, and then they turned into four. He started to become sleepy but knew to fight it.

I just want to know one thing. Why did you not trust me?

Bro, that is not who you think it is.

Whoever it is, it has been nothing but evil from the start.

Travis knew he was not the one who thought that thought about Jesus. Something about it, however, felt true. Then crows came out of the ceiling and flew down onto him on the bed, flooding him completely to his spine. He could not remember Zod anymore.

Oh, God, no, this cannot be happening! I have not been a bad person. I have tried to make sense out of your Word even though somebody put in there that it was inerrant, Travis prayed.

That was your big mistake. We are trying to fix it for you unlike you, rang Ophelia's voice with a bitchy undertone.

Travis was shocked. *That cannot possibly be how those people are,* he thought.

It is. Most of them. I cannot believe some of the things I have seen, but I know where my bread and butter are. You could try not playing for the same team as them until the end for all I care. Do you remember what I told you about a possible alternative? thought Karen.

I had no idea that woman was that pathetic or else I would have left the two of you alone to resolve this, Ophelia's bitchy voice echoed.

I really cannot say that I care about that other spirit now. It is obviously untrustworthy, thought Travis.

You could not have done this more absurdly. I and everyone else like us will let you go to bed.

Travis might have been unconscious for five minutes. As he left the waking world, he traveled to a night island. Here it was explained to him by other spiritual beings that there was only one future he should want to continue into. He wanted to know what these beings were, and then tropical birds flew by. This bothered him because of something disturbing he had experienced while he was awake not too long ago. He heard someone say, *Now do you trust me?* He was trying his hardest to stay asleep without controlling the landscape, but that creepy voice had followed him to this sacred place. He could not help but think that it must be the Demiurge and not God or anything else in Christian scripture.

Uh, I followed you here too, and this is Ophelia. Somebody is pathetic. You could have explained your visions better.

That girl is annoying. Travis had awakened after what seemed like five minutes of sleep and could not remember anything about what the hospital staff had given him to help him sleep, but he knew never to go back. This was where the Ashurans played. Ugh! Every gift from them had come at a heavy cost.

"I am out of bed already. And I am cutting the lights on," said Travis.

"Nobody else cares. We have been without sleep as long as you have the past few nights."

"Okay. That was a person next door. I can never go back to sleep," said Travis.

Shh. Use your telepathic head voice if you're going to be up.

"I did, and I need to turn on the lights. I do not want to keep myself up with a utility light and the curtains back until I see the morning light—"

Stream in.

"Please do not—"

Finish your thoughts for you?

"This is—"

Evil.

Travis stopped talking, and he stumbled around from his bed to the wall to cut on the light. He did not open the door. He knew he needed to sleep. He also needed to not sleep. So instead he paced the room back and forth in a straight and sometimes curvilinear direction. It was almost entirely curvilinear, and he needed to keep from knocking into the walls. He would try to avoid that, but he still needed to leave. With those people sharing their room next door ready to tell him off if he woke them up, the most important thing was to not run into the walls.

Use head voice.

Don't think.

The door flung open at that moment, and his head was about eye level with the latch. "Dude, are you okay?"

"What shift is this, and how soon is breakfast?" said Travis.

"It will be a while. The sun is up though."

Do they not get your vitals before breakfast while it is still dark out? Today marks the start of your second week in here.

Travis acknowledged that none of these were his thoughts and told the telepaths as well as the alien visitors he had mistaken for demons to piss off.

That guy is trash in this one. That is where we will be. I wasn't certain. Now I know for sure, thought Ophelia.

Most of them will say he is going to hell before he can be born again, thought Karen.

That's the breakfast tray, thought Travis. *They have skipped vitals for me.*

You can have that when you are ready. I knew that other one was going to bail on you. I know what I saw when I investigated your future all those years ago. You need to trust me. This needs to happen. There are a lot of things that Christian clairvoyants have been fighting for years, and after what I saw last night, no one else would blame you if you thought they were some of the worst people in the world.

Karen had left. Travis was feeling better even though he knew it was not over. His last friend had left him, other than Karen whom he had not seen in ages until all this mess got started, and it was basically because of those nutcases dabbling in clairvoyance and not really knowing what to make of what they were seeing. He was going to sit up on the bed until it was time for breakfast and try to read. There was no point in reading the Bible if there was going to be hell to pay regardless of how hard he repented—no point in conducting research on the arguments of theologians ever again. Whatever it was he was going to have to face, it needed to be much more glorious than going back to normal. He did not deserve to suffer anymore at the hands of those hateful destroyers of life.

"You can come on out. Your breakfast is here."

As Travis walked out of his room and down the hall to the atrium of the pavilion, he noticed that, once again, things had returned to normal for the day's activities. He looked at the whiteboard and was glad that he had told his family not to come and visit him. He could wait until this was resolved and his debt was paid. "The doctor will be visiting today."

"Which one? They don't normally make the rounds on Saturday," said Travis.

"Dr. Uganda."

"There is nothing else?" asked Travis.

"There's your breakfast. You can try eating it for a change."

Travis walked over to the tables lined up in what served as the unit's common area. The nurse, or tech, he couldn't remember him from before, brought his food over to him. They had allowed him to eat later than everyone else who were either in their rooms or in the sitting area playing games on the Sony PlayStation. He ate his food in silence. No one said a thing to him, nor did he say anything to anyone else. They were talking about the game. He got up and walked over to a tech and said, "I think I will get cleaned up by myself."

"I didn't know you needed help before."

"Don't talk down to me like that. I need my personal hygiene supplies." The tech handed these to Travis, and he walked back to his room. He brushed his teeth and showered one-handed so that he would be ready for a good meeting with Dr. Uganda. "I will also need to wash some clothes up for this week so I have something to change into."

"Later," said a tech

When Travis was done getting cleaned up and had settled onto his bed, he opened a book to read. Three lines into it, he heard Karen talking to him again. *Hey, I found some new people. They are doing something more mainstream than the other group was. It is still good orthodox New Testament Christianity. I think they might be able to help you get back with Ophelia. You should at least hear what they have to say. Before you respond, remember that you cannot guard your thoughts from us.*

Is that the guy you wanted us to guard from demons today? This does not look like it is important. I have the day off, and I do not want to spend it here.

I didn't ask you to. That was Karen's idea. I know what those are, thought Travis.

Got it. That kid doesn't want to be helped. He could have read that other book while he was in here—you know, the good B-I-B-L-E—and got it right. That is still how we teach it at our churches, and he doesn't do it so.

You are so full of it. It is much harder to say that certain passages in it are relevant today than in, say, the Koran, thought Travis.

Are you a closet Muslim, Travis? Are you secretly following the Koran for a messianic vision of utopia on earth, living it up away from the mosque as an extremely liberal Buddhist?

No one who knows me would accuse me of not being openly Muslim. In fact, I am Isa reincarnated, thought Travis.

You are sick. You cover for the mistakes of religious leaders who have gone before you in other faiths while we do not require you to do that in our own. What a great idea of ours to never read the Bible and let our leaders interpret it for us. Oh, that's right. It's Muslims who don't read the Koran. You do not make it easy for people to mimic your spiritual beliefs. Nobody follows Islam and has Buddhism as a philosophy of life. Have you seen anybody showing up at Baha'i faith gatherings? Was that your first choice when you decided to get spiritual?

Who cares at this point? Burn the system down. Capitalism must die! People should get to read what they want to read. You all take a few problems seriously, and yes, you would try to destroy someone who may not even be a Baptist or a New Testament Christian over missing the Baptist response to Baptist hot words. Know when to respond and when not to respond. You people don't matter to me. See if a Muslim immigrant cares after talking with a Baptist. I think I'll head to Europe. Our social programs have a time limit, and the Republocrats join forces to remove anything that works for the betterment of the working class. Americans have nothing now. The cost of living will continue to increase, and the minimum wage will be stagnant if we do not have a little socialism in the economy the next time the left rises, Travis pontificated.

I guarantee you that American Baptists will succeed at intimidating Black Christians into voting for the centrist that they prefer, with or without a prophesied economic crash, and your hopes of getting a revolution with steep tax rates will get backed up until 2028.

According to him, we are not relevant anymore anyway. Every time we try to discipline our weakest member, all we do is just dig our hole deeper for ourselves. Is it just in our heads that we have the trump card for keeping society rigged to promote family success? You do not act like Jesus is arriving in the clouds any day now and say that nobody cares about the end times and what his kingdom will look like when he arrives any day now. You need to get right with God. Jesus will not arrive without bringing the least among us, Travis Marx, into the fold. Even if it means waiting until after you die to get here to claim the rest of us. Who have you really convinced that we are all self-important busybodies on a mission to destroy what many have called the deep things of Satan? You'll have to figure that out for yourself.

You must try to end telling everyone to leave the welfare of people in the hands of the church and in the hands of her many unforgiving families and within an unregulated market system that devours what the church spares, argued Travis.

There you go. That is the new Christianity. It is like that game, the Last Stronghold. There is a mysticism surrounding American imperialism and the threat against the White Christian social order of the United States. It packs auditoriums full of the swine the reincarnated Nazis are bringing up to remove the undesirables from this overpopulated earth with abusive-narcissists-turned-sociopathic White men. Both President Hampton and the presumptive Democratic nominee, Vice President

Libby, were roaming across the United States inciting the masses to hate with their own distinctive brand of racism. People have never felt as free to drop racial and anti-religious minority epithets, let alone use every hate-filled chauvinistic word to threaten the most populous segment of America. They are not trustworthy characters, and they go prowling around the country looking for trouble until they can run another racist candidate, thought Ophelia, trying to mimic Travis.

I know why nobody wants to deal with him now. I am going to go get more Christian clairvoyants from within OUR movement across the nation and let them see this and tell us if that looks correct. This person wants to ruin everything. We must win this fight. We are entitled to kill those who convert from Christianity. It may not say as much in the Bible, but I am sure some prolific writer wrote that at some point.

I was a lifelong Democrat, Karen added. *I know how hard it is to get the kids to show up at our churches with this nonsense going on. Frankly, I don't care anymore. Southern Democrats who still pay their religious leaders attention look ridiculous right now compared with Progressive Democrats and Green Americans whose lives do not revolve around their church and who do not have wandering church members in their families. This is a buffoonish way to act. That way of life left in the 1950s. It is so unimaginably stupid to expect it to return. It probably sets off a French Revolution.*

There is nothing wrong with 1950s values for the social good. You go to work. Sometimes the wife goes to work. You go and talk to your neighbors. Except now that is done far away from the workplace and Main Street and the town squares in our best states. The only difference is that Southern rural communities are more vibrant and alive because they have an emphasis on devotion to a faith community in town. This would be with a strong emphasis on being Christian.

Jerks! You people are full of it. You do not care about community as much as gossip or finding the next neighbors to be your scapegoat or else you would hold communalist values. There are refugees on the run from Southern slave drivers again, and there are young people leaving to see the country and find out whether they can come alive again. When the social upheaval continues, then people would be open to community control over public utilities, schools, hospitals, police, banking and business operations funded by community development banks, and you would never mistake Puritanical offshoots for people with a normal face, one without two sides, ever again. Nobody wants your faith communities looking for trouble endlessly. Everywhere else they are all on board with helping your offspring leave your area and urbanizing this nation for sustainable development. In the context of a socialist society, the most antisocial and judgmental bigots will be left behind to siesta in the Southern heat. The panic of aging bigoted baby boomers is much more effective for greening the grid anyway. Social security is going bankrupt, and the stock market will crash again. It will happen quicker with President Hampton, and it will force these jerks in the baby boomer cohort to see how greedy and self-serving their own value system was. You know what everyone else knows about most of them here now. They are not mentally equipped to handle a deep economic depression the way their parents and grandparents were. They will behave with unimaginable animus toward those who do not allow them to wreck their lives next. Those weeds of that cohort played their part in the story, and they were a lot of jerks toward young people who don't trust them anymore. You lied about everything when you told your children what they could expect from life and about what was worth fighting to get. What are you sharing about what you desire, and what are you keeping hidden? You stay away from me for the rest of my life, Travis ranted manically.

I really cannot do that. That is not how our generation handles things. I must end it for you.

Karen spoke soothingly, *Travis, you don't have to worry about those malicious Pharisees. You can move soon. All you have to do is not give them any ammunition to say you are just an oddball Christian from their community who can't really get liberal right.*

Would you allow me to share secret knowledge if I pointed to how things are done in other areas around the globe? If I showed case studies where ideas not formed within the profit-above-all-else predatory capitalist system survive and work to share them with the geographically and anthropologically illiterate? Travis asked.

Many people are going to want to mock you because they are greedy and self-serving. Hopefully you can develop a thick skin. I am still bringing more men over here to see this.

This young man should not have been allowed to become a clair-voyant. He cannot leave the area. If he does, we are outed as bigoted and backward.

I hope that idiot is not pretending to be my father, Hank Marx Sr. He was fine until I went into the hospital.

According to everything you told me, if he lives any longer, he will break the law. I am wondering if you can get your mother to confess that you never struck a blow against your mother or your father.

Your father exaggerates when he speaks about you being violent. He hit you with words.

He is not going to try to control me forever, thought Travis.

You have no idea how far he would go to do exactly that. There is a private you who is open to heresy, and in private, he wants you to die off as young as possible. Has he ever told you to go ahead and kill yourself and make the lives of your parents easier?

That was back near Thanksgiving. I got work on the West Coast once, and they lied and told me that I would need a car, and they did not free up money from my trust fund to help me pay for what would be expected for me to get to do something different in that area for a change, thought Travis.

They are not concerned about your well-being long-term and haven't been awhile even if they try to look as if they are.

I will stay away from them. They are thieves, thought Travis.

They are stealing your best years because of the economic disadvantages they have saddled you with starting out. Break contact with them.

I will go grab some of the demons, Pastor.

Did one of their women just say that?

They don't care anymore if this doesn't happen the way you want it to go through. That's a nightmare for us. That's not how we were. We know you will not break free from our clutches if we show you how little we think of you all over the nation.

You are talking like you are fighting the Antichrist. That's odd of you, a puzzled Travis thought.

I need for you to be quiet for a few and let me fight these people, thought Ophelia. *I am nowhere near you in this geographic vicinity. You are, however, safe for now.*

"The doctor is in. Are you ready to see him?"

This could not have come at a worse time. I can't do anything like that now. That guy does not know what he is doing anyway, thought Travis.

He probably does. He needs to dope you up until you love Christ as much as God and start doing his thing finally. You know the one—the one where he brags about calling himself the Nutcracker and mocks his patients to changing meds to meds they don't need to be on either. I will walk you through your meeting with him. Talk like a capitalist.

I will not do that. You do not have to do that all the time, thought Travis.

IF YOU DO NOT DO THAT HERE AND NOW, YOU WILL BE HOSPITALIZED HERE IN THE AREA A VERY LONG TIME AND BE SO SCREWED UP THAT YOU COULD LITERALLY DIE FROM IT. HAS HE THREATENED TO CHANGE YOUR MEDS BEFORE ON RECORDING? REMEMBER THE PEN! NEVER TRUST HIM AGAIN. CHOREOGRAPH A LITTLE DANCE FOR THEM TO DO AND WATCH THEM TRIP REPEATEDLY.

IT SOUNDS LIKE THINGS MUST GET WORSE BEFORE THEY CAN GET BETTER, shouted another telepath.

That is undeniably true. I have heard doctors accused of quackery who have had no business being picked on for standing against the line of the AMA. They dredge the bottom of the barrel with shrinks. Travis walked down the hall toward the doctor's meeting room. He was hearing jeers from the fundamentalist Pharisees.

Let us have our way.

You are crazy.

Hank is radiant like Jesus.

He is the real victim here.

As Travis walked into the doctor's office, the doctor asked Travis how he had been this week with the staff leaving him alone on Thursday and Friday.

"I am doing well. I tried something unconventional to get into the hospital, but I am glad that I have some distance from my parents. My mother was even starting to walk back promises that she had made to me. She looks so bad and suspect for some of the things that she has said."

Dr. Uganda paused and said, "I think I have a good drug suggestion to help you cope with things better."

That could not be more obvious. That is how they think they help. Behave conventionally or suffer the consequences. That is it regardless of where they bring them in from when they bring them into this broken health-care system, thought a woman. *"Let's make more money,"* and *how are they making it? They can only make more money by making it off more sick and dying people. Make sure that you mess with him as well.*

I am going to do that. These are presumptive jerks who think people will shut up even though all the racket that they make is helping them accomplish all the items on their agenda to accomplish, thought Travis.

"I would like you to try Latuda. It is obvious you have more of a problem with bipolar depression now. If I wanted to mess with you, I would tell you that this sticker I am giving you for progress is a teleportation device."

"How are you getting that out of everything you have observed?" Travis asked.

"It's been hard figuring out what the problem is now. I think it is mostly that you don't know that you have to kiss ass before you can kick it, and you don't know that."

"I wonder if you know that most conditions can be treated effectively with psychedelics and all conditions with vitamins, exercise, meditation, sunlight, and a diet rich in tryptophan and magnesium and low in sugar. You can even get sound healing and ayurveda done to lift serotonin levels or dampen dopamine levels if needed. Psychiatric treatment is only meant for a short duration, and many doctors will taper their patients off medicine once they have changed their lifestyles," said Travis.

"The hospital will bring a case against you that you should be held under conservatorship. You do not show proper respect by refusing to take your meds. I must be kissed up to properly by all the inpatients. But since you have been quiet most of the past two weeks,

I thought you were depressed and did not want to be a jerk. Surely, that is the last thing you want us to call you."

I have grown sick and tired of all your insults. How does that work when you got this crap started? I will be a plague upon you until you stop exploiting people. They should pull the recordings of this, those you took on your pen. I bet that you are destroying those records, Doctor, thought Travis.

"It seems to us like we have the law on our side. We will just get a conservatorship for you. This way, we do not have to call out the military and shoot guys like you in the head the way that would've happened in *Schindler's List*. You cannot imagine how dumb that stunt of yours was this time. We have everything we need."

"You don't have a thing just because you take a broad license with what the medicine is capable of doing. Everyone whom you have ever screwed over will pile on top of my accusations along with me. You are despicable. You wallow in slime, you filthy pig! If you try to make it a conventional life here or with my family upon discharge, then I will be living on the West Coast and taking the medicine I believe I should be on. In the meantime, you can find something better than Latuda just because it's new and a drug rep put you up to it," said Travis.

"You are not going to do that. There is a reason people from the East Coast are snobbish toward the people on the West Coast. We have it better here."

"And what happens if I do that exact thing?" asked Travis.

The halls burst forth with laughter. "In this place, you must play by our rules, and we have zero tolerance for unconventional people."

"Or what?" Travis asked.

"We can call the police. We wish that we could jail people like you. Now are you going to vote for Vice President Libby and make us all happy?"

"I am just asking because you should not have me on one of those for mania or, in other words, the SLEEP DEPRIVATION YOU HAVE BEEN CAUSING THAT I GET TO USE AS MY

EXCUSE. Do you know what else? If I had been Black, that is the point where you would have killed me," Travis said a bit incoherently.

"Oh, get him up and give him the Haldol. I believe in my heart of hearts that after he takes this, he will wake up the sweet Christian boy his mother told us he was."

"Screw you! Every one of you here have mountains of karma to burn off. I am revoking your access to my mother. She misinformed you. IF YOU TRY TO FORCE ME TO GO AGAINST MY BELIEFS, I WILL DESTROY YOU. YOU WILL BE ALIVE LONG ENOUGH TO WATCH EVERYONE TURN AGAINST YOU. IT IS HIGHLY UNETHICAL TO RESPOND TO ACTS OF DOMESTIC TERRORISM AS IF THEY WERE A MENTAL HEALTH CRISIS," shouted Travis.

"That is a douchebag. We have the best health care in the nation in this state. Everybody looks to us to try to replicate our success. It is also true for our police force we have called here. As far as I am concerned, you may call the mother again and believe every word she says," said Dr. Uganda to the nurse Travis liked the most.

Travis felt betrayed. *Not you too, Maria! You little blonde blue-eyed EVA BRAUN CLONE. YOU TWO-FACED VIXEN. What a sad end your career in health care has come to,* he thought.

Dr. Uganda smiled. "THAT IS THE MOST THRILLING SHOW OF POWER I HAVE EVER SEEN DONE TO ONE OF OUR SOCIALIST MEN. IF THEY WON'T LEAD BY EXAMPLE, THEN THERE'S NO HOPE. Keep it in your mind always and never again doubt that even when push doesn't come to shove, we will ruin you for you withdrawing your support for the status quo that birthed you."

"I NEVER gave you DOUCHEBAG. YOU LIE ABOUT ME. I have the right to contradict that lie of yours every time you give it to people," Travis replied angrily.

"It is for our protection as well as yours."

"I would be sent back home dead if I had to go back home at all," said Travis.

Dr. Uganda's smile turned into a frown. "I do not like that. Of all the possible futures for you to live into, I like that one the least. I was not the person for you to tell that to."

I am staying out of this. That doctor is playing with Travis because things are heated with Christian clairvoyants right now, and he thinks he can get away with it. He is also new, thought Karen. *The Big Blue Guy is here to help.*

Travis said, "I am not going to exist to pay doctors and extra administration more than we actually need to pay them. I do not think my family ties it together the same as me, but they should not have sent me to college if they did not want me to end up radicalized. I pick up on everything, and I cannot forget. I also don't want to work for a life like theirs. It was made off the suffering of others. How does a system work where the capitalist profit incentive is to make money off more sick and dying people?" asked Travis.

"It goes on endlessly and mercilessly because the people are threatened by the idea of remaking the economy. Watch the other nuts in here whom you have already cracked going along with it already. You believe you cannot help us out if we want to remake the economy or abolish the current socioeconomic mode," said Travis, answering his own question.

"When you are realistic about your prospects while being a socialist, I do not have to screw you over so hard that you could potentially die."

Just so you know, you are brilliant. I do not know any other people who do well with the languages and arts so quickly as you. YOU CRAZY BASTARD.

Travis ignored it. He did not think he even giggled. It sounded like the bad end of a good relationship.

"I do not want any additional drugs to cope with these problems. I will meet with you later when you make sense. Some problems just require sleep. I'm going to my room to sleep a bit," Travis said abruptly.

Travis went to sleep, and he awakened two hours later furious. He had no idea how he was going to get out of the hospital.

Travis got up and walked out of his room. He knew that he had an audience of clairvoyants on the other side who were going to push thoughts into his mind that did not belong there. They might be humorous and inappropriate thoughts. Instead, he was remaining absent of thought. As he closed the door, he began pacing the room from front to back. Every now and then, someone would drop by to offer an insult and a jibe; but at a point, he was in an altered mental state and nothing was reaching him. He looked up out of the window and saw that it was dark, and the twenty-four-hour period he was promised a resolution within was about to come to an end, but nothing had been attempted by Karen again.

How was that not a thought? said a menacing spirit.

It is time you started calling us what we are again, all that good stuff.

We are demons, and there are many of us.

Oh, I am so scared. At least you are not interstellar time travelers. If you were, I would be at a serious disadvantage, thought Travis.

You SHOULD BE SO SCARED.

You think dumb for me, and you waste time on stupid ideas I would never care about, and then you talk about me like you know me. That makes you think dumb. I have gifts, the likes of which you have never seen. Everything you once thought was sheer nonsense is about to be used by me to DESTROY YOU, YOU WICKED CHRISTIAN CLAIRVOYANTS. Listen to yourself and where you place emphasis. I DON'T GIVE A CRAP ABOUT ANY OF THAT! I DON'T THINK I AM GETTING ORDERS FROM JESUS IN THE SKY! Travis yelled.

Are you sure you have not heard the voice of God?

NOT IN THIS LIFE. WHAT IF I AM ISA REINCARNATED! I WOULD BE PISSED OFF. I HAVE TOLD YOU ONCE I DID NOT DIE. I AM GOING TO TELL YOU A SECOND TIME I DID NOT DIE. I AM JUST A GUARDIAN OF THE WORLDS, AND I AM PISSED OFF. YOU CANNOT GET RID OF ME WITHOUT DIVINE RETRIBUTION BEING VISITED UPON EARTH, thought Travis.

Liar! You forget that I can go back and grab your old memories. You have an interstellar time traveler helping you out. You may have two.

YOU have never been one. The only problem is that supernatural things happen around you when you are mad and we get caught up in it. Who else was that last night?

I DO NOT KNOW ANYTHING ABOUT THAT ONE OTHER THAN THAT HE IS MISCHIEVOUS AND A SHAPE-SHIFTER AND DOES THE GOOD WORK OF CONFUSING PEOPLE AWAY FROM THE CHURCHES, thought Travis.

Yep. Do not think we cannot handle this. You are a forgetful idiot. You know that murderous ideas have crossed our minds before. Until you can keep all your memories available to you when you need them, regardless of how horrifying they are, the bad guys and girls of the world have the ability to destroy you instead.

I will retrieve all my memories if I must. I didn't know you were going to be such a-holes about it all, thought Travis amid the intruders.

Who told you that you had not heard God before?

If you have not heard God before, then that means people can fall so far from grace that they can get crowned the Antichrist. I refuse to believe that you weren't saved at some point.

That has been a big thing the past couple of weeks. Look, I don't care. If you want me to, if you need me to, I can wreck your world and send you on a new trajectory, trajectories that you never thought possible. I can show you how to travel through space using just your mind, said the Big Blue Guy.

Some of us are already doing that.

I have IDEAS, and then they happen, JERK, thought Travis.

Are these gifts from God and the angels and not some of the unpleasant characters, you know, demons?

You absurd person. There is a God who has so many worlds to tend to, and he needs for all of you to show some agency. Speak to God and be quick about it. No one likes a complainer! thought Travis.

What if we only have the one life? How does that not make it easier to be religious?

If you believe that God only gives you one life to live, you probably are vengeful whether you are an atheist or a monotheist. You should let the universe right itself through its own natural laws. For every wrong action you do, there is an equally wrong action directed to you later, thought Travis.

I am not vengeful, Travis. I do, however, want the old ways. If you do not give us the old ways, we are going to have to get rid of you!

Who am I to give you anything? thought Travis.

You are a good teacher and not a demon. I will stay and help you with Karen.

We all remember that other one, and he says he is God. This one is only outwitting all of us by continuously choosing the smuttiest arguments against our ways of life.

That guy is the Antichrist! We get to have that! Let's go ahead and give it to ourselves.

You don't even have it right what my train of thought sounds like. You are some dumb Christian clairvoyants on the hunt for a scapegoat, thought Travis.

Oh, say it out loud. Talk out loud! Come on already. We've even been doing it for you and modeling it for you. It is appropriate. Talk out loud if you love Jesus!

That is not what I am going to have to deal with the rest of my life. I won't even see you again! exclaimed Travis.

Oh god, this isn't happening. I wanted the other so bad. You should have given us the other. We would have known what to do with the other. That person isn't a nut. He needs to be a nut now and not an evil guy callous enough to let in all the offensive thoughts that agitate us enough to make us get involved. We sound odd if we call him evil, but we basically must do it. For Jesus.

For Jesus.

I think I know what you are in for, and I will tell you it would have been better for you to have picked a different mental take on the matter your very last night in our world. If you were going to go with Christianity, you should have done it the way we wanted you to do it. Just Jesus.

You can stick around on the astral planes, said the rumbling bass voice he knew as the Big Blue Guy. *You need a clever Avatar. How about the Bloody King?*

I think I know what happens from now on. It just goes south, thought Travis.

Are you looking into the one and only future for you now? It could get better. It depends upon your attitude, said the Big Blue Guy.

Nuh-uh. You should have to suffer a bit more too, Travis. That seems fair to us. We are very angry that you are not giving us some exclusivity as the best people on earth.

I'm back here again, thought Karen.

Are you just going to keep trying new blasphemous things each night?

Tonight you die, Travis, thought Karen.

Has this happened before? Have I ever been this fed up and this flippant before? No, I haven't. This is a new special gift meant for all of you, thought Travis for everyone.

Obviously.

What do I need to do to stop the crazy, life-destroying Christians? thought Travis

I will walk you into the one where they suffer more than you for starting this and taking it this far, said Karen.

Fire the laser cannon! said a girlish voice.

Travis chuckled; he kind of giggled at the end of it.

What's so funny, you dog! I really am a demoness, and I have a laser cannon. I am going to fire it at you if you don't do everything I tell you.

I do not see a laser cannon. I know you're just making crap up at this point, thought Travis.

Well, fine, I will leave and let the real demons handle it because that's obviously what the other things are.

I may too, thought Karen.

It isn't because I have done anything wrong, is it? thought Travis.

No. You have done everything right, Travis. You kept your sarcasm in check enough.

Now you are making me sound self-righteous. I know I am not a son of God and not to go around talking like I am a son of God. It seems completely blasphemous, thought Travis.

You could call God Allah, said a childlike visiting space creature.

I don't have a job in that one, I don't think, but I am over it already. I am going to have to figure out how much of that memory I need to share with you when they arrive, thought Karen.

So you are leaving me too? thought Travis.

Before the night is over. You need to be strong and remain resilient—especially if you are going to stay around and watch over us. I will be back, and I will remind you of one of our meetings. Do not make the mistake of thinking it is me after that.

Whatever you do, don't do what the demons tell you to do, said the magical space creature.

She just left. That was another woman clairvoyant complaining about golden opportunities to behave sadistically that were slipping out of her hands.

There's more than one demon here, thought a Christian man clairvoyant.

I hear you, and I do not care, thought Travis.

You people were screwing things up badly, and we do. We have to put an end to this.

I still do not care, added Travis.

Then don't walk near us, and we won't go near you.

Okay, I will walk back and forth and not go near you, Travis replied.

Dude, I don't care anymore. I am just going to go ahead and do it. You need to be ruined for this because you did do something like that.

I did not try to sell my soul to Satan for clairvoyance, responded Travis.

No one thinks that is what you did. You cut a deal with one of us. You get to join the extradimensional beings for an eon or two now. Some of us are nice. Others not so much.

Did you try to sell your soul to Satan for clairvoyance when you were a teenager? shouted a shrill Baptist lady at him.

I was not like that then, Travis countered.

Wrong! You are like that now, and people don't change!

How are we all coming to these conclusions? You are reading way too much into all this rebelliousness on my part, and I am convinced it isn't in my best interest. When I leave here, I would like to be safe, thought Travis.

I just posted a video of your entire life to YouTube from the moment that Blue Guy showed up as it was seen through your eyes. What are you going to do about that?

You can't do things like that with clairvoyance, thought Travis.

There are a lot of things you would have thought were not possible five years ago that are now possible. There's a scientific breakthrough every day. This one is designed to stoke panic in the hearts of everyone— the same as the atomic bomb. Thanks for doing your part, Travis. You did it. You fixed everything.

Is that really what I just did? Oh well, I guess I am all right. I don't want this world anymore, Travis said.

But why? said the childlike space creature again.

I am kind of with her. The intelligent thought creator, it settles itself this way. This world was way offtrack. I, too, was not certain whether you would continue in the same direction you were heading in when you were in the eighth grade, but obviously, you needed to keep it up after Thanksgiving. I am glad we came back around this way. We don't always decide to settle things this way. You know, with you and with everyone who has ever known you.

I am not an Antichrist! insisted Travis.

Don't be a wuss about it if you are, Travis. Wear the mantle with pride. If people want to look at your whole life, it will be up there in one form or another. That company will always have the long version. Don't you worry about a thing. You were a decent guy a lot of the time. It provides you with a lot of insulation others don't have.

That is not what people in God-fearing rural areas will think after tonight. Am I supposed to live in a city the rest of my life? Travis asked.

You shouldn't have to live anywhere at all. You can stay with us after tonight.

We are heroes for sharing all your personal information. I guarantee you that is what the American people, old and young, go with about you after tonight, Mr. Antichrist.

Well, okay, but they're not really that way there, thought Travis.

Why are you walking slower?

Because I have been up walking for most of the past week and my back hurts. I have a rash between my legs like somebody who just went from walking nothing to twenty miles, Travis complained.

Maybe you could stop and stand still. Your human friend will be dropping by soon.

Travis stood still and counted the minutes until forty-five had passed.

I need for you to remember something I got out of you during hypnosis.

Why did you go there? inquired Travis.

You let me do that once.

Travis had a flashback to his sixteenth year when he was first meeting with Karen. He and his parents had taken a trip to see Dr. Samedi in her office over in Charleston in the neighboring state, South Carolina. They had waited in the reception room for an hour and a half double visit they were not expecting to have to pay for. Karen had brought him back into her office and was asking him about his life and what he was doing to keep himself busy. She knew he was a clairvoyant but had no idea why he was not using his gifts. Clairvoyants had surrounded her since she decided to go exploring.

"Tell me why you think your mom is hypercontrolling."

"You are very inquisitive right now," said Travis.

"Well, Travis, women do not usually change as they get older the same way guys do. They get stuck someplace in high school and stick with that one for the rest of it. If a woman is more independent then, she usually gets more liberal. If she is very dependent, then she often gets very conservative. I can tell you that your mother is the type who is dependent, and she will do the most agreeable thing here with your father, and she will always be like that."

"What an illuminating insight you provided today," Travis told her.

Karen frowned. "Travis, I like to get results from my practice. I would like to speed things up. I would like to know something."

"What?" asked Travis.

"Are you a Christian?"

"Does being a Christian mean believing everything you were taught since you were baptized? Because that is not how a whole lot of people see it," said Travis.

"I know that many people think you are bound up with them from that point onward because that is when a person gets the gift of the spirit. Most Catholic and Orthodox communion people who believe faith and works are the exact same. If they give you a saint's name and keep it registered, they may think they have a claim to you. Your group does something strange there when they convince you to be baptized at ten like that is really a thing for faith and works families anywhere anymore. The Catholic and Orthodox communions do not do that, and they have too many members globally to be considered a cult. Those Restorationist groups are as odd as they can be. I see that messing with a kid's worldview later. That is especially true if they do not take advantage of the internet to get informed with all the defunding of the public education system that has occurred.

"If you do not make time for historical lectures and geography lectures, then a child from that background would become a dumbed-down adult only capable of entering the workforce to be perpetually indebted and a religious capitalist until unemployment finally skyrockets at the end. That was a bold move of yours to leave a private school so that you could get a proper education in *scientific* life sciences and astronomy. Most people ignore scientific studies now if they are not being reported on in the centrist mainstream American media and popular with their town's religious leaders. That is comparable with cultures without the internet where the population is much easier for the wealthy and the state media to control. I think your parents have done some interesting things with you and your brother when you have visited natural and historical sites as you have traveled, but they do not do a lot to challenge you to think about options available to you outside of entering the workforce as a laborer if they are not thinking you should be working now. You are an exception to what I see normally from that background. I was wondering whether they have spoken with you about getting you banked eventually when they decide you can work?"

"No. They did not speak to me about providing help in that area. The counselors in the state have been the same," said Travis.

"It is a shame that they are not even doing that. There is not a lot that can be done here in this country unless you want to live in a group home, and then they usually want you to stay there for the rest of your life. I was hoping one day you would decide there was not any difference between living with them and living in a group home. Anyway, will you let me hypnotize you?"

"All the social upheaval that we are undergoing may end up making them as stupid, I mean ignorant and foolhardy, as the rest of their religious community and catatonic by the end of the next decade. I was really wanting them to do more than the other middle-class families that they live and work with. There are people who have lived in rural areas who are knowledgeable and not content to stay who have left. I figured I would end up that way eventually," said Travis.

"Your parents do not care, Travis. They understand them down here more than they do you. It is only a bit of hatred, and your family is all right with the way the community handles it."

"I thought that having me as a son would have an effect on them," said Travis.

Travis, get a clue.

"I do not see a group of them doing well in the real world when the cultural revolution leaves the South impoverished," said Travis.

"Do you know how you are going to handle the loss of that way of life when it is time?"

"No. I am only sixteen. I am not worried about the necessity of a French Revolution in order to make any actual progress," said Travis.

"Will you let me hypnotize you? It may help. Here, this is my watch. Look at it sway."

Travis was out of his right mind at that moment.

"When did you hear God?"

"Never!" exclaimed Travis.

"Does your group call on the name of the Lord?"

"Is that really a thing?" asked Travis.

"Would you ever do it if somebody called you on not having done it yet? In one future, somebody a bit like God talks to you, and yet you are not really the type to do Christianity like those guys."

"Makes sense," said Travis.

"Was it any different from when you prayed as a kid? Any different from the first time you asked God to show agency for you?"

"I have never heard back from him. I have seen that in my life and in that of those who are praying the most fervently. He is giving them a world that is hostile to their teachings and is not giving them a convenient world for them to live into. I hope the adults in this small town I am stuck in a while are not malicious to me when they realize I don't want to spend more than one life with them. I think some of them are trying to end the world for him," said Travis.

"Have you ever hated God?"

"What a dumb thing to waste time on," retorted Travis.

"I need you to let me guide you. I'll ask a different question. Have you ever turned to other gods, Travis, other religions, Satan?"

"I asked a spirit once if I could have telepathic abilities—stupid thing to do since I haven't heard back from him since then," said Travis.

"That spirit, the Big Blue Guy, did you ask it for any other abilities?"

"What other clairvoyant gifts are there?" Travis asked.

"You should've done research and asked what else was on the menu. Just stay asleep and let me find out more."

Karen told Travis that she had viewed his entire life from the point that spirit contacted him until its likely end. It was not easy finding the correct thread, however, if he was going to follow the science and observe interstellar space travelers and not presume malice on their part. The one showing up with high probability to help Travis set the world right again was the Big Blue Guy.

"I know I outlive you, Travis. I had no idea how vicious the other clairvoyants were going to be or why your eyes looked at the things and people they looked at. You have a remarkable amount of curiosity."

"I change my views all the time. Whenever I read, I keep an open mind and can carry on a conversation about science," Travis explained.

"And when does it go too far for you as opposed to people in your community and that cultlike sect your family belongs to? If someone sat you down and explained to you, say during a foretelling, that you could trap us all in a nightmare, a world no one wants, would you still continue to follow the evidence, however startling, that things are not the way you had conceived them to be originally with less information, the way a scientist would?"

"It would be wrong if I was not going to broaden my mind after seeing the possibility of a new universe being caused by any resistance to accepting new scientific discoveries," said Travis.

"You do not talk an awful lot, and then that mother of yours discourages it. The last few weeks of your life were very confusing, but I definitely know what I saw through your eyes at the end."

Travis was coming out of hypnosis and was not sure what she was talking about, but she was continuing to talk. *I kind of want that one to happen as well. I can't have discussions honestly as a medical professional, scientist, and clairvoyant without being considered a heretic at church, so I will be there to help at the end, I think.*

Those last three sentences could not have been her. She would not do that to me when I needed to be brave, thought Travis.

You mean you couldn't tell how you were going to die tonight. You never can while you are awake. People still are not sure what it is they are seeing. If it's not some avant-garde movie, there are parts of it that look like Dada. If it goes on the whole dozen years and people skip around in two to three hours, there's going to be a riot.

I am just going to stand here and clear my mind of thought, Travis decided.

Travis thought to others unintentionally no more. After counting out thirty more minutes, he began seeing things that should not have been on the walls. He knew what it was meant to resemble. There really were no black flecks of ash falling from smoke clouds all over the globe even if they were increasing, and why would he want to see that? Those were people accessing his life story on YouTube. He had lived a good life. He could cut the light off and crawl in bed.

As he got into bed, he realized that the bathroom light was on, but the curtain was shut enough that basically only a little light was shining through. *I need to sleep* and *keep knocking away bad spirits.* He saw the light streaming between the curtain and the door, and it seemed to be dropping down further to the floor the deeper he breathed. *I really did not want for anyone to think Ophelia was more relevant than she turned out to be,* thought Travis.

Oh. She hates you. Let me tell you what she saw when she looked at it tonight.

"I would rather just drift on into unconsciousness and not do it slowly. I don't have enough energy for this," said Travis.

Travis went to a night puddle. It was about the best way to describe it. There were literally thousands of people who were coming up with new types of devious pleasures, all at the same time in the same place.

This version seemed holy somehow. *We want nonviolence, and the household is still a place where fights are going to continue and pathologies will continue to form in individuals. When are we going to see an end to religion and the family? Sexualize the violence! Do not carry it away from your intimate others.*

Are you even sure all these people are in the same world system as ours or the same universe? That's not how the people I go to church with talk, thought Ophelia.

You are not supposed to ever do more than a few acts. We settled that a long time ago. You must be restrictive there first so you can be violent against everybody else from the moment you wake up, thought somebody at him.

All you have done is made it possible to have one's rights met without adequate compensation. I am not sure how that is going to go, thought another person.

I despise everything about the polyamory movement and the peace movement, thought still another person.

You are obviously a malevolent alien. I am ready for you to leave the planet if you do not understand this is in our best interest, thought Travis.

I like that mainstream journalists, religions, and tabloids shame serial monogamy and polyamory, and I hope it continues. Are you sure you want to leave the world like this? Why are you participating now in it being more liberal than we want? thought Ophelia.

Travis was awakened from night swimming; he saw this for what it was.

You need to go away and let me deal with my final hours, thought Travis.

I will go away now, Travis. I'll live on in the flesh and hopefully be able to help you out with some of this. At least I will be doing the popular thing here in the South, the place that matters most to me, thought Ophelia.

What if we could find you a physical transportation device? asked Travis.

Clairvoyants from all over town were awake and shouting at Travis.

You're type gives Christians and New Agers a bad name.

If you are the Antichrist, we will destroy you.

You are not supposed to exist. That was the big thing about Travis that I thought we could use to ruin him.

Are you not perturbed at all?

"I don't care anymore. As long as people are panicking and as long as the lies from that crowd outnumber the truths, I am happy. I knew that was how they conducted themselves a long time ago," Travis said decisively.

Are you like that, Travis? That's how I thought you were. We are going to get a mob started. I do not care if there are still a hundred thousand gnomes outside the hospital.

Try to shut up like Travis said. You may be living a nightmare here on this world before too much longer—even as I steal him away from here, said the Big Blue Guy.

It is a shame that you will not live to see your prophecies come true.

Do you hear that? That is the banging open of the hospital doors outside. They are coming to get you. Nobody cares about that anyway. They don't understand how you can make a deal out of it. You must make lust a problem at some point, and it should be enough to keep you at the center of attention. They should get it in the real world, and then we can all shame them publicly if someone gets pregnant or contracts something we didn't want to cure, thought Dr. Strangeglove.

You all are in the movie too, said the Big Blue Guy.

"Okay, that started two hours ago. I am going to stay quiet and listen," said Travis.

The door burst open with hospital security, and there were extra police with them. "Whatever that was, it cannot continue. Grab him and drag him away. If he fights back, beat him up."

"You don't have to make it that. You can't have seen it all. I will go with you peacefully," pleaded Travis.

"We are taking you outside for the public to have their way with you. No one cares about giving you Miranda rights." They pulled his hands behind his back and put them in handcuffs.

"Can you not cuff them in front?" asked Travis.

"That's not a thing. *You* may not even get a trial. There has never been as much hatred stockpiled in the world as there is now. We need you to satisfy our bloodlust."

The militarized police force for removing undesirable people pushed him from the back through the behavioral health unit while two guards opened doors and moved to the side. They carted him through the atrium's pavilion and out into the night. There were headlights. There was a helicopter shining a light on him. The local news station was there to film the incident. They had parked minivans, and soccer moms were sitting out in folding chairs. He felt an ominous feeling—not like he was gone for good but like he was about to be executed by these people for their entertainment. He passed the corner of that building before he reached the police car. He held his head high, glad he was spared a crucifixion. The two guards in the front stopped, and the one behind him knocked him to the ground.

"KILL THE ANTICHRIST!" rang through the air, as did the first person's knife. She had flung it into his waist. He turned to look at the people there. That was his family and a cousin standing over there; she appeared to be leading the charge on a megaphone.

"WHAT A DUMB CHOICE TO MAKE!" said his father as he dug a knife into his son's sternum, missing his heart and puncturing a lung.

"YOU HAVE RUINED SO MANY LIVES!" That man there was his brother. His knife went into the back of his body and hit a kidney. He slumped to the ground, bleeding profusely and in intense agony. All he could think to do was press the sticker on his shirt.

"I WILL TAKE CARE OF IT AND FINISH THE JOB!" Viviane walked right up to Travis and slashed his throat open. They had stopped and backed away and were watching him die. He looked comatose. He knew he would not look any different from any other dying person.

As the blood poured out of his neck and he lost his sense of place totally, he went on an OBE. He looked at his blank brown eyes on the asphalt. They had turned red, and he was glad that his blood had been shed without serving any purpose other than vengeance. He had a vile family—one that was not even worth staying around and haunting. He had also harbored a secret desire the family unit would go away someday along with religion. It did not look like it was going to happen soon. Maybe their treatment of him will nudge younger people in the direction that removes *all* forms of oppression. It might not happen, and he might have difficulty expanding their consciousness, let alone preparing the human body for interstellar space travel. Families should be abolished. There stood a genuine chance of there being no suffering in life if we'd abolish the family unit. He could hear people talking around him about how nice it was to kill him finally but that it had ended too quickly like a fireworks display. They were obviously in the wrong, and if they knew it would look bad later, they did not care now—at least they had one another. He had no interest to stick around and see what became of it.

Before the lights started turning off in his mind as his brain was losing its firepower, Travis looked at a hallway stairs' Exit sign and moved through that doorway into the great beyond. He was teleported onto an alien spaceship and had his head and arms covered in red nodes for replacing blood while his throat was sutured up touchlessly with an electric device in an operational ward on some foreign spacecraft. They were going to implant a new kidney. They had his lungs back to operating normally. He left the people who should never have happened, and he left the town that would go away. He left…with the Big Blue Guy.

ABOUT THE AUTHOR

R. B. Batson currently resides in the Deep South with his beloved family.

He has a master of ministry in ministerial counseling and history of biblical interpretation and theology, which he received with honors; a master of professional studies in community development; and a bachelor of arts in geography.

He is an Eagle Scout; and in his spare time, he likes to backpack, sing, and draw.

He is currently writing another novel and owns a handmade, sustainably produced, and organic soap-making business.

Milton Keynes UK
Ingram Content Group UK Ltd.
UKHW040314080224
437360UK00001B/98